The *Blazing Star*

Thomas Conrad

PAGE PUBLISHING, INC.
Conneaut Lake, PA

First originally published by Page Publishing 2020

ISBN 978-1-6624-0925-7 (pbk)
ISBN 978-1-6624-0926-4 (digital)

Printed in the United States of America

Also by Thomas Conrad
The Reunion

1

Winter 1871

The match flared, illuminating an unshaven face beneath a wide-brimmed, snow-covered hat. Smoke billowed from the well-used corncob pipe as the mounted figure drew from it in long slow breaths. The man brought the glowing bowl to the top of the saddle horn, holding it in both hands and feeling its warmth, his dark eyes never leaving the conflagration in the near distance. The horse shuddered beneath him, shedding its blanket of snow to the knee-deep accumulation on the ground.

"What's goin' on?" came from a voice at his side. The horse jumped, and the man nearly dropped his pipe in surprise at the sound.

"Goddammit," he growled as he looked down to see a boy standing a few feet away. The young face glowed yellow from the light of the burning building down the street. A drop of water fell from the brim of his hat to hang briefly on his nose before falling to a well-worn wool coat. He never looked at the horseman but reached out a hand to the horse's flank and steadied him. The man kicked out at the boy's hand in anger, but it was already gone. The lesser figure had moved away like a windblown tumbleweed through the snow, his raggedy flapping outline melting into the commotion. The horse pawed at the snow then shuddered again, still unsettled.

Chaos reigned in the street when the boy approached, as horses with and without riders raced in all directions. He melded into the fray and stopped to watch several men take turns running to splash water at the inferno. The heat, like a shield, kept them from getting close, but their ineffectual assault continued. Tossing the flour sack containing his few possessions at the stoop of a church, the boy moved to join the line of citizens passing water-filled buckets hand to hand toward the blaze.

The area in front of the building was a slippery mess, as melting snow mixed with the bucketed water. During a moment's gap in the chain, the boy looked around at the illuminated buildings of the town. Taking in the scene, he missed a dark movement at his side and collided with a large woman wielding a full bucket of water, knocking her to the ground. In a cocoon-like mass of muddy wet fabric, she rolled in the slop in front of him. He stepped forward to help but lost his footing, landing on top of her, great melon-sized breasts cushioning his fall.

"You little shit," she said, bringing a fist hard onto his left cheekbone. The sharp pain stung him, and he fell, dazed, back to the soft pillows beneath him. The woman's struggle, now more difficult with the boy on top of her, added to her fury and thus her strength so that she clumsily rolled over on top of him. He began to regain his senses, though not his sense of direction, while trying to breathe within the murk of her dress. His original mission of rescue had become one of escape, and he struggled to crawl away. Having cleared the sodden petticoats, he regained his footing, the left side of his head throbbing and his vision blurred. The swelling around his eye gradually forced it closed.

The woman, still furious, spotted him and started in his direction when they heard the scream. It had the dual quality of an echo and seemed to rise above the pandemonium with increasing volume. The boy eased away from his nemesis in her distraction and crossed the street facing the blaze. His face ached, his clothes were soaked, and he didn't notice taking a step forward toward the warmth of the burning building.

He saw the twins a moment after he heard a gasp from the crowd. Through the smoke on the second-floor veranda, they appeared, silhouetted in the eerie orange glow. One coughed and cried; the other half covered her face with a handkerchief while looking side to side, up, and down the street. They were dressed in identical show gowns: scarlet satin trimmed with white lace where the neckline dropped to outline cleavage and ivory-white skin. Their long dark hair hung in pipe curls past their shoulders, framing pretty faces that were barely visible. Standing close together, they moved as one to the railing and looked down to the citizenry.

The boy wiped his single seeing eye with his sleeve and squinted hard at the double vision before him. The twins! He had traveled 1,500 miles to see them and almost arrived too late. He couldn't know if everything he'd heard was true but now knew they were real, at least for the moment. Mesmerized by this apparition, he didn't notice the large woman as she continued her pursuit of him from his blind side.

"Look at my dress damn you," she growled, her hammer-like fist cocked for another blow. The boy easily ducked beneath the punch, though momentum carried her forward, and his face bounced again into her bosom.

"I'm sorry…" he sputtered. But sensing an apology was wasted time, he spun away and ran as fast as he could into the burning building.

The Blazing Star was the largest saloon and brothel in Alamo, Montana. Built of brick and wood, its two stories towered above the town's other buildings. The saloon on the main floor was spacious and featured a long and ornate mahogany bar, backed by the biggest mirror the boy had ever seen. He'd been in many saloons but never in one as well-trimmed-out as this. The walls were covered with antlers, mounted heads, and skins representing the wildlife of the Mountain West. Intermingled with these *trophies* were lavish examples of Western art, to include paintings and hand-carved figurines, all of it now smoldering or melting from the heat. Across the room from the bar, a large potbelly stove glowed red in front of a wall fully consumed in smoke and flame, its share of the treasure already lost. The mirror's reflection completed a volcanic effect and reminded the boy of his mother's prediction that he would burn in hell for his laziness. She'd laughed when she said it, and he knew she wasn't serious.

Chairs were overturned on tabletops, and there was a mop in a bucket near the bar. Holding his sodden hat over his nose and mouth, his only seeing eye cried from the smoke. Staying in a low crouch, he moved toward the staircase at the back of the room and began to climb. On the third step, he slipped and fell forward into a smeared stream of sticky black liquid. Skirting the murky flow, he started up the steps then changed his mind and turned back to follow the dark path. The trail led to the shadows behind the bar where a young woman lay on the floor staring at the ceiling, the front of her gown saturated in blood. He gently closed her eyes, his fingers lingering to caress the still warm skin of her cheek. A bald man in a blood-covered apron lay just beyond the girl, his body also drained of life. The boy stood up slowly and again surveyed the room. "Bad, bad," he said to himself, "bad, bad, bad."

In a feline stalk, he moved back to the stairway and rapidly climbed to the second floor. A hot cinder hissed as it landed on his back and sizzled in the damp wool of his coat. Smoke rose through the cracks in the floor, and the heat burned his feet through the thin soles of his boots. The two doors to his left were open; the blood trail to the stairs came from that direction. The two doors to his right were closed and at the front of the building, so he moved toward them. He entered the first room and moved through it quickly, grateful not to find more bodies. The door of the second room was locked. The boy pounded on it with his fist and heard distant voices in reply. The twins reentered the room from its street-side balcony, came to the door, and banged in response.

"The door's locked!" the boy yelled, shaking and turning the knob.

"We know," came a calm voice in reply. "The bartender has the key."

"He's dead," the boy called back, throwing his weight into the door, bouncing off it ineffectually. "Wait there," he said, immediately thinking, *that was dumb.* He ran back to the first room and groped through its dim light for something to use as a battering ram. Finding a chair jammed up under the knob of the door to the veranda, he grabbed it and turned to leave when the door opened behind him and in walked the twins.

"We hoped you'd figure that out," one of them said.

"Why, you're just a skinny boy," said the other. "No one else came to save us? We were afraid we'd have to jump."

The boy stared at them, still holding the chair. "We better get going, ma, ma'am," he stuttered. "I mean ma'ams."

"Yes, let's go," the twins said in unison.

They moved quickly to the stairway and collectively raised their arms to shield their faces. Casting flashing silhouettes, the twins followed the boy closely, one looking in horror at the spectacle, the other focused on the descent and their escape. At the bottom step, the boy glanced toward the bar and slipped in the blood, falling hard to the floor. The twins following closely were unable to stop and tumbled forward, landing on top of him.

For the second time in ten minutes, the boy found himself under skirts and petticoats. Having never touched a woman's undergarments before, this was not the experience he'd imagined it would be. Nor had he considered that it would smell so fine, something he hadn't noticed beneath the large woman in the street. Drawing from that previous incident, he knew the best method of escape was to stay low and crawl out. He emerged to see embers and flaming planks falling on them as the ceiling began to collapse. The young women screamed under burning material as he scrambled to his feet. Reacting instinctively, he rushed to them and pulled and kicked the fiery boards away even as the rain of hell fell around them. The twins writhed and thrashed as their gowns ignited, their tandem effort to escape seeming to fan the flames. His hands scorched, the boy peeled off his damp and muddy coat, threw it over them, and fell to the task of beating and rolling to smother the flames.

Together they stumbled to the street and fell into the muck, sucking in the fresh air. Smoke and steam mingled from their charred and smoldering bodies. The townspeople, shocked to see them emerge, closed in like concerned parents. Someone brought a bucket of water from the relay, and the twins drank greedily in turn. A wagon was brought forward, and the town's only doctor supervised as the twins were loaded onto it for transport to his office. An explosion of sparks looked like so many fireflies as the roof of the Blazing Star fell to its foundation. The bucket wielders backed away as the futility of their effort became obvious.

A flurry of ash and snow was falling when the boy returned to the church to reclaim his belongings. With hands cupped full of snow and his gunnysack tucked under one arm, he moved slowly through the dark toward a stable his nose told him was close by. He entered through a back stall and made a nest behind a stack of moldy hay. Lying down next to a family of deer mice, he closed his eye, wiped his nose on a sleeve, and went to sleep.

Morning broke in Alamo and found most of its residents napping after a sleepless night. The smoldering ruins of the Blazing Star hissed and popped as it cooled. Its brick walls had confined the heat and flames within the structure like an oven and kept it from spreading to the buildings on each side. Half a dozen men sat across the street at the Lobo drinking coffee and discussing the night's events.

"Reminded me of when the Jubilee burned over at Gilmore."

"Burned five dead that one."

"Thankful the twins is alive."

"Who was that boy?"

"Dunno, but he's a brave sort."

"When you goin' in, Walter?"

The sheriff spat toward the base of the wall, squarely hitting a strategically placed spittoon. He took a long draw from his coffee cup in no hurry to answer. "Be this afternoon, I s'pect, before it's cooled off enough." He leaned back in his chair and looked at his deputy. "Delbert, you keep an eye on it. I don't want nobody in there before us. I'm goin' back to the jail and sleep for a few hours. Come get me at ten." The sheriff checked his pocket watch and stood to leave. The deputy nodded and glanced across the street to see a magpie briefly light on one of the two standing walls then drop out of sight into the ruins.

Sheriff Walter Becker turned his collar up against the breeze and walked into the new day's light. He crossed the street on his way to the jail and entered Frank James's office. Asleep in a chair by the stove, the old doctor jerked awake and reached out to the wall to steady himself. He adjusted his spectacles and focused on his visitor. "That you, Walter?" The sheriff stomped the snow off his boots and walked in to stand with his back to the warmth.

"It's me, Doc. How're they doin'?"

The doctor leaned forward and yawned. "They're asleep. I gave 'em a good dose of laudanum, so they'll be out for a while. Burned 'em pretty good, but they'll be okay if I can keep the infection away. There'll be scarring, but nowhere it'll be seen whilest they got clothes on." He stood and shook the empty coffeepot then set it back down, seemingly confused as to what he'd set out to do. Running his hand through his thin white hair, he brightened at a new thought and went to his desk to remove a whiskey bottle and two glasses from a bottom drawer. "Any idea what happened to that boy?"

"No, but if he's burned like these girls, he's prob'ly feelin' a might uncomfortable by now." The sheriff accepted his drink and sipped it slowly. "Can't figure how he got them out of there."

They drank in silence until the glasses were empty, then Becker moved to the door and paused to look over his shoulder. "Let me know if you see him."

The doctor nodded to the sheriff then leaned back and closed his eyes. Walter Becker shuffled through the snow to the jailhouse. He put a couple of logs in the stove then laid down on a cot in a vacant cell. The vision of the Blazing Star scorched his inner eyelids and burned into his dreams.

The boy, too, dreamed of the fiery hotel and the two beautiful women. He awoke shivering from the cold and burning from a fire within. Crawling out of the stall, he ate several handfuls of snow and let his fingers linger in the frozen pack until it gradually dulled the pain. His head was in a fog as he backed into the straw and tried to count the mice watching him from a top rail. He located his gunnysack and managed to get the cord that bound it around his neck. Retracing his steps from the previous night, he staggered outside, made it to the front of the barn, and fell into the street.

2

The twins drew men from all over the West to Alamo, Montana. Townsfolk of all stripes crowded main street to watch them take their daily stroll down the boardwalk. It was well-known that they were committed to their health and made the trip except in the worst weather. Neither drank nor used tobacco, which was uncommon for women of their type. Impeccably dressed and made up to perfection, they were unusually beautiful. They reveled in their celebrity. Curious about everything, they were in continuous conversation. They especially loved children. Unfortunately, and perhaps naturally, the town's mothers were their biggest detractors. At twenty-one, they were at the apex of their lives. Though they had never been abused, their path had never been certain.

Summer 1849

Born into a family of ten children in Spanish Fork, Utah, their mother, despite a well-traveled birth canal, did not survive the experience. The family's patriarch—a stern, religious man—held the girls responsible. He had been a demanding and cruel husband and was concerned that his wife's burden would now become his. What he had failed to notice was the share of the feminine chores his oldest daughters already carried. Their mother had trained them well, and the addition of the twins was barely noticed. With so many siblings and three milk cows on the premises, their welfare was never in doubt. They were healthy babies, each with her own parts, but firmly joined at the hip. Their adoring sisters named them Chastity and Prudence, and the twins thrived under their care.

Prior to the birth, Chatham had spoken to an elder of the polygamist sect in the valley and had plans to join up. His eldest daughter was almost seventeen and a comely girl, and he was looking to make a trade. Zelda had fought off his sexual advances with such vehemence that he was forced to back off lest his adventure be broadcast to the family. He had no confidence a new wife would take to the freak twins, and he intended to get rid of them.

But what do you do with Siamese twin babies? For one thing, their popularity was a serious complication. The stream of visitors was already more than the man could tolerate. He could probably charge admission and they'd still come—hardly possible in Spanish Fork, but the idea inspired him.

The solution arrived one day when the *Phantasmagoric Circus & Sideshow* rolled into town. Better known as the P&S Circus, Colonel Phantastic was planning a three-day stay. His twelve-railcar caravan was scheduled for a four-day show in Salt Lake City, followed by the long trip to the West Coast, and the troupe and animals needed a rest. Spanish Fork was far too small a venue to justify the erection of their big tents for the presentation of the "Greatest Show in the West," but they did put together a respectable parade in appreciation of the community's hospitality.

The man forbade his eager family's pleas to see the rare extravaganza but made a trip himself to the circus's camp on the second day to seek out the Colonel for a private conversation. His proposition was straightforward. The twins were for sale and *without a doubt* would be a tremendous asset to the P&S's line of unusual attractions. He emphasized their youth and good health and that the circus could expect many years of service.

The Colonel was interested. He had been a slave owner, so the sale of humans presented no ethical issues, but this was different. This could be considered kidnapping, and a passing circus would be a logical place to look for such creatures. Not only that, in order to attract an audience, he'd have to advertise that he had them. The situation was fraught with complications, but the Colonel smelled money and knew he could come up with a solution. First, he had to deal with this rube. The man was probably right about the long-term value of the babies to the circus. If they were as healthy as he professed, the Colonel could keep them their entire lives. Why, they could even be a draw after their deaths with some decent taxidermy. The asking price was probably a bargain.

"First of all, my good man, one hundred dollars is out of the question. I'll give you twenty-five dollars, after inspection, of course. You say their mother is dead?"

"Yeah, she died when they's borned."

"So you're their legal guardian?"

"No, I'm they's pa."

"Yes, yes." *What an idiot*, he thought. It was ridiculous to think of giving this dislocated cracker anything for the children. Life in the circus would be far better than what they might experience in his care. "I'll want to legally adopt them. I'll not tolerate a conflict with the law. Bring them to my railcar at midnight. It's the last car on the line. Come alone. Can you sign your name?"

"Yeah, I can. But I gotta have fifty dollars for 'em."

"We'll see about that. Have them there at midnight."

After the man left, the Colonel walked into Spanish Fork, wired an attorney he knew in Salt Lake City, and asked him to meet the train for an urgent matter when it arrived the following day. The request was specifically vague, knowing there was no such thing as a confidential transmission. Next, he had to prepare the troupe for the earlier-than-planned exit. He walked among the performers and animal keepers and gave instructions for a 12:30 a.m. departure. The train's engineer and conductor were notified. Their combined effort had booked three carloads of cattle and four cars of lumber for the trip north. This additional freight was vital to cover travel expenses for the P&S, and the Colonel was pleased to hear that leaving this early could be managed.

Back on the farm, the man reentered his daily routine thinking through his escape plan. The getaway would be simple. He would take the twins from the house while the rest of his clan slept, but this was where things fell apart. The Colonel's insistence that he go to Salt

Lake to sign adoption papers took away his plan to claim they'd been kidnapped. When morning came and he, the twins, and the circus train were all gone, there would be no doubt about what happened. What would follow was less certain. Chatham was having second thoughts.

3

Winter 1871

"Sheriff, sheriff, we got that boy."

"What? Where?" The sheriff's hat fell from his face, where it had shielded his eyes from the morning's light. His toes were cold, and his back ached when he swung his boots to the floor. *What the hell's he talking about? What boy?*

"He's at Doc's. Jesse found him in the street in front of the livery."

"Okay, I'll head over." The sheriff pulled out his pocket watch, squinted at the dial, but couldn't make it out. He shuffled to the front of the jailhouse and shook the coffeepot on the woodstove. There was still liquid in it, but how old? He took a sniff then poured it out through a crack in the floor. *What is that smell?* It wasn't the coffee, burned as it was. He was used to that. He walked to the window and looked down the street to a small group of men and women staring at the smoldering remains of the Blazing Star. "Oh yeah," he mumbled.

The forgetfulness had been getting worse. At first it had been just an annoyance, but he knew it had been affecting his work. For how long, of course, he couldn't be certain, but it had crept into his conversations, and he was sure it was being noticed. He'd learned that reacting slowly often gave him the opportunity to get the gist of where a discussion was going before he responded. Delbert was aware of it, and he intended to talk to Doc but hadn't found the time. Or had he... The lack of a night's sleep wasn't helping. When the jail cells were full, he had to sleep in a chair. What would he do without this job? He had less than sixty dollars saved and no place to go except that shithole of a ranch in Utah.

"Goddamn," he said, then opened the door and walked outside.

The pong hung thickly in the air, and wisps of ash still wafted skyward from the smoldering building to mingle with the falling snow. The resulting pall merged with the dark overcast sky somewhere on the horizon. The spectators would later discover that their clothing would be permanently stained gray from the sticky soot that settled on their shoulders. The sheriff waved at his deputy, standing between the ruins and the onlookers, then walked in the opposite direction toward the doctor's office.

"Doc."

"Walter."

"Whadda we got here? If somebody told me, I already forgot."

"Sit down and have some coffee. We'll go through it."

"Thank you, sir."

The sheriff sipped and listened while his friend described the events of the previous night to the most recent hour when he first saw the scorched skinny boy.

"We got three survivors. Any idea who's missing?" The doctor took the sheriff's pulse while he waited for a response.

"No idea."

"When you goin' in, Walter?"

"I reckon as soon as I'm done here. She's still smokin', but it's prob'ly cooled down enough. I'll want to talk to the twins and the boy as soon as I can."

"That'll have to be tomorrow. No sooner. The boy's got pneumonia, so maybe not even then. I'll send word when they're ready." The doctor poured more coffee. "You need to sleep yerself. I'll tell you what. You come back here tonight, and we'll let it out that you're protecting the patients. It'll likely be more peaceful than the jail."

"Thanks," the sheriff said, standing up. "Maybe I'll do that."

Alamo's main street was quieter than usual at midday. Walter got a few nods from the group in the street when he approached Delbert. Playing Doc's version of last night's events over and over in his mind, he had a good-enough handle on what happened to know what had to be done.

"You ready, old son?"

"Yes, sir." Delbert nodded. "Neither Charlie Burk nor Mabel Monroe's been seen since last night."

"Okay, let's go."

They entered the ruins in the middle, the sheriff scanning to the right, Delbert to the left. Hot spots and occasional flaming embers limited their access and guided their way. The stench was intense, with all manner of combustible materials adding to the fumes. In his twenty-three years as a lawman, Walter Becker had been in many burned-out buildings. Chimney fires, cooking fires, and the occasional arson were a constant threat to structures that were made primarily of wood. Once started, they were almost impossible to put out and usually resulted in a structure's total destruction. Firefighting efforts mostly focused on keeping the blaze from spreading. The sheriff tiptoed toward the cast-iron stove and the masonry chimney to which it was attached, both still intact. He grasped the stove's open door, pushed it closed, and heard it latch securely. "Hmph," he grunted. "That ain't right."

"Sheriff. Over here."

Delbert was standing in the wreckage where the bar used to be. With the second floor, the ceiling, and the roof remains all in the pile, nothing was recognizable. Balanced on a smoldering beam, gloved hand against his face, the deputy stared through a gap in the debris at a blackened skeletal hand.

"Looks like we found either Charlie or Mabel," he murmured.

The sheriff stumbled through the debris to join his deputy, wondering if he'd ever get the stink out of his head. He looked up as the snow flurries charged them in a cloud of white, the blackness beneath winning that fight with a hissing laughter. "When I get to hell, I'll recognize it by the smell," he said.

"You ain't going to hell, sheriff." The deputy coughed. "Somebody in this town is though. This fire was no accident, was it?"

"No, I believe it was not."

They stared at the hand in silence for a full minute.

"Go get Charley and Gunner, Delbert," the sheriff said quietly. "Bring shovels and a pry bar and two canvas tarps."

"I need to talk to that boy," he said to himself, backing away from the hand. He moved carefully so not to disturb anything, wanting witnesses to his part in the search. Climbing through the debris, he stumbled in the direction of Charlie Burk's room in the back-southeast corner of the ruins. He'd always been amazed that anyone could live here. Sleeping in a jail every night was bad enough, but who could tolerate living in a saloon? Yet Charlie had been doing it for ten years, ever since the Star was built. He was not the owner, though he might as well have been. A hardworking, decent man, he took care of the place as if it was his own.

"Charlie, I'm gonna find out who did this, if my brain don't turn to mush first." The sheriff choked. He covered his mouth with his handkerchief and hacked into it.

In a gruesome effort, the two bodies were removed to Evan Grove's Mortuary. Doc was called to examine them, and he left with a grim expression and a shake of his head, not certain if the limbs even belonged to the torsos they'd been grouped with. There was no evidence as to the cause of death other than incineration. The undertaker placed the parts in coffins and flipped a coin to decide which corpse was which.

"We got two missing persons and two bodies," Doc told Walter Becker. "There's no proof they're the same. What you wanna do?"

"We're going to have a service and bury 'em," the sheriff replied. "I'll have Delbert see what he can come up with for next of kin. How's that boy?"

"Well, not takin' into account the pain he must be in, I'd guess he's havin' a pretty good time. The twins went and got him and are keepin' him in bed with them. There's a lot of gigglin' going on."

4

Summer 1849

The house was settled in for the night. The older girls had the family fed, the kitchen cleaned, and the babies in bed. Three of the oldest boys would be off to labors across the valley before dawn and were well into their night's slumber. The man had little to do but prepare for his midnight rendezvous. He entered the barn and went straight for his Mason jar. His confusion over the details that had been added to his plan had him rattled. *Sign a paper! Did the Colonel think I was stupid?* The man could go to jail! Selling babies had to be against the law. And what did he say? Twenty-five dollars? The more he drank, the madder he got. Let the Colonel go to *Simeeze* and get his own twins. The stiffness in his pants would miss the new young wife, but he'd figure another way. After all, he had lots of daughters.

"Pa, Pa, the twins're gone!"

"What?" The man sat up and brushed stems of hay from his face. His head ached, and his mouth was full of dirt. Streaks of early light shined through cracks in the barn walls, throwing stripes of yellow across the faces of two of his children. The man squinted at the distortion in front of him adding to his confusion. *The Colonel. The twins and the train at midnight.* But he didn't go; he was sure of it. "Gone? Where's they gone?"

"We don't know, Pa. They're not in the house!"

"Don' be stupid," he said, getting to his feet as the children raced away. "They can't be gone," he continued to himself. "I been here all night."

But the twins were indeed missing, and the house was in an uproar when he stepped inside. "Fetch me some water, Israel," the man said as he staggered into the kitchen.

"Pa, Joseph went for the sheriff."

"The sheriff? Go stop him right now!" He gulped the water that had been pressed into his hand. "How long did he go?"

"Just before we got you, Pa."

The family stared at the man in disbelief. They were desperate and scared and couldn't understand the delay. The man sat at the kitchen table and drank more water. His addled brain panicked at the thought of the sheriff in the house. But the Colonel had come into the man's home and stolen two of his children. *Oh, the outrage!* He knew he was complicit in the crime even though he didn't know how. But he slowly came to realize that there was nothing here to connect him to their disappearance. Nothing anywhere really. There might have been witnesses to his conversation with the Colonel, but they could have been talking about anything. Let the sheriff come. Let him be the one to ask the questions. Who else would want Siamese twin babies but a circus?

The agitated children surrounded him in their distress. "Who should go, Pa?"

"Never mind, never mind. Fix me somethin' to eat."

5

Nothing good ever happened in John's life, so he was surprised when he'd been given the badge. It was quite a promotion from sweeping jail cells and emptying shit buckets. When he pinned the heavy badge through his work shirt, it ripped a hole in the thin fabric and the five-pointed star fell to the floor. His chest still hurt where the pin punctured his skin when the sheriff poked it through to his long johns on the second try. He was given an old cap and ball revolver that he stuck in his pants since he had no holster. The rope he used for a belt dug into his skin where he tied it tight to keep the heavy pistol from pulling down his pants. It had misfired three of the five times he shot it, and when he took it apart to clean it, he couldn't get it back together again. Sheriff Becker had laughed at him.

It was his first week on the job, the sheriff was preparing to leave town, and he was nervous. *A kidnapping!* Young John Walker was far from prepared to deal with such a serious crime. He caught up the sheriff's mare, which would have been impossible had she not already been in a stall. "How come you had your baby and stayed so fat?" he asked the old bay horse. The month-old colt whinnied and stomped at her side, not happy at this intrusion into its new life. The saddle he'd been left to use had a broken horn and was missing a stirrup. He let out the cinch to the last hole then snugged it against the mare's distended girth. She kicked out at him as he walked behind her, but he was well out of the way, having anticipated her reaction. He slapped her on the butt, and she laid back her ears and reached out to bite him. It was embarrassing to have to ride out with the mare and her foal, but walking would have been worse. John would be a pitiful sight when he arrived at the Chatham place with all its pretty girls.

The door opened as he approached, hat in shaking hand. Four young faces and one beautiful young woman stared at him as he walked toward them.

"John, what are you doing here?"

"Your little brother came and said there's been a kidnapping."

"We sent him for the sheriff."

"Yes, ma'am, but the sheriff can't come. I'm the new deputy."

"Oh my, Pa's not going to like this."

"Yes, ma'am, I figured that."

Zelda Chatham knew John Walker from school. He was two years older than her when he finished eighth grade, his last year in Spanish Fork's one-room schoolhouse. They'd had a crush on each other, as much as that was possible for children in those days—their exchanged furtive glances often prompting shy blushing smiles. This was the first time either had ever spoken to the other.

"Well, come in," Zelda said. "Let's get started."

6

Seemingly a difficult place to pull off a kidnapping, the room had no direct access to the outside. The space was small considering its use. Not only was it the kitchen but also the dining room and bedroom for the youngest children. It was the original log cabin the man and his wife built and had been added to on all four sides as the family grew. It was the heart of their community where there was warmth and constant activity. The three oldest girls slept in the upstairs loft, and the four oldest boys had moved into the woodshed two years ago. Even though it was hard to justify, the man kept a room for himself.

"Whozzat?" the man spoke with a mouth full of bread and cheese then picked up the bowl that contained the gruel he'd just finished and slurped down the remaining milk.

"Pa, this is Deputy John Walker," Zelda said, speaking with as much confidence as she could muster. "The sheriff's out of town, and the deputy's here to help find the babies."

The man stared at them in disbelief. "You get your ass outta hea' boy and come back with the sheriff. Is that train gone yet?"

"The train, sir?"

"The circus train, you idiot. Who else would take Simeeze twins?"

John looked at Zelda bewildered, and she responded in kind. The investigation had taken off at a rapid pace, and the investigator hadn't asked a single question yet. But Mr. Chatham had raised an interesting point. The man stood up from the kitchen table, noticing the eyes in the room had shifted from the deputy to him. Had he said too much?

"Yessir, I'll be lookin' into that. Before I leave, would you mind if I looked around a bit?"

"You do what you want," the man said, taking a softer tone. "Just get them babies back here." Then he stormed out of the room.

7

Winter 1871

The sheriff woke to the smell of decent coffee, which immediately confused him. He didn't recognize where he was and thought he might be dreaming. But there was Doc sitting on a nearby stool holding two cups of the steaming liquid. "Mornin', Walter," the older man said. "How'd you sleep?"

The sheriff swung his feet to the floor and reached out to take one of the cups. He sat quietly taking in the unfamiliar surroundings, watching the man across from him. The hot liquid coated his parched throat, and the caffeine gradually warmed his thoughts. The sheriff looked around the small room to be sure they were alone and got to the point. "I been having some trouble lately, Doc."

"I know, Walter."

"I ain't thinkin' clear. Seems like it's getting worse every day."

"Yeah, I know."

"Can you tell me what's goin' on? Is there anything you can do for me?"

The doctor looked at his friend, weighing his answer. Their occupations had brought them together years ago and had kept them close. The doctor was blunt. "It's in your head, Walter. Your brain's aging faster than it's supposed to. It's not going to get better."

The sheriff stared at the cup in his hands, slowly shaking his head. "What should I do, Doc? How much longer can I be sheriff?" A single tear rolled down his cheek. "I ain't got nothin' else."

A shaking hand reached across the short distance to the sheriff's knee and held there until the tremor subsided. "I got issues too, Walter. How'd you like this shaky hand here stichin' up your next cut?"

"Dang, Doc." The sheriff shook his head.

"Fortunately, Jeanie's been helping in this place for so long she's been better'n me at doctoring for a while. I look over her shoulder to keep her on track, but mostly she already knows what I know. I'm here, and we'll get through this. If things get too complicated, you can come live with us. We've got room and have already talked it over. Best you can do is stay busy and don't worry." He stood and put his hand on the sheriff's shoulder. "Now let's go talk to my patients."

8

Summer 1849

Zelda led John through every room of the house. They circled the building twice and stood together at the yard gate surrounded by twenty chickens and ten goats. There wasn't any mystery about how the intruders got in. There was only one entrance, which was never locked, and none of the windows had been tampered with. The paths to and from the house and around the outbuildings were well-worn with no unrecognizable footprints. With all the human and animal traffic, it was a busy place.

"Has anybody unusual been here in the last few days?" John asked.

"Not anyone we didn't know," Zelda replied.

"No one from the circus, I guess."

"I can't believe Pa said that."

"You think he knows somethin' about what happened?"

"I hope not." Zelda turned away so the deputy couldn't see the anger on her face. After the repeated sexual assaults, she knew he was capable of anything. She'd been able fight him off, but it was just a matter of time before he attacked her sisters, and she was determined to protect them. Was he capable of hurting the babies? Absolutely!

"Miss Chatham, there's not a lot to go on here. If you don't mind, I'm gonna have to take what yer pa said as the only clue I got. That train did leave in the middle of the night. I heard it. I'll go down to the depot and ask around, see if anybody's got anything to say."

"Thank you, John. Will you let me know what you find?"

"Yes, ma'am'."

"Please call me Zelda," she said, putting her hand on his arm. "Thanks for coming."

Deputy Walker blushed full red in the face, tipped his rag of a hat, and turned to leave. Walking away from the house, he touched his arm where Zelda's hand had just been and felt the fire left behind. He imagined holding that hand, and his heart jumped. It was the first time he'd had physical contact with a girl. Sufficiently distracted, he wandered too close to the old mare and got kicked in the leg. Stumbling backward, he regained his balance in time to keep from falling but not in time to stop the pistol from slipping through his belt, down his pantleg, and into the top of his boot. Taking advantage of the cover proffered by the fat old horse, he retrieved the gun with one hand, and fended off a bite from the enraged colt with the other. Feeling the fool, he looked over the mare's back toward the house to see Zelda wave, seemingly unconcerned by his predicament. Determined not to let his built-in incompetence ruin his high, he mounted the mare and hung onto her mane with both hands as she crow-hopped down the lane.

The train station was unremarkably quiet for a midweek morning. Since no rail traffic was due until tomorrow, there wasn't much for the Mid-Northern Flyer's only employee in Spanish Fork to do. Doyle Dance was repairing a section of rail fence near the loading chute when the deputy approached.

"Gimme a hand here, John."

"Dang, Doyle, what happened?"

"The goddamned circus, that's what happened. These corrals was meant for cows, not goddamned elephants. Next time I see the mayor, I'm gonna let him know what I think of his idea to invite the goddamned circus to spend a few days with us."

The two men set poles and spiked rails for the next hour then broke for lunch. Doyle stoked the fire in the stove in the depot's storeroom where he lived then retrieved a slab of bacon wrapped in burlap from a wood crate outside the building's back door. A rolled-up newspaper contained a half loaf of bread that he inspected for mold. Finding a few colorful areas that offended him, he scraped them off then used the newspaper to wipe out his frying pan. He cut the bacon into smaller pieces, threw them into the pan, and licked his fingers before wiping them on his pants.

"I heard Walter deputized you last week. How you like being a lawman so far?"

"Feels like I got a lot to learn, Doyle. The Chatham twins was kidnapped last night."

"Them Simeeze girls?"

"Yessir. I was out there this morning. You didn't maybe see anything 'spicious at the train before it left last night, did ya?"

"Hmm, I get yer drift." Doyle broke the bread into crumbs, threw them into the frying pan, and stirred them into the grease. The smell wafted through the room, and the stomachs of both men growled loudly. "I cain't say I saw anyone loadin' up a bundle of babies. I can believe that asshole colonel might put 'em in one of his sideshows to make a buck. When's Walter due back?"

"He left this morning. He's going to Mapleton first to look at a horse, then he's going home to check on his ma. I hope he's back soon."

"Talk it over with him, John. He ain't gonna like a baby kidnappin' goin' on in his town. No, sir. He ain't gonna like it one bit. When's the last time you ate?"

"Yesterday mornin'," John replied. "I believe I'll step outside and wash up in the tank."

"Don't be too long. I might eat it all," Doyle laughed. "See if you can find an apple pie while yer out there. I ain't got nothin' for dessert."

9

Winter 1871

"They're probably asleep," Doc said in a loud voice. The two men stood outside the curtain-covered doorway and smiled. The muffled sounds of fumbled bedding mixed with low laughter came to them from the small room. They entered to see the three patients lying beside one another with their eyes closed. The doctor cleared his throat, and the three pairs of eyes opened at once. He checked for fevers then spoke to each to determine that their pain levels were under control.

"Prudence, Chastity, you know Sheriff Becker." The girls nodded and smiled in acknowledgment. "Sheriff, this boy's name is Samuel Shines."

"Girls, it's good to see you again," the sheriff said with a nod to each. "Son, I'm glad to know you." He extended his hand toward the boy then withdrew it at the sight of the bandages. "I'd like to interview each of you individually, if you feel up to it."

At that, the twins giggled and said, "Sir, I don't think that will be possible."

The sheriff blushed and replied, "Well, yes, I understand that. I meant you two girls separate from young Samuel." He glanced at the doctor. "Can the boy be moved to another room?"

"Yes, of course," he said, stroking his long mustache. "His feet were not injured. There is a burn on his ankle."

"Nothing below his belt was harmed," the twins added laughing. "We hope this doesn't take too long, don't we, Samuel?"

The boy sat on the edge of the bed, pulled a white cotton gown over his head, and gave the twins a stern look. Then he stood with his back to the men and walked sideways from the room.

Barely able to contain their amusement, the girls declared, "Pull up a chair, sheriff. You're next."

"I'll be right back, Walter," the doctor said, following the boy out. He, too, caught up in the levity of the moment.

The twins sat up in bed and let the sheets fall to their waists, exposing four perfectly shaped breasts. They did this together, the movement coming from the same thought. Though their bodies functioned independently, they were so in tune that many things they did and said were synchronized. Their senses took in information individually, but it was processed collectively in their brains. Except when in conversation with each other, they often spoke in unison. To be in their presence was an extraordinary experience, and it overwhelmed most people.

The sheriff, who had known of them longer than anyone in Alamo, was no exception. Failing to react with the expected rapture at the sight of their combined naked beauty, his gasp sucked the tobacco from his cheek into his windpipe, cutting off his breath. He staggered sideways, ricocheting off the wall and falling to the floor. The combined scream from the twins brought the doctor who quickly accessed the situation and jerked the sheriff to his feet with a bear hug from behind. The girls winced as the tobacco plug sailed through air, striking the wall, then covered their faces to hide their mirth.

"For God's sakes, will you two cover yerselves? This old man is not up for your shenanigans."

"Doc, we love this old man and would do nothing to harm him," Prudence said.

"Sir, we are whores," Chastity continued. "Baring our breasts is far down on our list of shenanigans, but we apologize to you and your friend. He's our friend too, you know."

Walter Becker coughed twice, took a few shaky steps to a chair, then carried it across the room. He pulled his handkerchief from his pocket then sat in the chair and bent to collect the tobacco from the floor. "Sorry. That was embarrassing," he said, putting the kerchief in his pocket. "I'll be saving this for later."

There was a momentary silence until the sheriff turned around with a smirk on his face. The doctor chuckled as he left the room to tend to the boy, who was watching from the doorway. The twins laughed in a rollicking response. "Don't bother saving any for us."

The sheriff brought the chair to the bedside and stared at the girls. "I been scared a few times in my life, but when I saw you two on the balcony of that burning building, I damn near died. This whole thing bothers me more'n I can say. I'll appreciate it if you don't say nothin', but it looks like Charlie and Mabel was murdered. They was killed before they was burned. Tell me what happened that day, ever bit."

The girls started to cry. "Why would anyone kill Charlie and Mabel?"

"I don't know." The sheriff shook his head. "But I'm gonna find out."

Doc came back into the room and sat in a corner to witness the conversation as planned. He leaned against the wall to steady himself then retrieved his pipe and tobacco pouch. He searched his pockets for a match and scratched it to life on the coarse boards of the floor. The flame danced in his fingers until he pressed his hand against the wall and brought his face close enough to ignite the coarse leaves. He puffed, the smoke billowed, and he inhaled a cloud. The fire in his lungs was almost more than he could stand, but he held it in for a full second then gasped as he let it out. He didn't like the light-headedness that accompanied the treatment, but the smoke temporarily calmed the tremors. Jeanie could not tolerate this assault to their dedicated health regime, but he would accept whatever damage he was doing to his lungs for the relief to the walking earthquake he'd become.

The sheriff spent the next hour listening to the twins describe what to them had been an ordinary day. They slept late as usual, bathed, dressed, and ate breakfast at noon. Their early afternoon walk through town was unremarkable, except that it was shorter than normal because of the heavy snowfall. After returning to the Star, with little else to do, they helped in the kitchen for a couple hours. Back in their room by 4:00, they prepared for the evening. Their song and dance performance lasted from 6:00 to 7:00, and they met their first customer at 7:30. They entertained ten men that night and were done around 2:30 in the morning. Seven were regulars, and three new. There were no problems with any of them.

"When did you first realize something was wrong?"

"The key," Prudence said.

"Yes," Chastity added. "The key to our room was missing from the door lock when we came back upstairs for the night. We lock it when we have a customer, and we lock it whenever we leave. As far as we know, Charlie had the only other key. We went back to the stairway and called out to him to let him know it was gone, and he said he'd come up and lock our door before he went to bed. He said we'd find the key in the morning. He and Mabel were cleaning up."

"A little while later, we heard the door lock. We called out good night, but Charlie never responded," Prudence said.

"Which he would have done," Chastity added. "He would have said good night."

"What about the door to the balcony?" the sheriff asked.

"It locked with a latch from the inside. There was no key," they said together.

"It was a silly lock," Prudence continued. "There was a window in the door, so if anyone wanted to get in, all they had to do was break the glass and reach in to open it."

"And the balcony reached across to the room next to yours?" asked the sheriff.

"Yes," they answered.

"And that's how young Samuel got to you, by opening the door to the balcony from that room?"

"That's right."

"Hmm, okay." He turned to look at the doctor and shrugged, then looked back to the women. "How do you feel?"

"Better," they said.

"What will you do now?"

"We don't know. We have some money in the bank, but everything we owned is gone."

"Jeanie wants them to stay with us until they figure things out. There's no hurry," Doc said.

"First we'll need to make ourselves new clothes."

"Yes, yes." The sheriff stood. "Do you know why anyone would want to hurt you?"

"No!" they chimed together. "We're adorable, don't you think?"

"Indeed I do," said the sheriff.

"Our customers love us," Chastity enthusiastically replied.

"We don't let them go unless they're satisfied," Prudence added.

"Okay, thank you both. I'll keep Samuel busy for a while, so you can get some rest."

There was laughter in the room as Walter Becker stood, approached the doctor, and helped him stand. They entered the hallway, pulled the curtain closed, and walked the short distance to the building's small office. Reaching into the bottom drawer of his desk, Doc retrieved his whiskey bottle and two glasses. They leaned back in their chairs and sighed, each sizing up the brown liquid before taking a sip. The doctor spilled some on his shirt.

"Better keep this place locked up, Doc. I'll be damned if I know why, but I think those girls were the target of that fire."

"I will. Maybe you should continue to sleep here for a while."

"Yeah, that's a good idea. Delbert can stay at the jail. All we got there is the Grimes brothers, and they ain't hardly criminals. They just got nowhere else to go." The sheriff drained his glass. "Doc, you got paper and pencil I can use? Ain't no use in askin' questions if I cain't remember the answers. You got enough to do without followin' me around bein' my memory."

The doctor slid the writing materials across the desk as they both stood. "Jeanie is making us all something to eat. I'm going to go give her a hand. We'll be back shortly," he said.

"Okay, Frank, thanks. Thanks for everything."

10

The sheriff entered Samuel's room and pulled a chair close to the bed. He straightened the paper on the clipboard he'd been given, pulled out his pocketknife, and whittled a point on the pencil. He spoke slowly while he worked.

"That was a brave thing you done the other night. Put the rest of the men in this town to shame. I'd like to think if I was twenty years younger, I'd a been in there with you, but I wasn't. Those girls mean a lot to this town. Some folks wouldn't say so, but it's true." The sheriff touched the point of the pencil to his tongue. "Where you from, son?"

The boy answered the sheriff's questions in brief segments, not appearing to hold anything back but not offering more than asked. He was unemotional, calm, and matter-of-fact. *Overly mature for a fifteen-year-old boy*, the sheriff thought, knowing that was not uncommon in this part of the country. He was born to a prostitute in St. Louis and lived with her in a bordello, working for his keep until she died last year. From there, he was eventually hired on as a swamper on a steamboat from St. Louis to Ft. Benton. The walk to Alamo had taken him three weeks.

The sheriff slowed the boy down when he began to describe the interior of the Blazing Star. Writing as fast as he could, he sensed another presence and turned to see the doctor standing in the doorway behind him. Relieved, he looked at the scratch he'd produced and folded the paper and put it in his pocket. Unconsciously, he reached into another pocket for his handkerchief, retrieved his tobacco plug, and packed it against the inside of his cheek.

36

Unlike his reticence to speak of himself, the boy covered the details of the fire and his rescue of the twins without prompting from the two men. He spoke uninterrupted for half an hour, leaving the men dumbstruck and staring. A tap on the doorjamb broke the tension, and the men exhaled.

"Lunch is here," Jeanie said. "If you two will serve the girls, I'll change Samuel's dressings before he eats. The trays are in the office. Yours is there too."

"Thank you, dear. We'll do it," the doctor replied.

The two men thanked Samuel then left to attend to their chore.

They met Jeanie in the short hallway. "Care to join us?" the doctor asked. "There's a heck of a story to hear."

"No, thank you. I've got bandages to wash," she said.

She kissed her husband on the cheek, and he patted her behind as they passed.

"Don't know what I'd do without her," he said.

"You're a lucky man," the sheriff said then thought of his own wife and the too-short time they'd had together. Though he'd never been a religious man, he held onto the belief—the possibility—that he might see her again. He believed knowing her had made him a better lawman. That such a woman had loved him bolstered his self-confidence and gave him the courage to go into situations where common sense might have held him back. He missed her so much.

They settled into chairs at the desk and leaned forward to inhale the aromas from the plates before them. The doctor brought out the whiskey bottle and shakily splashed the amber liquid toward a glass.

"Here, let me do that," said his friend, reaching over to take the bottle. "Aren't we just a pair to draw to?"

"If we were attached, we could be Siamese twin old men!"

"With a murderer to catch."

Walter Becker held up his glass, while the doctor picked up his with both hands, getting most of the drink to his mouth.

11

Summer 1849

Within an hour of his lunch at the train depot, young John was sitting in the outhouse behind the jail in gastronomic distress. Doyle's rich fare was far beyond what the deputy's empty stomach could tolerate. Using his shirttail to dry his hands and face after washing up at the stock tank, he'd looked up to see a man a hundred yards beyond the railroad tracks walking through the cottonwoods in the creek bottom. He stepped back into the shadow of the outhouse and watched the dark figure, pretty sure he was looking at old man Chatham.

Two days later, his head was still crowded with thoughts of missing babies and the beautiful Zelda as he moseyed across the street to Heaven's Café. He checked his pockets at the door and stared at the single quarter he held in his palm. Head spinning, he made his way to his favorite table in a back corner prepared to spend it all. A teenage girl in a two-tone blue dress with matching bonnet arrived immediately. She smiled and handed him a piece of paper with the day's specials, handwritten and priced in descending order. The deputy scanned the menu and made a show of letting his eyes linger at the top of the page, knowing he'd be ordering from the bottom.

Though his formal education had been limited, he took advantage of every opportunity to further it on his own. He read everything that came his way—including wanted posters, newspapers, menus (of course)—and kept a list of words he couldn't define in his room. Opportunities to cipher were everywhere, including making change, calculating mileage, and tracking the days of the month on his calendar. He hoped to someday have a pocket watch. "I'll just have the pea soup with bread and butter, please." At twenty cents, he'd be able to leave the girl a nickel and still temper the anger in his stomach.

"Would you like something to drink? The buttermilk is fresh and cold." Looking back at the menu in his hand, he realized he could afford the extra five cents but, in a proud moment, said, "No, thank you. This'll be good."

Not an attractive girl, the waitress was of an age where she should have been married by now, but there were many females in her family, and she hadn't fared well against the competition. Her father had been trying to negotiate a trade with other church elders, but the only offers he'd gotten so far were for maidens even harder to look at than his own. His latest negotiation for a middle-aged mule had stalled. Feigning disappointment, the girl made a slight curtsy, smiled, and left.

No sooner had she turned than John jumped from his seat and dashed out the back door to the privy. *Dang, Doyle, you're killin' me here,* he thought as he paged through a catalog of sewing notions. He'd not recovered from Doyle's lunch two days ago. Still dizzy, he left the tiny building and went to the well pump for a drink and to clean up.

"Ma'am, I didn't order these." The deputy stared at the hard-boiled egg and tall glass of buttery milk that had been added to his supper.

"Well, they were leftover from lunch, and I thought rather than throw them out, you might enjoy them. There's no charge."

"Ma'am, I can come by later and pay you."

"That won't be necessary." She curtsied and blushed. "My name's Sarah," she said and walked away. Glancing toward the kitchen, he saw several bonneted heads watching him, heard them giggle then disappear. He salivated before the feast, forcing himself to eat slowly, savoring the wonderful flavors. As he ate, he drifted to the new experience of female attention and wondered what was going on. *Must be the badge,* he thought, glancing down at it hanging dangerously close to the soup bowl. Tomorrow he'd wear his other shirt, the green plaid, the one he saved for special occasions. He wished he had a better hat.

Sheriff Walter Becker stood and walked around the corner to look at his mother asleep on a straw mattress in a cell. Somehow both she and the old buggy had survived the trip on the rocky trail through the narrow red rock canyon. It had been his intention to surprise her on her eightieth birthday, but when he arrived at the old log house, neither she nor his older brother, Norbert, were there. Standing outside, he heard a raspy chopping sound and walked around the house to see a figure digging in the family cemetery a hundred yards distant. *Dang it, Ma. Couldn't you wait to die till I got here?* Head down, he followed the family's path of sorrow until he was close enough to see it was her who was waist-deep in the hole.

"Ma, what're you doin'?"

"What's it look like I'm doin'? I'm diggin' a grave."

"I thought it was Norbert diggin' that hole."

"Shoulda been Norbert. It's not my intention to be the last person alive in this family."

"Never been any doubt you'd outlive us all, Ma. Where is he?"

"He's in the barn with a gunnysack over his head so the magpies don't get his eyes ate before I get him in the ground."

"What happened?"

"I dunno. I found him there this mornin'." Then she started to cry.

"Come on, Ma. I'll finish that. Let's get you home."

The sheriff half-carried the old woman down the rise of the hill. The door to the house was open, it was cold inside, and there was a layer of red dust on everything. Walter guided her to bed and pulled three quilts over her thin body. "Ma, you stay here. I'll be back in a minute."

Bess the cow, Hammy the pig, and six chickens called to him as he walked the short distance to the barn. Everybody was hungry here. "Hold on, hold on," he spoke in a steady voice. "I'll get to y'all. I gotta have a look around first." The animals were calmed by his presence; the intensity of their anticipation was palpable. Something was missing—somebody was missing. The biggest appetite with the biggest voice was not in the barn. Norbert's horse, Jupiter, was gone. Walter walked to the stall of the big old horse, opened the half gate, and flushed half a dozen magpies out of the barn and into the paddock. He knelt next to the stiff, cold body of his brother and removed the bloody gunnysack from his head. The sheriff stood and took in the small space then followed the blood track outside into the paddock. A steel T-post lay in the dirt at the end of the trail, traces of blood and hair caught in its rough edges. He brought it back inside and placed it in the corner of the stall. *Not surprisingly*, he thought, *Jupiter's saddle and tack were gone, but nothing else was amiss.*

He pitched hay to the cow, grained the pig and chickens, then looked through the other outbuildings and around the barnyard but found nothing out of place. Before going back to the house, he gathered half a dozen eggs and retrieved a variety of items from the root cellar for them to eat. He built a fire in the cookstove, brought in three buckets of water from the well, and put them on its large surface. On a well-stocked herb shelf, he found rose hips, nettles, and chamomile to add to the tea pot and let it steep. When it was ready, he took a cup to his mother and sat her up in bed to drink it.

"Ma, tell me what happened to Norbert."

"Did you bury him?"

"No, Ma. He's wrapped in a tarp and lying on the hay wagon in the barn."

"He was in Jupiter's stall. He had a bloody lump on his head, and I couldn't wake him up."

"When was this?"

"I think it must have been yesterday," she said, sipping the tea. "Or maybe the day before. I put a gunnysack on his head…"

"Yeah, Ma, you told me. To keep the magpies off his eyes."

"Oh dear," she said in a small voice and again began to cry. "I've got to pee."

The sheriff leaned over to kiss her cheek, touching her hair, which was matted and full of the red dust that covered everything in the house. The smell of piss and shit was strong on her clothes.

"Come on, let's get you to the outhouse, then I'll pour you a nice warm bath."

After his mother was bathed and fed, Walter changed her bedding and tasked her with packing clothes and anything else she'd need for a couple-week stay in Spanish Fork. He was under no illusion that she'd ever be coming back here but did not want to have that conversation tonight. The last two hours before dark, he spent outside searching for anything unusual. He covered the obvious places, the trails into and around the property, even the secret places where they'd played as boys. Any tracks had been blown over. There was no sign of anything strange anywhere.

In the morning, he spent an hour cutting and whittling down an old shovel handle to replace a broken spoke on the family buggy. Jupiter had been a big horse, and his harness required several holes punched to size it down for Freckles, the sheriff's gelding.

"Here, Ma, let's get your coat and hat on. I already got your bag."

"What about Norbert? I gotta finish digging the grave."

"It's done. He's in the back of the buggy. We're gonna bury him, then I'm taking you to town."

"Did you build him a casket?"

"No, Ma. He's wrapped in the quilt you made for him. It's what he'd want. I'll have a marker made, and we'll bring it back and set it."

They drove the buggy up the hill to the Becker family cemetery, and together they laid Norbert near his father and his four brothers and sisters and covered him up. Mrs. Becker sobbed quietly, and Walter, not a religious man, failed to offer a prayer. He spoke of Norbert's strength and steadfastness but failed to mention his lack of enthusiasm and laziness. He didn't say that as a child, Norbert refused to go back to school after two years or that he'd never made any attempt to find a wife, learn a skill, or try to read a book. Their mother had felt an obligation to stay on the farm to look after him after the rest of the family was gone. A naturally curious woman, she'd longed to move to Spanish Fork when Walter became sheriff, where she might have found a job. She'd grown weary of carving red dirt from beneath her fingernails years ago and knew she had little time left to harvest the life's joy that had eluded her. Sitting sideways next to Walter as they drove away, she watched her home until it disappeared, her sad bundle of possessions in the wagon bed behind them. They stopped at the Jordan place, where the sheriff inquired about any recent sightings of a rider on Jupiter and received a negative response. Mrs. Jordan could barely contain her joy when he told her to retrieve the cow, pig, and chickens for their own in exchange for keeping an eye on the Becker Ranch. The sheriff wrote out a bill of sale to the desperately poor family of ten and suspected Hammy might not live through the night. *So be it…*

12

Sheriff Becker was at the jail when the deputy returned from the café. After hearing John's story, he sized up his deputy and wondered if he was up to the task he had in mind for him. "When did this happen?"

"Two days ago."

"And you think he was headed to Salt Lake to get those little girls?"

"Well, sir, his reaction to the news that they was gone was not sorrow. He wanted to know if the circus train had left. Then he asked out loud, 'Who else would take Simeeze twins?'"

"Who's in charge out there?" the sheriff asked.

"Well, sir, Zelda is the oldest of the daughters. None of the older boys was home."

"Okay, tomorrow I want you on the train to Salt Lake, and you snoop around that circus and find out where those twins are. Don't get caught, and don't let Chatham see you if he's up there. My brother's been murdered, and his white horse stolen. The timing would be about right. The horse will be pink from the red dirt he's lived on all his life—unless the son of a bitch who took him gives him a bath. I doubt Chatham was plannin' to walk to Salt Lake City, and our place is on the way. Send me a telegram if you see him or the horse or can find out anything about those babies. Now go out and tell that Zelda what you're gonna do and tell her to keep her mouth shut about it. Ask if her pa said anything before he left." The sheriff pulled his wallet from his hip pocket and took out three ten-dollar bills. "Here's twenty dollars for expenses and ten dollars against your first month's wages. Buy yerself some new clothes."

"Sheriff, can I take your horse? That mare ain't fit to ride."

"Get the clothes first. The horse just had a long walk."

Young John looked in the mirror of the Good Shepard general store and barely recognized himself. "I reckon these clothes will last me the rest of my life," he said proudly.

Mr. Shepard smiled, admiring the result. "That might depend on if you're done growing. Someday you might gain a pound and won't look like a fence post."

"Yes, sir," the deputy said, turning sideways, hoping to get a look at his profile. "I like this hat, but it might be too tight." He gave it a sideways tilt, testing the rakish result.

"It'll stretch out. You get anything bigger, your ears will become permanently folded down. You don't want to look like a hound dog, do you?"

"No, sir." He had spent twice the amount he'd been allotted, but Shepard let him put the balance on account, pleased at the boy's transformation.

The sheriff walked out of the cell where his mother slept and addressed the man standing at the door, "What can I do for you?"

"What do you think?" said his deputy with a mile-wide grin.

"I'll be goddamned! Ain't you just a dude!" The sheriff laughed for the first time in days. "Don't tell me you got all that for ten bucks."

"No, sir. Mr. Shepard said I could pay him later. I sure hope I can keep this job."

"Well, we'll see how you do on your assignment. Now go out and talk to that girl."

13

Well-dressed and riding a good horse, Deputy Walker was brimming with self-confidence when he dismounted at the Chatham place. He sidestepped a pile of manure, opened the gate, and sauntered toward the house.

"John, is that you?"

"Yes, ma'am," the deputy said, unable to hold back a smile. "I got some new clothes."

"Why, yes, you did. You look very handsome. And please call me Zelda."

"Zelda." He removed his hat and blushed. "Is yer pa around?"

"No, he's not." She looked down at her hands and shook her head. "He left after you did and didn't say where he was going."

"I saw a man that looked like him walking north along the tracks a couple mornings ago. Do you think it coulda been him goin' after the circus?"

"Yes, I do." There was anger in her voice. "He doesn't care a lick about the twins. I doubt that he's ever touched them, which is probably good. But he's furious that they're taken. If he finds them, he won't bring them home, but he'll exact his revenge on the kidnapper."

"Zelda, the sheriff wants me to go to Salt Lake after your sisters. He told me to come out here to tell you. He asks that you don't tell anyone I'm goin', but he wants you to know."

"What are you going to do when you get there?"

"I guess it'll depend on what I see. I'm supposed to send him a telegram. The sheriff's pretty mad."

"If you find them, you tell the sheriff to come here and tell me. I'll go get them. He's not near as mad as I am."

"I will. I'll tell him for sure."

"Oh, John."

"Yes, Zelda?"

"You do look very nice."

14

The sheriff loaned him a coat and tie (the coat hung on him like a tent), a holster for his pistol, and advised him to keep his badge pinned inside the coat where it wouldn't be seen. After securing his seat, Deputy Walker stepped off the train to help a woman with seven children load baggage while she attempted to herd her herd into their coach. Fortunately, it was not the one he was riding in. It was his first train ride, and he was beyond excited. Once they got underway, the noise and smells of the giant machine melded with its rocking motion to complete the physical experience. He smiled and waved at three boys who ran alongside trying to keep up as the familiar landscape slowly passed. Soon the scenery was new, and he removed his hat so he could keep his face close to the window.

"Excuse me, is this seat taken?"

"Uh, no." The deputy reached over to take his hat from the empty seat next to him without turning his head. A minute later, he felt an elbow poke him in the ribs.

"Aren't you going to say hello?"

"Zelda?"

"Yes, it's Zelda. Yesterday I thought you fancied me."

"Why, yes, I do. I mean, what are you doing here?"

"I'm going to Salt Lake with you to get my baby sisters. Are you surprised?"

"Well, yeah," he said and turned his head to the back of the car, then to the front. Several passengers were watching them.

"Don't worry, John. We don't care what anybody thinks. This is important."

"Yes, ma'am. I know it is, but…"

"Here, put this on." She opened her bag, took out a small velvet pouch, pulled a drawstring, and poured two gold bands into her palm. Putting the smaller of them on her left ring finger, she said, "Give me your hand. No, the other one. These were my parents'. Pa never wore his, and mom doesn't need hers anymore." She slipped the ring on his finger and smiled at the perfect fit. "When we get to Salt Lake, we'll pretend we're married. No one will know us. We'll stay in a hotel room, and I'll sleep on the couch." She laughed. "You better close your mouth, John, or a bug will fly in it."

The deputy's shock was complete. He stared at the young woman as if for the first time, dumbstruck by her beauty. Her dark-blue dress accentuated an hourglass figure, modestly concealed beneath a gray-and-black waistcoat. She pulled back the veil of her hat and leaned forward to flash him with long lashes over bright blue eyes. Dark-brown hair neatly pinned above her neck, she smelled like a rose garden. She smiled when he glanced down to be sure his hat covered his enthusiasm.

"The hat was my mom's," she said, touching it lightly. "She made it from turkey feathers. I made everything else, except the shoes. They were mom's too.

"You're amazing," he said, shaking his head. "I don't know what to say."

"Why, thank you, my pretend husband." She laughed again. "Won't this be an adventure!"

15

Winter 1871

"Sheriff, sheriff, wake up. He's here!"

"What? Who's here?"

"The horseman. I smell his tobacco."

"What're you talking about?"

"From the night of the fire."

"Tobacco?"

"Yeah, his pipe tobacco. I remember it. Different than Doc's. Really strong."

The sheriff sat up on his cot, and the boy sat next to him and retold the story of his arrival to town and the Blazing Star. He talked fast, trying to both wake the old man and rekindle his memory of their conversation from the day before.

"Sheriff, he's outside right now. We gotta go!"

The boy moved quickly around the small room, gathering boots and pants awkwardly with his bandaged hands. The old man moved at his own pace, getting dressed, buckling his gun belt, then following the boy to the door.

"You stay here," he said then stepped out onto the boardwalk. He stood quietly in the cold and let his eyes adjust to the night. Music was coming from saloons down the street, the sound amplified by the surrounding silence. Across the street, the ruins of the burned-out hotel were silhouetted like a misshaped tombstone against the light of a million stars. A layer of wood smoke hung low against the rooftops. He breathed in that familiar smell but turned his head toward an acrid, stronger odor. The snow crunched beneath his boots as he walked to the building's corner and looked into the alley.

"Hold on there!" he yelled to a shadow before it disappeared around the building's far end. He drew his pistol as he stepped into the darkness then broke into a slow trot at the sound of the back door crashing open. The unified screams of the twins came to him through the wall, followed by a gunshot and more screams. He grabbed the building's edge as he made the turn, but his boots slipped away, and he crashed into the snow. Crawling on his hands and knees, he made it to the opened back door and struggled to his feet. The sheriff— covered in white—stumbled inside, effecting another scream from the twins, followed by another gunshot.

"Stop shooting! It's me!" he yelled.

"Sheriff, there's a man in here."

"Shush for a goddamned minute!"

The sheriff walked to the back door, pulled it closed, then searched the rest of the building. At the opened front door, he looked up and down the street then pulled it shut. He found a lamp, lit it, and walked back to Doc's patients.

"What happened in here?" he asked.

"There was a man," the twins cried excitedly. "Samuel shot him!"

"He's not hit," the boy said.

"Where'd you get the gun?"

"From my poke."

"What else you got in there?" The sheriff paused, wondering where the question came from.

"Nothin' much." Samuel watched him in the dim light.

"Did you get a look at this man?"

"Yes!" the girls exclaimed excitedly. "He was huge!"

"I did," the boy replied.

"Was it the man from the night of the fire?" The sheriff went to the table and adjusted the flame in the lamp.

"Yessir."

"What'd he do in here?"

"He tried to kill us!" the twins cried in unison then insisted. "Samuel shot him."

"I just wanted him to keep movin'. There'll be a hole in the ceiling. I'll patch it in the mornin'."

The sheriff wandered back and forth the length of the building. "He won't be back tonight. Y'all calm down and get some rest. We'll figure this out. I'll be right here."

He sat at the table, laid his head down, and fell asleep.

16

"Jesus H. Christ, Walter, what happened in here last night?"

The sheriff pushed up from the table and groaned, unable to straighten his head.

"Hold it right there." The doctor moved in behind him, placing both hands on his shoulders, then gently massaged his friend's neck until he heard a sigh of relief.

"Thanks, Doc. I gotta remember not to sleep like that. Seems like we had a mess in here last night. Let's get the boy to tell us, then I'm goin' to get Delbert, and we'll go over it all again." He looked to the front then the back of the building and added, "I'll send the Grimes brothers down to fix these doors."

The sheriff stepped out into the cold morning, buttoned his coat to the top, and pulled his hat down to cover the tips of his ears. He retraced his movements from last night down the alley and back, shaking his head. "I gotta get this guy," he mumbled as he shuffled off toward the jail.

Smoke was pouring from the jailhouse chimney as he approached, and the smell of fresh coffee greeted him when he opened the door. "Mornin', sheriff," said the voices, not quite in unison.

"Mornin', boys," he said, stepping to the wall to get his cup off its hook. He sat at his desk, leaned back, and slurped some coffee before removing his wallet and pulling out two dollar bills.

"I want you boys to stop at the café and get some breakfast," he said, looking at the Grimes brothers. He handed each a dollar and continued, "After you eat, go to Doc's and see what it takes to fix both the front and back doors. They been broke down. I want new locks on both. Get what you need at Miller's and bill it to me. Delbert, you come with me. We got a fresh crime to investigate. If we hurry, we can still get breakfast from Jeanie." He opened the top drawer, pulled out his notes and a pencil, and stuffed them in a used but still usable large envelope. "Lock the door behind us, old son. We got us a snake in the grass."

They arrived at Doc's in time for breakfast in the office, while Jeanie and the twins cut and sewed fabric for dresses in the back. Samuel described the previous night's events again, leaving the men with the consensus opinion that the strong-smelling pipe tobacco was their best clue to the identity of the arsonist-murderer. The obvious flaw with this evidence they knew was that the suspect could quit smoking his pipe, and they would have nothing.

"How long has it been since the fire?" The sheriff put down his pencil and looked around the room.

"Five days tonight," Doc said. "Today's Wednesday."

The sheriff did the arithmetic on his fingers under the desk.

"Delbert, go to the livery and both hotels and ask about who's new in town since Saturday. Ask about a strong pipe tobacco. Samuel, you remember if the rider you saw that night had his bedroll on his horse?"

The boy thought a moment and said, "Yessir. I think he did."

"Okay, let's say he just got to town that night. Might be wrong, but we gotta start somewhere." He looked at the boy. "You think you can leave those girls long enough to do some detective work with Delbert?"

The boy blushed and said, "Yessir, I can try." They all laughed.

"I'm not sure I could do it if I was you," the sheriff said. "Take your nose along. You can be our bloodhound. We gotta find this sons-a-bitch."

17

Summer 1849

The conversation during the first couple hours of the train ride north was one-sided. Zelda chatted away about life on the Chatham farm, giving John more information than he needed to know or would have ever imagined to ask about. She mentioned all her siblings by name, describing each in detail, clearly missing them already. Sobbing uncontrollably, she talked about her mother. A hardworking, intelligent woman, she'd raised her children to be curious about everything. She'd scoured the community for books to borrow or trade for, and she read to them, and they read to one another. Mrs. Chatham and Lupita Hernandez, whose family lived and worked on the many-acred apple farm adjacent to their property, taught each other's children to speak the other's language. When her husband ordered his wife to cease, she refused. "We live in Spanish Fork! Our children shall speak Spanish!" she'd said.

Deputy Walker and Zelda arrived in Salt Lake City late in the afternoon and booked a room at the Depot Hotel, three blocks from the train station. The young desk clerk offered a paternal smile when they registered, accepting them as the young married couple they appeared to be. Having never seen a hotel room before, John nervously climbed the stairs not knowing what to expect. Zelda unlocked the door and held it for him as he carried their bags inside. Unable to speak, he scanned the room for the couch that wasn't there, having decided earlier that she would have the bed no matter what. He would sleep on the floor. His bedroll, a blanket tied closed with a rope, held his green shirt, shaving kit, toothbrush, and a pair of socks that left more toes exposed than covered. His original plan was to search out a livery and offer the keeper a quarter to share a stall with a gentle horse. To instead be sharing a hotel room with a beautiful girl was far beyond anything he could have imagined. Zelda was better prepared. She opened a carpetbag and removed a feast of fried chicken, bread, cheese, carrots, and a cherry pie. While they ate, she told him of the family meeting she'd held the night before. "Pa doesn't know we keep money from him. He's so drunk most of the time, we could dress like Indians and speak French, and he wouldn't know the difference. My four oldest brothers have good farm jobs, and my sisters and I sell vegetables and the clothes we make. They all agreed that I go with you to get the babies and that we would pay expenses. When we find them, you will protect us and bring us all home."

John sat up straight, feeling the weight of this responsibility. He glanced at his pistol on a table in a corner and wished he'd fired it a few more times. This *adventure*, as Zelda described it, had become considerably more complicated from where it had begun. He turned back to see the girl looking at him. His face flushed red, and she reached forward and held his hand. "Where shall we start, John?"

The hand that held his was feminine yet strong. He turned it over and saw callouses and a cut on the right index finger. There was no doubt that this girl worked as hard as any man and carried more confidence than most. "I suppose we should find the circus and look around," he said, not ready to let go of the hand. "But I'll bet they keep the twins well-hid. Zelda, the sheriff's brother was killed and his horse stole a couple days ago. I won't say your dad was involved, but the time would have been right, and he would have passed right near the sheriff's family ranch on his way north."

"Oh my Lord, John," Zelda gasped and covered her face with her hands. "He did it. I know he did."

"Well, it does give us something else to look for. The horse was big and pink. Can't be too many of them around."

"The horse is pink?" She laughed.

"White horse and red dirt." He smiled. It was the first time he'd heard her laugh; and it, like everything else about her, was charming. "We can check the stables on the way."

"I agree," she replied. "Let's go."

Arm through his, she leaned in to the deputy as they walked out of the hotel and onto Front Avenue. Lamplighters on both sides of the street worked against the coming darkness amid passersby on their way home from work. Horse-drawn wagons and buggies added to the commotion, the dust cloud trapped between buildings taller than either had ever seen. Zelda pulled the sheer veil of her hat down to cover her face. "My pa could be anywhere. We should watch everyone," she said. "He won't be expecting us, and I doubt he would even recognize you, especially in those clothes." She lifted the veil so he could see her smile. "Let's look for a quieter street."

They turned back toward the train tracks and blended into a considerable stream of folks flowing toward the fairgrounds. While this pedestrian traffic produced less dust, it was no less raucous, as families with enthusiastic children paraded toward the wonders of the P&S Circus. They passed two stables where John checked for any horse matching Jupiter's description. A worker stacking hay bales told them he'd seen a rider on such an animal the previous morning.

"If we find the horse, the murderer can't be far behind," Zelda said.

"And the murderer is in pursuit of our kidnapper. We may need some help," John responded.

A dozen colorful circus railcars sat on a track siding that ran the considerable length of the fairgrounds. Several breaks between the cars allowed for a continuous flow of workers, trainers, and animals from the performance and exhibit area to the holding pens and housing tents on the opposite side of the tracks. Delightful food aromas and the rank smells of animal waste and machinery produced a rich bouquet that was both savory and repulsive. Breaking away from a line of spectators that angled toward an enormous canvas tent, they backed into a space between several stacked wooden barrels to watch the activity unnoticed.

"Where do we begin?" Zelda asked.

"I don't know. There's so much to see," John responded, noticing that she was holding his hand. "Your pa must have made a deal with someone at the circus. The Colonel hisself would be my guess. Since he left town the day after the circus, makes me think the Colonel double-crossed him and stole your sisters in the night."

"That makes sense," Zelda said. "Would the Colonel keep them in the train after he got here?"

"Not if he thought it would be searched. Not if he thought the law would ever be after him." Deputy Walker looked into her eyes, feeling the weight on his shoulders.

"Or if the twins' kin would follow after him," she said and squeezed his hand. "That would be us."

"And yer pa."

"Yes, the Colonel might expect him, but he likely won't expect us. Let's look around."

They walked past the big top, games, and food booths and came to a stop in front of an archway that read FREAKS OF THE WORLD. They walked beneath the gaudily painted sign and entered a circular group of tents. A barker stood before each, wearing a straw hat, waving a cane, and touting the wonders of the creatures inside.

THREE-LEGGED MAN!

MERMAID!

TWO-HEADED CALF!

ELEPHANT GIRL!

WORLD'S FATTEST MIDGET!

"Oh my," Zelda gasped and started to cry. "Could they be here?"

"I don't think so," John said. "Not yet."

"It's awful."

They looked back across the crowd to the Big Top where a barker stood on a large box with a megaphone, announcing the many fascinations of the show that was about to begin. Two clowns stood near the tent's opening, one juggling large knives, the other taking tickets. An emaciated tiger lay in a cage next to them, panting heavily, eyes closed. A young father standing close by lifted his son to see the big cat, prompting one of the clowns to lean toward the cage and growl loudly while poking the animal with an unseen stick.

Perhaps on cue, the tiger rose in a rage to charge the clown then raced around the cage, sending urine-soaked sawdust and feces through the bars and onto the closest spectators. The little boy was especially hard-hit, getting an ample sample of fresh shit in his face and hair, to the great amusement of the clowns. The assembled crowd was at first shocked and afraid of the animal's ferocity but soon joined the clowns in laughter at the spectacle.

"Hey, hey! What's goin' on here?"

The attention of the group shifted at the arrival of a tall man dressed in fringed buckskins, knee-high spit-shined black boots, and a wide-brimmed black hat garnished with a perfect eagle feather. A bushy brown mustache and long brown hair would distinguish him from his contemporary, Buffalo Bill Cody, whom he despised. The group parted for the showman, who went directly to the clowns for an explanation.

"Caesar got excited, Colonel, and sprayed us all," said the ticket-taker.

Taking in the scene, the Colonel focused on the still-sobbing boy. "Get a bucket of fresh water and a towel and clean him up. See that his family gets free tickets to the show."

"Yes, sir," said the juggler, and he disappeared around the corner.

Zelda ran into the commotion and called out, "Where are the Siamese twins?"

The Colonel spun around and said, "Who said that?"

John caught up to her, grabbed her by the arm, and said, "Zelda, I don't think this is a good idea."

"I did," she snapped back at the Colonel.

"There are no Siamese twins here, young lady. Where did you hear such a thing?"

"A man on a pink horse told me so."

"A pink horse," he roared with laughter. "I know of no one with a pink horse, but I wish I did. Jasper, give this woman and her friend tickets to the show and escort them to my railcar afterward. I want to hear more about this man with a pink horse." He continued to give Jasper further instructions in a low voice.

They filed into the huge tent with the rest of the patrons and took their seats in the grandstand. "Zelda, I don't like this one bit. We gotta get outta here."

"No, that Colonel's got my sisters, and we're going to get them back."

"Listen to me. If he's got the twins, and I believe he does, he's not going to admit he kidnapped 'em and turn 'em over to you. I also think he knows about your pa and the pink horse. I don't know what kind of deal they made, but he must know he can't buy you off. We're in trouble here."

"Oh dear! You're right. I made a mess of this, didn't I?" she said and wrapped her arm around his. "I was just so mad."

"Don't look now, but there are men watching us on both sides. Let's move to the middle."

There were four sets of grandstands under the Big Top, and each was fully occupied. A parade of elephants, horses, and four camels—all with costumed riders—entered the arena, circling in different directions. Acrobats flew above the hoard on trapezes in a dazzling performance.

"Do you think you can squeeze through these bleachers?" he asked her. "As soon as everybody stands for applause, we need to make our move."

"Yes, I can," she replied. "Tell me when."

The Colonel appeared in the center of the extravaganza as if by magic, unnoticed by the audience as they focused on a beautiful girl outfitted in sequins and feathers flying through the air on a trapeze. Gaining speed and altitude, she launched herself forward in a double summersault to be grabbed by her catcher in a seamless display. The culmination of the performance brought gasps from the crowd as the girl was released into yet another summersault to land on the back of a running horse. The amazed multitude rose to their feet with roaring approval. "It is my honor," the Colonel exclaimed in a booming voice, "to welcome the fine people of Salt Lake City to the Phantasmagoric Circus & Sideshow's 'Greatest Show in the West.'" The applause continued when the Colonel launched himself onto the back of a galloping gray stallion and rode alongside the beautiful girl, hand in hand, as they rose to stand on top of their saddles. They rode to the center of the arena and were surrounded by the show's remaining animals and riders. The crowd went wild in an ovation that lasted a full two minutes! When they finally sat back down, John and Zelda were gone.

18

Winter 1871

The sheriff opened his envelope and spread its contents on the desktop. "Lookit here, Doc. Help me put this together." It was a jumble of details that didn't make much sense, but with a series of arrows, he directed names to places, accompanied by numbers to give it order. "Looks like my brain after too much whiskey," he mused.

The doctor spread the pages out and rearranged them like the puzzle pieces they were. "Except for what happened last night, it looks like you've got the details correct." He pulled an ink pen and some fresh paper from a drawer and began a new list. "Here, let's try this differently. If we ever intend to read this, you're going to have to write while I dictate." And so they worked together to create a document that was both accurate and legible.

"Walter, you've known those girls since they were babies. Why would anyone want to kill them?"

"Well, not for any reason they deserved. But they've caused a ruckus ever where they've been. They're pretty derned unusual."

19

Summer 1849

The sun broke in a sliver of light through the curtains in the room's only window. John gazed into Zelda's dark silky hair, wishing she'd turn over so he could see her face. There had been no sleep for him. He'd relived the night a hundred times and pressed it into his memory so well that if there were a thousand other nights with this woman, he'd never forget a single moment of this one. It was so amazing! Reluctant to leave, he put on his pants and shirt, grabbed his toothbrush, and shuffled down the hall to the bathroom. On his return, he smiled as Zelda approached from the ladies' room at the other end of the building.

"Good morning, my soon-to-be husband," she said, wrapping her arms around his waist.

"Good morning, my beautiful girl," he replied and kissed her lips. "Hmm." He sighed and kissed her again. "We need to talk. Let me go down to the lobby and see if there's coffee."

He returned shortly with a pot of coffee, warm biscuits, butter, and marmalade. Two shiny red apples sat together on the tray. They sat on the bed with their breakfast between them, neither able to stop watching the other. "Darlin', I'm afraid you caught me at a weak moment last night," John began. "Don't get me wrong. I really had a good time. It was by far better than all my nights ever put together. But you deserve better 'n me for a husband. Zelda, I ain't got nothin'. Heck, I don't even own these clothes. I just don't see how I could take care of you."

"John, I don't have anything either 'cept a big family, and I'm ready to start a family of my own." She fixed a biscuit and held on to it while he took a bite. "We can do this. You've got a job, and I'm a hard worker." She put the biscuit down and placed both hands on his cheeks. "Don't you love me?"

"Yes, I do. I think I've been in love with you for forever."

She smiled and said, "Well then, I think we should talk more about this later," and she began to take off her nightgown.

20

Despite her insistence that they seek out a justice of the peace, John took them back to the stables they'd passed the day before to look for the pink horse. After a good start, the deputy's day continued to improve when they walked into the first barn and stopped to stare at the animal. The swaybacked old gelding gave them a sideways glance before returning to his hay.

"Say there," John called to a man braiding a rope by a haystack, "where'd you get this horse?"

"Who wants to know?"

"John Walker, deputy sheriff, Spanish Fork." Zelda came up to run her arm through his. "This horse belongs to my sheriff, Walter Becker."

"Good. Tell the high sheriff he owes me two dollars for his keep. Tell him his horse wouldn't look so poor if he had some basic maintenance on his feet and his teeth."

"The sheriff knows how to take care of a horse. This horse was stolen. Where's the man who brought him in here?"

"I dunno. The horse was here two days, was gone yesterday when I got back from supper, and was standing outside the gate this morning. Musta come back on his own."

"Did you get the man's name?"

"Said his name was Smith. Didn't say where he was from."

John walked over and handed the man two dollars. "Somebody'll be back for the horse. His name's Jupiter."

Zelda tugged on his arm. "Ask him."

The deputy reached out to shake the man's hand. "Sir, can you tell me where I can send a telegram?" Zelda kicked him in the shin.

"And where can we find a justice of the peace?" Zelda could not keep quiet.

"Well, young lady, you're in luck. The telegraph operator is also a justice of the peace."

"Oh my! Thank you, sir," she replied. John blushed.

They left the stables with directions for the short trip to the rest of their lives. "Zelda, are you sure about this? You don't even know me."

"Yes, I do. And I love the man I know. Will you please calm down and enjoy the happiest day of your life!"

> TELEGRAM: SHERIFF WALTER BECKER, SPANISH
> FORK, UTAH
> FOUND YOUR HORSE.
> COLONEL KNOWS WE'RE HERE.
> INSTRUCTIONS?

The telegram was sent, and while they waited for a response—which might or might not arrive that day—they got married. The JP's wife cried while she sang a medley of suitably joyous religious songs. Their three children giggled nearby, anxious to be doing something else. The ceremony lasted no more than fifteen minutes, which made it obvious to the officiating couple that the newlyweds were not members of the Church of Jesus Christ of Latter-day Saints. In the LDS church, marriage was a much bigger deal and not officiated by a justice of the peace. Anxious to guide the handsome couple toward a life of righteousness, John and Zelda were presented with a leatherbound copy of the *Book of Mormon* as their first and only wedding gift.

The newlyweds meandered down the boardwalk and stopped at a café for lunch. Both overwhelmed by the events of the last twenty-four hours, they alternately watched each other and looked at the menu. The waitress arrived, and Zelda ordered the daily special for them both: pot roast, mashed potatoes, mixed vegetables, and a tall glass of milk. "You're going to need your energy when I get done with you, pardner." She laughed and spun the wedding ring around on his finger.

"Zelda, I wonder if us finding Jupiter was a trap."

"Well, so much for high romance!"

"Yeah, I'm sorry," John said. "But think about it. That guy at the stable knows a lot about us. If the Colonel put that horse there for bait, we walked right in and took it. He can ask the guy a couple of questions and find out we're waiting for a return telegram. He could have someone waiting for us when we go back there."

"Okay, but first we have a marriage to consummate."

"Consummate?"

"I promise you'll like it. After we eat, we'll go back to our room. We'll make sure we're not followed."

They returned to the Depot Hotel without accompaniment. Zelda led the way, circling each block, doubling back at least four times. John followed her, using alleys and entering shops periodically to watch her progress from behind. It took forever, but he was convinced they were not followed. He was certain the danger existed, but they would be vigilant.

The newlywed's afternoon exceeded their expectations, leaving them exhausted and asleep in each other's arms. The evening presented them with few good options (other than staying in the room), and the deputy didn't like any of them. The circus would be leaving for the West Coast in three days, and so far, all they knew for sure was the whereabouts of Jupiter. He had to check the Western Union office, but that might be the most dangerous thing to do. He wondered if Sheriff Becker noticed the word *us* in the telegram.

"Zelda, I'm going to the telegraph office, but first I'm going to talk to that stable guy. I have to know if he set us up. I'll be straight back after that, and we can decide what to do. I shouldn't be more than an hour. Please stay here, and keep the door locked."

"Okay, but be careful."

Deputy Walker approached the stable from an alley and melded into a haystack. A familiar voice was talking to another familiar voice, then he heard the first voice say his name.

"If that sheriff gets up here and talks to his deputy, I don't want to be around to answer their questions. They don't know nuthin', but they could get the local police involved, and we could be standing in a pile of shit. After all, we are still in possession of the sheriff's stolen horse. Eddie, I want you to get rid of him. Is Jasper still at the telegraph office?"

"Yessir, he's across the street at the café, readin' the paper. I reckon he's got it damn near memorized by now."

"I didn't know the tripe head could read," the Colonel said with disgust.

"Yessir, I believe he went to the eighth grade. You want me to relieve him? He's been there all day."

"No, I want you to start checking hotels. Those two aren't camping out."

John Walker felt a gun barrel on the back of his neck then heard the hammer of a revolver pulled back to the cocked position. His wrist was pulled around behind his back and thrust up between his shoulder blades. Head bent forward, he was pushed into the barn to stand in front of the small group. "Colonel, I got something here you ought to see."

The Colonel burst out laughing. "Oh, ho, ho, ho! Son, you just made my life a whole lot easier! Eddie, take a walk around and see if his girlfriend's here. You can't miss her. She's real pretty, with a real big mouth. Search him, Jack."

John was spun around to face the haystack, hands against it. His frisk lasted a few seconds when his gun was pulled from its holster.

"Jesus Christ, boy! Where'd you get this antique?" the Colonel exclaimed, holding up the old revolver for the small group to see. "Does it shoot?"

"Give it back to me, and we'll see," the deputy said, holding out his hand.

The Colonel stepped forward and hit him hard in the cheek with a gloved fist. "Say another word, boy, and I'll close yer other eye."

But the Colonel had misjudged his advantage. The armed man at John's back had drifted away, and the deputy put all his weight into a left uppercut that sank deep into the Colonel's ample gut. Quick as a blink, he followed with four left and right haymakers to the older man's face, knocking him to the ground and leaving him gasping for breath. He dove for his navy revolver, rolled twice to his right, and cocked and fired it three times into the air. The explosions of the old weapon were deafening, and the smoke blinding enough to cover his escape. He ran hard to the street, slowed to merge into the traffic and headed straight for the Western Union office. The café across the street was busy at this early hour, bustling with couples out for the evening, enjoying the popular fair of the quaint little eatery. The tables were fully taken save one, occupied by a man with a newspaper, watching the street. John entered and walked up to the man, taking the paper from his hands, folding it in half, and laying it on the table. He took him by the arm and escorted him outside, all the time with a smile on his face. They turned the corner into an alley, then John pushed him against the wall and repeatedly pounded the man in the stomach. The man fell to the ground and lay there gasping.

"Tell your boss you saw me, and the next time, I won't be alone. I'll bring every lawman in this city, and we'll go through your circus train until we find what we're looking for." The deputy kicked him hard in the ribs and went across the street to get his telegram.

21

"Ma, you awake?" Sheriff Becker asked the old woman, who yawned and looked around at her unfamiliar surroundings.

"Yes, where am I? In jail?"

"Yeah, Ma, I had to arrest you."

"For what?"

"Ma, you robbed the bank." The sheriff made a pistol with his thumb and index finger and pointed it at her nose. "After I take you to the outhouse, we're going to the café for some soup, then I'm taking you to a tree I got out back for a good old-fashioned hangin'."

"You better have some help. I ain't going easy."

"Posse will be here in an hour."

"Hmph."

Walter was surprised at how nimbly she moved on their little journey to the café. The diminutive and frail little woman he'd seen at the ranch seemed to have been left behind. She ordered freely from the menu and ate with enthusiasm, including the number 5 dessert special, which was a meal itself. After they finished, Walter ordered coffees, leaned back in his chair, and let his belt out a notch. He focused on his witness.

"Ma, you know Norbert was murdered, don't you?"

"Yes."

"Tell me what you remember."

"I'd been sick," she said, eyes welling. "I asked Norbert to get me *the carry bucket* 'cause I had to go and didn't think I could make it to the outhouse, and he left and didn't come back. And then I messed myself, and I got so mad." She was sobbing now. She reached for her coffee, tipping the cup, spilling the dark liquid into the saucer.

"Here." Walter reached across the table, deftly lifting the cup and saucer, pouring the coffee into the cup, and setting them back on the table.

"You didn't spill a drop," she said.

"Neither did you," he replied, gently pushing the delicate porcelain service close to her shaking hands. "Try it again."

She drank slowly now, holding the cup in both hands, visibly more relaxed. "I got out of bed, gathered my gown around myself, and walked to the sink to clean up. I looked out the window and saw a man walking toward the house. It wasn't Norbert, and I got scared. I couldn't see Norbert anywhere. I ran to the bedroom, climbed in bed, covered up, and closed my eyes. I heard the door open, and heavy footsteps walked through the house. He got to my room and said, 'Whew, Jesus Christ!' Then he walked out and slammed the door."

"Would you recognize him if you saw him again?"

"Of course, I would. He was looking right at the house when he was walking to it."

"What happened next?"

"Well, I was still a mess, and felt terrible. I went to the sink and cleaned myself as best as I could, but I only had a half bucket of water. I got into clean clothes, which didn't make much sense since I wasn't really clean."

"I understand, Ma. Did you see anything going on outside?"

"No, I didn't. I was watching the whole time I was at the sink, but never saw the man again."

"And didn't see Norbert or Jupiter either, right?"

"Not while I was at the sink. You think I wouldn't mention that?"

"Ma, I'm trying to figure out what happened up there, so I'm going to ask some stupid questions. Please be patient."

Walter asked as many stupid questions as he could think of but never gained a better picture of what happened to his brother than what he already knew. He moved his mother into the boarding house where he lived and told her they'd find a place of their own as soon as this business about Norbert could be settled. She seemed satisfied with the room and liked the idea that they would eventually have their own house.

22

The telegram left the sheriff unsettled. *Not much information here*, he mused. Young Deputy Walker had found the sheriff's brother's horse but had blown his cover and was now being pursued by a dangerous man—maybe two if old man Chatham knew he was up there. And what did he mean by *us*? Who was he with?

A myriad of thoughts filled his head as he walked to the telegraph office. There would be complaints by some county commissioners about the money being spent on this travel to Salt Lake, but he'd taken a pledge on their *Book of Mormon* to *serve and protect*, and none of them could complain about the peace and prosperity he'd maintained in their community the last eleven years. He had his own money in the bank and a ranch that could be sold. There would be justice served to his brother's murderer and this kidnapper of babies even if he had to pay for it himself.

23

John entered the telegraph office out of breath. He'd learned as a boy that a punch to the belly of an adversary often did as much damage as a sock in the face and was a lot easier on his fists. The exception he'd made for the Colonel was reflexive. The threats and insults to Zelda had infuriated him, and he wanted to hurt the arrogant bully where it would be visible. He fingered the tooth he'd pocketed from the dirt under the Colonel then looked at his fist and the corresponding cut on his middle finger. Since there was a customer at the caged window, John drifted to the glass in the door to check the swelling of his eye. In the reflection, he noticed a familiar shape sitting in a corner of the room behind him.

"Sheriff Becker, what are you doing here?"

"If you'd check your mail occasionally, you'd have known I sent you a telegram yesterday to meet me at the train station this afternoon. I guess you've been too busy getting married and getting in fistfights to do your job."

"Sir, I can explain everything. You won't believe what's happened. But right now, we've got to get back to Zelda. I'm late."

"Zelda's your wife?"

"Yessir, she's the twins' older sister. I can explain everything."

They began walking back to the hotel, Deputy Walker talking as fast as he could, trying to describe what had happened in the last two days.

24

Winter 1871

"What'd you find, Delbert?" Sheriff Becker asked, sitting near the woodstove in Doc's office.

"We talked to everybody we saw, sheriff. No witnesses, and no one had anything to say about bad-smelling smoke except from some stale cigars," he said, hitching up his pants and snapping his suspenders. "Show him, Samuel."

"Yessir." He reached into his pocket and pulled out a leather pouch. He handed it to the sheriff and said, "This was on the eastside brick wall of the Blazing Star."

The sheriff took the small bag, opened it, and pulled out a corncob pipe. He brought it to his nose, winced, and put it back in the bag. "Here's our evidence and our best clue. The sons-a-bitch is stayin' ahead of us." He ran his fingers through his thick gray hair and noticed everyone watching him. "Delbert, before you go back to the jail, check and see what kind of job the Grimes' are doin' on these doors. You're a better carpenter than the two of them put together. Samuel, how're your hands feelin'?

"Fine, sir."

"Sure, they are. Go check in with the doctor then ask him to come out here to his office so I can talk to him."

After they had gone, he pulled his notes from the old envelope and read through them twice. He was missing something, and he was pretty sure it wasn't in these pages.

The old doctor shuffled into the room and sat behind the desk across from his friend.

"Doc, you know I have some history with the twins. My first job as sheriff was in Spanish Fork, Utah, where they were born."

"Yes, Walter, you told me that," he said, pulling open the desk's bottom drawer and grasping the whiskey bottle with a shaky hand.

"Here, let me do that," the sheriff said, standing to lean over the desk.

"That'll be good. There are clean glasses over there by the water pitcher."

The sheriff retrieved the glasses and set them close to the bottle. After a generous splash in each, he walked back around the desk and sat on its corner. He tapped the glasses together and said, "Here's to us!" Then he poured one down the doctor's mouth and the other down his own. "They were kidnapped when they were babies, and I think what's goin' on here has everything to do with that," he began. "Might even have something to do with me."

"Maybe we ought to have another before you get started," Doc said, managing to get his feet to the desktop as he leaned back in his chair.

"Excellent idea," said the sheriff before he poured and served. "I can't remember what day it is, but I've still got a pretty clear picture of the far back past. How do you account for that?"

Doc just shook his head, which already was in a mild tremor. "I don't know, Walter. I say ta-take advantage of it and make your brain do the work. It'll be good exercise."

"Well, let's see," he began. "It would have been twenty-one years ago, since I know that's how old the twins are. I would have been thirty when they was born."

Walter Becker covered the details of the days the circus was in Spanish Fork, his mother, his brother, the pink horse, and the mission he sent his young deputy John Walker on to Salt Lake City. It was a complicated, whiskey-induced tale that kept the doctor captivated until after the fourth round when the sheriff lost track of the details and began to repeat himself.

"Here, Walter, why don't you lie down on the cot in the next room for a few minutes while I check my patients."

"Doc, I should get back to the jail."

"No, I want you here in case our outlaw comes back. We may need protection."

"Well, yeah, that's a good point."

25

Summer 1849

"She's gone!"

Both men entered the room and looked around the tiny space as if they might not have noticed her at first.

"Is there anything missing? Besides your wife?" the sheriff asked.

John walked around and looked at her luggage but shook his head. "Her purse, hat, and a shawl, I guess."

"What did you say to each other when you left?"

"I told her I was going to check for a telegram but that I would go by the stable first to see if your horse was still there. I figured the circus people would be looking for us at both places. I told her to wait here and that I'd be back in an hour. That was about two hours ago."

"Okay," the sheriff said. "She got worried and went to look for you. Let's backtrack and see if we can spot her. Did you reload your pistol?"

"No, sir."

"Do it now, and let's do this." He reached into his coat, unclipped his badge, and pinned it over his breast pocket. "We're a long way from home, but nobody knows that. Let's try and look important."

They stopped at the hotel's front desk and asked the clerk if he'd seen Mrs. Walker leave. Yes, he had, about a half hour ago. No, he didn't notice which way she'd gone. They stopped at the telegraph office next, but she hadn't been there.

At the stables, Jupiter's stall was empty, and the proprietor was visibly nervous. "Where's my wife?" Deputy Walker had the man by the collar of his shirt, pushed up against the wall.

"She went to the circus. She was looking for you."

"Were the circus guys here when she was?"

"No. They left after you did. They took your horse, but I don't think they'll keep it."

"Is the saddle still here?" the sheriff asked.

"Nope, it went with the horse," the man replied.

"How far is it to the sheriff's office?"

"It's a couple miles. The police station is a lot closer."

"I'll start with the sheriff. I know him. I'll need to rent a horse."

"Make it two. We're in a hurry," the deputy added.

"John, we'll go to the circus and find your wife, then I'm gonna get Sheriff Jenkins," Walter said. "We need to search the train for those babies, though I doubt we'll find 'em."

After they were mounted, John looked down at the stable keeper and asked, "You haven't seen the man who brought in the pink horse, have you?"

"I have," he mumbled. "He was standing across the street in those trees when your wife was here."

The deputy was off his horse in a heartbeat and had the man pinned to the wall again with his hands around his throat. "Why didn't you tell us that before?"

"You never asked." The keeper choked. John shoved him hard and turned away. "Sheriff, your deputy's crazy."

"That man's a wanted murderer. If he did anything to my deputy's wife, I'm gonna bring him back here and watch him beat the shit out of you."

They rode at a fast-walk through the busy street traffic toward the fairgrounds. "You think Chatham would hurt his own daughter?" the sheriff yelled over to his deputy.

"I don't know, sir!" John yelled back. "He tried to sell his own babies. He might do anything."

A city policeman stopped them at an intersection to let several buggies and wagons pass. Pedestrians moved in all directions in total disregard to the flow of larger traffic.

"And now he's your father-in-law."

"Yessir. I hadn't thought about that."

"He killed my brother. My ma says she can identify him." The traffic started to move. "If we get him back to Spanish Fork, we'll give him a fair trial and hang him."

"Yessir. That'd solve my problem."

26

Winter 1871

"Frank, you suppose you could do something about that snoring? It's scaring the cat."

"Yes, dear," he said, holding the desk and chair for simultaneous support to stand up. "This was my fault. Walter got to telling a story, and I fed him too much whiskey to keep him going. I'll go roll him over."

"Whoa, Doc, what happened? Why am I in bed?" the sheriff sputtered.

"We were drinkin' whiskey, and you were tellin' me about when the twins were kidnapped," the doctor said, patting him on the shoulder. "I had to tend my patients and told you to lie down here for a minute. I guess you dozed off. Supper will be ready soon."

"Thanks, Doc, but I could use a cup of coffee if there's any sittin' around."

"Let me see what I can find. Why don't you come back and gossip with the girls for a minute? They've got new clothes to show off."

Jeanie met them at the door, coffee cups in each hand. "I thought this might be appropriate."

"Yes, dear," her husband said. "You think of everything." She gave one to the sheriff and carried the other for her husband.

They walked past the patients' beds into the operating room, where the twins were setting the surgery table for supper. They brightened upon seeing the men, twirling carefully in the small space, pleased to be seen in the dress they'd created.

"My, my, don't you girls look beautiful." The men both smiled.

"Thank you, sirs," they chimed.

"We have two more that are close to done," Prudence said.

"Yes," Chastity added. "Once we get some decent clothes to wear, we'll be moving out of here."

"Well, I'll want to hear more about that," said the doctor. "But first, Walter, we need to talk about tonight. Come back out in the front room and sit." He walked across the room, picked up a chair, and sat across from the sheriff. "What would you think about asking Samuel to sit out on watch tonight? Maybe across the street in Yokum's Dry Goods. We could talk to Joe about it. He could watch from the window on the second floor. He'd have a good view of main street and us over here, and he'd stay warm to boot. Just think if this arsonist of ours started this place on fire. He could pick us off coming out the door."

"Hmm, yeah. The boy could at least get off a warning shot like he did last night. Maybe I ought to do it."

"No, Walter, I'll feel safer if you're in here. Samuel," the doctor called out, "come in here."

The boy walked in, and the sheriff patted the space next to him on the cot. "Sit down, son. We want to talk to you. Samuel," he began, "we'd like you to be our lookout tonight. This arsonist isn't done yet, and we're still his target. If you could sit in the store across the street and watch out for him, we'll all be safer."

"I'll do it," the boy replied.

"I thought you would. Just after dark, go into town but circle back through the westside sagebrush. I'll meet you at the back door of Yokum's store and let you in. You'll have a good view from upstairs." Joe Yokum was more than happy to cooperate with the night's plan. He put an extra log in the stove and outfitted Samuel with a coat and hat from the slightly used rack.

Back at the jail, Delbert reported that his inspection of the new doors at Doc and Jeanie's little hospital verified that they were sound and secure. He volunteered to take a walking patrol every couple hours, and the sheriff agreed to the same, allowing some sleep for both men. Samuel's position at the window did indeed give him an unobstructed view of Frank and Jeanie James's hospital. A small move to the right or left allowed a clear view up or down main street. Curtains and a dark backdrop made his silhouette invisible, and the ladder-back chair he'd been provided was uncomfortable enough to keep him from dozing off. He palmed his pistol and laid it on the small table next to his chair, by the cup of coffee he'd been given. His instructions were straightforward: if he saw anything overly suspicious, he was to open the window and fire a shot. Owing to the presence of innocents and lawmen, he'd been told not to shoot to kill.

27

Autumn 1870

Samuel, or Sammy as the twins had taken to calling him, smiled at the turn his life had taken since he'd left St. Louis. Listening to the drunken men in the saloon/whorehouse where he lived and worked describe the adventures of life on a riverboat convinced him it was what he needed to take the death of his mother from his dreams. It had been six weeks since he'd held her while she retched the last of her body's fluid into a bucket. He stayed with her through the night until three of her friends took her lifeless form from him, washed it, and wrapped her in a white linen sheet. Samuel borrowed a shovel and pulled her in a fruit cart to the city cemetery where he buried her. He etched her name and the date on a board he found and set it on the grave with the collection of white river rocks he'd given her. The wood would crumble, but the rare stones would forever mark the place and the loving woman who slept beneath them. His heart broken; he wasn't prepared for the loneliness that swept over him.

In the muddled world where he lived, his mother's strength had been his security. She protected, guided, and educated him to the extent she was able. He learned quickly and soon assumed a certain responsibility for their little family, such as it was. When he was seven, he moved out of the rooms the girls occupied and into a broom closet on the main floor. A single chime on the bell behind the bar was his summons, and he could return from anywhere in the building in seconds—except when he was fleecing the whorehouse clientele while they fucked. He had visual access to most rooms through holes he bored or through ceiling or floor cracks he discovered. Stealthy and quiet as a snake, he never took more than would be noticed and split his plunder with the girls. Nothing happened in the building without his knowledge, and some of what happened was not good.

Samuel recognized the whoremongers at the Lewis & Clark Saloon early on. He knew which girls they liked and how they treated them. He was naturally most interested in his mother's customers and watched her door closely. Mostly they were nice guys; he had even met a few. One man named Chester Maxwell said he had a son about his age and gave Samuel a penny after every visit. His mother's working name was Penny Shine, which made Chester laugh, as he would proclaim in his booming voice, "You are your mama's shiny penny."

Chester's pennies, the money he'd stolen, and the tips he made after being promoted to bartender added up over the years. Penny started a bank account in his name and added the meager amount she was able to contribute. She obtained a document from an amused teller stating the boy would be able to obtain a wire transfer of funds to any bank in the country based on his signature and an account number, which they both memorized.

Penny never talked to Samuel about her clients. He knew she liked Chester by the way she smiled when he came through the door. She even granted him a *free roll* after he took Samuel home to meet his son one afternoon after school. School—a place her own son had never been. Penny also liked the young boys with their nervous excitement as they walked up the stairs in front of her. This made Samuel jealous, though he knew he needn't worry that they would hurt her. Not so when Mr. Courtney walked in. Penny Shine would visibly shrink at the sight of him and glance around for a means of escape, but she was never fast enough. Mr. Courtney would seek her out as he came through the door then walk over to her with his big smile and press a dollar between her breasts to place his claim on her time. Then he would strut over to the bar for a shot and a beer while he scanned the room to be sure he was the best-dressed gentleman in the establishment, which, of course, he always was. The first time he made the connection between Penny and Samuel, he winked at the boy while saluting with his middle finger and its large diamond ring. Samuel glared at him defiantly and would not look away. He waited until the couple went upstairs then followed to watch from Lucy's room next door since it was not in use. None of the whores at the L&C had ever attempted to cover their nakedness in front of him, including his mother, but he did not watch them while they worked. He pressed his ear against a crack in the wall in a corner of the room, but the muffled conversation was impossible to understand. Then he heard a slap, and his mother cry out. His instinct was to run to her door, but he stood silently and watched through the sliver of light. Mr. Courtney's hairy nude body passed across the room to the door, which he jerked open. He stepped into the hallway and returned seconds later before propping a chair under the doorknob and returning to the bed.

Looking for me, Samuel thought. There was anger in the big man's voice now and another slap, followed by his mother's cry. Samuel stood with clenched fists and returned to the bar.

"He's hitting her!" he told Lester, the L&C's owner.

"Yeah, son. There's nothing we can do about it. Courtney's a county commissioner, and he could shut us down if he wanted to."

"I'm going to kill him!"

"Hush now. Someday someone's gonna do just that, and you don't want no one sayin' they heard you say it. Go on out back and chop some wood. I'll come get you after he's gone."

Samuel chopped, and he stacked, bitter tears rolling off his face. His hatred burned in his stomach, and he knew it must be satisfied.

"Hey, boy!"

The voice was unfamiliar, but he knew who it was.

"Come here."

He turned, still holding the axe, and took a step forward.

"What are you going to do with that?" Mr. Courtney laughed. "Chop me up?"

Samuel came at the big man swinging the axe with both hands, but his rage exceeded his combat skill, and he was easily disarmed. Still laughing, the man stepped into his smaller opponent, hitting him with a powerful backhand, the diamond ring cutting a deep gash across the boy's cheek.

"Now you'll remember me every time you look in a mirror, you little shit." Stepping back, he looked down at the front of his suit for blood. Satisfied that it was clean, he started to walk away but turned back and said, "Next time I'm here, I'll expect you to shine my boots."

"That ain't gonna happen asshole," Samuel coughed as he staggered back to the building.

"Jesus Christ, boy," Lester said, looking for a clean bar rag. "Get in here." He scanned the room until he saw who he was looking for. "Thelma!" he yelled, "get yer sewing kit and get over here."

Samuel was guided into a back room, and a couple of the girls worked at stopping the bleeding. "Mom," he said. "Someone's got to check on my mom."

Thelma emerged from the back room and cried, "I can't do this. This boy needs a doctor."

"Okay, calm the fuck down," Lester said, trying to calm himself. "Go get Doc Stiles. Nellie, get a mop and clean this mess up. Chrystal, go get Penny and bring her down here. What else…?"

He walked behind the bar and poured two shots of whiskey, drank one, and took the other to Samuel, who was holding a bloody rag to his face. "Here, boy. I'll bet that stings."

"Yeah, some," the boy said, slamming the drink down as he'd seen done a thousand times. He was still trying to control the fresh blood flow from his face when Chrystal ran into the room crying, "She's not breathing."

Samuel was on his feet and running up the stairs well before Thelma returned with the doctor. "Upstairs on the right," Lester called out. "The boy's up there with his ma, and she might be dead."

Two hours later, Doc Stiles walked up to the bar and asked Lester, "Who did this? The boy wouldn't say."

"Commissioner Courtney," Lester said.

"This can't stand," the doctor said. "Call the sheriff. I'll sign the complaint. That girl's going to die, and the boy is scarred for life."

"Doc, you know it won't do no good. There aren't any witnesses except the boy, and who's gonna believe him over Courtney?"

"Goddammit," the doctor said, slamming his fist on the bar. "Pour me a shot."

28

"Samuel, what're you doin' here?"

"Mr. Maxwell, Mr. Courtney killed my ma."

"What? When'd that happen? What happened to your face? Did Courtney do that too?"

"Yessir. Happened 'bout a week ago. I buried her in the cemetery."

"Oh God, son. I'm sorry!"

"I got more."

"More?"

"Yessir. I killed him."

"Jesus, son, don't say that," Chester said in a panicked voice. He stepped out on the stoop and looked up and down the street. "Come inside here. Sit down. Don't move."

He went to the kitchen to get the boy a glass of water and himself a whiskey. He sat down in front of the boy, then got up, went back to the kitchen, and poured himself another glass. "What happened?"

Samuel told Chester all the things he promised Lester he'd never repeat. "He broke her ribs and poked holes in her lungs. She could hardly breathe all night."

"Goddamn him to hell!"

"Yessir, he's already there. I sent him myself."

"What do you mean?"

"I beat him with an iron pipe. Started at his legs and moved up to his head. He's dang sure in hell now, the fucker."

29

On his weekly trip to the L&C to visit Penny, Chester acted dutifully shocked to hear of her demise. "Lester, what happened to her?"

"Commissioner Courtney beat her to death."

"Did you call the sheriff?"

"Of course I called the sheriff."

"And now Courtney's dead."

"So you heard about that."

"Everybody's heard about that. Where's the boy?"

"That's what I was just going to ask you, Chester."

"Me?"

"Yeah, you. He always liked you."

"Look, Lester, I don't know where he is."

"Well, the sheriff's looking for him. He wants to ask him what he knows about Courtney."

"That's ridiculous."

"Think so, do you? I wouldn't want that kid gunnin' for me."

"Well, if anybody knows that boy, it'd be you, Lester. He's lived here his whole life."

"Yeah…"

"Yeah what?"

"Yeah, I am gonna miss him, but I don't know where he is, and I'll bet you do. And I think he killed Courtney. And he did it with the piece of iron pipe that was found next to the body when he could have shot him."

"Shot him?"

"Yeah, my .44's missing."

30

"Captain Myers, this is the boy I was tellin' you about. Name is Samuel Shines. He's been a swamper at the Lewis & Clark all his life. He wants to go to Ft. Benton and will work for his passage. I'm vouching for him." Chester beamed. He held the boy in front of himself like he was giving the steamboat captain a Christmas present.

"Be here in the mornin' at five o'clock, boy," the captain said. "We shove off at dawn."

Samuel had stayed at Chester's house for six days. He was overwhelmed by the security and structure of life in Billy's home. School and the comradery of other children were like a dream to him. Samuel told the boy of his life in a bordello, including a description and the function of the women's body parts. It was more than Billy could comprehend. Samuel laughed when Billy asked him if he'd ever had a wet dream.

"There's no need to wait," Samuel assured him then sent him off to the outhouse with basic instructions and a hand-drawn picture of a naked woman. Half an hour later, Billy returned with a grin and a thank-you. They both laughed when Samuel refused to shake his hand.

Samuel memorized Chester's address and promised he would write. He told Chester of the $358 in his bank account and gave him the letter from the banker to keep for him. Chester counseled the boy to take thirty dollars with him but to keep it in his boot and not to bring it out until he absolutely needed it. He outfitted him with old but suitable clothes, boots, and hat from a closet of things that had been his when he was younger. "Billy will have to settle for new," he said. "You don't want to look prosperous."

Chester knew Captain Myers from his sole trip on the Missouri when they'd crewed together. "Myers is a good man, but he drinks too much. Keep your mouth shut and do what you're told. These will be the same kind of men you've seen all your life in the Lewis & Clark. Try not to kill any of them," he chuckled. "What will you do out West?"

"I'm not sure," Samuel replied. "I've heard talk about Siamese twin whores in Montana. I'd like to see 'em."

"Well, son, that sounds like a great way to start a new life," Chester said. "One last thing, take these scissors, find a mirror, and cut the stiches out of your face in three days. Everyone you meet will probly ask you about that scar for the rest of your life. Think up a believable story."

Morning on *Cleopatra's Tomb* was total chaos. It wasn't immediately clear to Samuel what his job was, since whenever he was tasked with one thing, he was soon pulled off it to do something else. Mostly he was a runner for the captain, delivering orders and keeping his coffee mug filled. It was Myers's first trip as captain, and he was clearly nervous, diluting the coffee with generous quantities of whiskey. His pilot, George Gravy, had made the trip twice, but each time only as far as the confluence with the Platte where the boats both hit cottonwood snags and sank. Samuel knew this because Amos Walker, whose main job was to tend the livestock, told him. They both bunked in a haystack, and from what Samuel could tell, Amos appeared to know more about riverboats than anyone on board. Amos, one of two former slaves on the boat, had been on both trips with Gravy and had been threatened by him to keep his mouth shut.

The steamboat was a four-year-old 100' × 30', low-draught, stern-wheel freight hauler. Based in Cincinnati, it had made five round trips to St. Louis and now, under new ownership, was beginning a new life in the West. Reinforced in the bow and hull to withstand the rigors of the great Missouri, it carried clothing, foodstuffs, guns, ammunition, ten mules, six bred cows, hay, tools, whiskey, fabric, tents, cookware, and thirty passengers (including four military wives). If the trip avoided hazard, Pilot Gravy told Captain Myers he expected to make it to Ft. Benton in seventy days, not record time, but respectable—especially, he could have added, since he'd never been there before.

By noon, the captain was asleep. When the boat was in motion, the pilot was in charge, guiding the big vessel upstream, so the captain was less necessary. Samuel took direction from both men throughout the voyage. From his duty station in the pilothouse, he was witness to the decisions that guided the boat upriver and the situations that made those decisions necessary. When he wasn't otherwise occupied, Gravy sent Samuel to the roof to watch for floating snags and worthwhile driftwood stacks onshore. Under the direction of the pilot, he made adjustments to charts of the river's everchanging sandbars, channels, rapids, and shoreline. By the second week of the trip, he'd made himself indispensable to the boat's two officers.

Samuel was in regular contact with Silas, the engineer in the boiler room, and kept the captain appraised of the wood supply. The *Tomb* departed St. Louis with ten cords of hardwood and five tons of coal. They would harvest cottonwood from the streambank en route. The problem, as Silas explained it, was anticipating the pressure the great boiler would produce, as each fuel type burned at a different temperature. Samuel thought this former slave might be the happiest man on the boat when the engineer hired for the job failed to show up and the captain gave Silas, the fireman, the promotion. He laughed and sang a little ditty for a week: "Ever-body knows if the boiler blows, the big boat glows! The big boat glows!"

Amos slid into the fireman job. He also worked in the galley, hauled water, and emptied shit buckets. The captain apparently had no idea how much a cow or a mule could eat when he bought their hay. Amos had to put the animals on starvation rations from day one just to keep them alive to trip's end. Still, he had to clean up after them daily to keep the deck from rotting. Samuel had never known a black man before, nor had he ever had a friend. Amos became both. They talked of their pasts long into many nights, both amazed at how the other had lived.

The trip was not without its troubled moments, including a mutinous night of too much whiskey and an argument over the curse the boat's name cast upon them all. The ensuing fight involved twenty-three men who beat the crap out of one another. A head count the following morning showed a passenger from Kentucky was missing. After a search of the boat, it was assumed he'd fallen overboard.

On day 43, the *Tomb* was ambushed at a driftwood pile on the north shore by a dozen Indians. The boat was greeted with a shower of arrows as it approached, one hitting Samuel's friend Amos Walker in the thigh as he was lowering the boarding plank. The attack so enraged Captain Myers that he called upon the sleeping whiskey-drinking buffalo hunters, who staggered to the upper deck with their .50-caliber long rifles and laughingly shot the Natives as they ran away, killing them all. The curse of the *Tomb* fell hard on Amos as he succumbed to a valiant effort by the cook to amputate his gangrenous leg on day 50. His passing devastated Samuel.

On day 69, the boat paddled in place midstream for four hours, waiting for a herd of buffalo to cross. The buffalo hunters amused themselves by killing ten and letting them float past the boat downstream. One of the hunters named Burger dropped a rope over a big bull's horns as it passed in an attempt to salvage the carcass but was pulled overboard when the rope looped around his wrist. Pilot Gravy let the boat drift backward for a full mile in an attempt to keep him in sight, but he was lost to the current and never resurfaced.

Cleopatra's Tomb made it to Ft. Benton on day 80, to the joy of everyone on board. The women seemed especially happy to end their river adventure. A hearty group, they had volunteered to help in the galley each day in exchange for hot water so they could bathe. The livestock, starving after their confinement and insufficient fodder, staggered down the ramp in a daze at half their boarding weight. The whiskey barrels received an ovation as they were rolled off the boat by all hands onshore, the celebration lasting most of the night.

Two days later, the boat was reloaded with furs, hides, gold, silver, and a hundred passengers for the return trip to St. Louis. Captain Myers and Pilot Gravy, anxious to begin, invited Samuel to join as a paid crew member. He'd so enjoyed his first river experience that he was tempted, thinking he might one day like to become a river pilot, but he knew he could not return to St. Louis. There was no doubt the sheriff there was looking for him. Too many people knew the truth about the murder of his mother and the scar on his face for this secret to be kept.

Samuel expected to make it to Alamo in a fortnight. Before he left, he bought a pair of buffalo skins to cover his boots, a wool coat and blanket, bear-skin mittens, hard tack, buffalo jerky, and a canteen. He fell in with a party of trappers traveling to Dillon, and in the twelve days he was with them, he absorbed everything they could tell him about the life of a mountain man. Unfortunately, they exacted a price for what they'd taught him and stole his winter clothes and blanket, leaving him with the well-used things he'd been wearing when he boarded the boat in St. Louis.

31

Samuel leaned forward in his chair on the second floor of Yokum's to look up and down the street. There was no one in either direction. It started to snow and reminded him of the last couple miles into Alamo the night of the fire—the eerie glow in the sky that led him in then the smell and the commotion. His reverie was interrupted by the prick of cold steel into his cheek and the awareness of a stream of blood coursing down his face.

"You move, boy, and I'll cut you a scar right here to match the one on the other side of your face."

32

Winter 1871/Summer 1849

"Walter, finish your story about the twin's kidnapping," Doc said. Jeanie, and the twins were there, everybody gathered around the wood stove, the men sipping whisky and the women knitting sweaters. Delbert had just left for an evening patrol of main street and would return in two hours. Doc continued, "Last you said, you and your deputy were riding rented horses through Salt Lake City looking for John's wife, Zelda."

"Zelda was our sister," the twins said.

"That's right, we were looking for Zelda, you girl's older sister," the sheriff began. "We knew she was headed to the circus, and from what the stable keeper said about her Pa being there, we knew he'd be followin' her. Nice thing about being on horses was sittin' up high like that, we could see pretty good. Bad thing was the circus people didn't want us ridin' through the crowd droppin' horse shit ever where. Made us wonder *what was the big deal*, after the elephants had already been through. Anyhow, we showed our badges and said we'd stay off to the side, and we did. But we knew Zelda and her Pa weren't there for the amusements, so we rode around behind the tents, split up, and sat ourselves at each end of the railcars. Now I didn't know Chatham well, but I knew it was him sneakin' around the caboose, and John saw him about the same time. I was at the other end of the train and headed that way at a trot, and when I got there John already had his father-in-law on the ground with his knee on his chest. 'Hold on there John,' I says. 'We can't be hangin' him here.'"

The sheriff paused, took a sip of his whisky, then walked over to the window to look across the street. "Doc, the boy is at Yokum's right?"

"Yes Walter, upstairs sitting in the dark at the window watching us."

"Good, I wouldn't want anything to happen to him. I wish we'd have set up some kind of signal. I can't see nothin' through that window." He sat back down and ran his hand through his hair. "I got a bad feelin'."

"So do I," Jeanie added.

"I suspect as long as he's not shooting that gun of his everything's ok," Doc replied.

"Get back to the story sheriff," Chastity chimed.

"Yes," added Prudence. "I want to make sure we weren't drowned! Or something worse!"

"No, you weren't drowned, but no thanks to us," the sheriff said. "Well, we got Chatham rolled over and his hands tied behind his back, stood him up, and told him he's under arrest. John, who I could see lacked a light touch, has the guy's face pressed into the side of the railcar and wants to know where Zelda is. Chatham tells him to go to hell, so John who's built like a telegraph pole, but strong as an ox spins him around and punches him hard in the guts two times. He tells the guy he'll break his arm next and I'm sure Chatham believes him, but since he can't breathe, he can't talk, so I says 'wait a minute, wait a minute.' Well, eventually he starts to breathe and coughs out, 'She's in the caboose.' A minute later we're bangin' on the door."

"Oh my!" The twins cried out.

"Yeah well," the sheriff continued. "It's mostly my fault. I never gave my deputy a minute of training and him being in love and all – he's got his gun out and goin' through the door before I can say 'open up!' I'm right behind him, and right behind me comes two clowns, the strong man, and the bearded lady. Inside, the Colonel's sitting on the side of his bed pointing a double barrel shotgun at us, and we got half the circus behind us and they got guns too. The Colonel says something like, 'How 'bout you boys lay your guns on the floor.'"

"Where were we?" The twins asked breathlessly.

The sheriff starts laughing and reaches out to the table for his whisky. "I don't know, somewhere in the city would be my guess. I know the Colonel wasn't in the mood to have two cryin' babies in that railcar with him. And he damn sure wasn't happy to see us in there."

He takes a sip and sets his glass down, pleased to be the center of attention, though not at all sure how close this story was to the true history of the event. *Let it be* he thought, no one here has reason to deny it. "So I'm discussing our situation with the Colonel, 'Hold on says I, we're the law here, and you're suspect for the kidnapping of twin baby girls. Their father's tied up outside, and their older sister was seen coming into this railcar. We're not leaving until it's been searched.'"

"'You're a good distance from your jurisdiction aren't you sheriff?' The Colonel replies, brushing down a mustache as big as a medium sized prairie dog to be sure it covers his missing front tooth, which I happen to know is in John's pocket."

"Salt Lake County Sheriff Bobby Jenkins is a good friend of mine," I says to him. "He knows I'm here, and Utah Penal Code Chapter 7, Section 49, covers the pursuit of a felony suspect beyond county lines throughout the state. Take your pick. We ain't leaving until this car's been searched."

"'I think you're full of shit sheriff, but I've got nothing to hide,' he says. 'Have a look around. When you get done, be sure and take your deputy with you when you go. We've been fighting that son of a bitch all day, and the boys here would be happy to shove your *penal code* up his ass.'"

"'Keep your gun pointed at Wild Bill there John while I search this piss bucket,' I says. The Colonel laughs. Calls me *a fool.* My deputy shoots a hole in the ceiling, and a lightning bolt later, has the barrel of his pistol in the man's ear and says to him 'say something else, I dare ya.'"

"I had to laugh, the boy could be a handful. Anyhow, I look through the car and didn't see any sign of babies or Zelda. Quite the palace though. Full kitchen, well stocked bar, biggest bathtub I ever seen, buffalo hides spread out on the floor. I end up at the back end of the car where John still has his gun pointed at the Colonel's head. 'We'll be back Colonel I says, I don't guess you'll be hard to find.'"

"Guns all seemed to be pointed to the floor when we turned to go. We get to the door and Deputy John turns to the Colonel still sitting on his bed and pulls the tooth out of his pocket and holds it up in the light. I had to smile when he says, 'Here *Buffalo Bill,* this belongs to you.' He tosses the tooth toward the bed, then walks forward to step on it. Then he says, 'You'll want to wash that off before you put it in your mouth. I got elephant shit on my boots.'"

33

Summer 1849

The sheriff and his deputy climbed out of the railcar and looked down the tracks to see their prisoner was gone. "Didn't you tie him up?" the sheriff asked.

"Yessir, but I don't remember tyin' him down," John said, shaking his head. "We was in a hurry."

"Don't worry, sheriff. I got him." There was a flash of fabric and motion, and Zelda was in John's arms.

"Zelda, where've you been? You like to scared me to death when I got back to the hotel and you was gone."

"Well, when you didn't come back, I got worried and went looking for you. What happened to your face?"

"I got in a fistfight with the Colonel and some of the circus boys at the stables."

"Ahem, ahem."

"Oh yeah. Sheriff, this is Zelda."

"Zelda is your wife?" the sheriff asked.

"Yes, sir. I'm the new Mrs. John Walker," she beamed. "I know who you are, Sheriff Becker. I've seen you in Spanish Fork many times."

"Yes, ma'am, you look familiar," the sheriff replied. "What were you saying about our prisoner?"

"My pa," she said, anger in her voice.

"Why, yes, ma'am, that'd be right."

"Call me Zelda, sheriff. And please accept my condolences and regrets for your dear brother. If Pa doesn't hang for murder, he'll suffer a worse fate at the hands of his own family if he ever sets foot on our farm again. He's a child abuser and a kidnapper, and I'll not have him back."

"Thank you, ma'am, er, Zelda," the sheriff said. He shifted his weight uneasily from one foot to the other, uncomfortable in the presence of such a beautiful woman. "Where is yer pa now?"

"Oh, yes," she said. "He's on the other side of the tracks tied to a tree. I had to hit him with a stick a few times to get him to move. He could tell I was mad. I tied that stick in his mouth to shut him up."

"I declare. You two are a couple of tough biscuits. If I ever get in a fight, I hope you're both there to help me out. I don't suppose yer pa said anything about yer twin sisters."

"No, sir, but I know he's talked to the Colonel. He was grumbling his name before I got him to chewin' on that stick."

"John, I'll take him and the horses to Sheriff Jenkin's jail for the night. I'll question him there and meet you at the stables in the morning. We'll make a plan then."

"Yessir. I'll help you load him up."

"Sheriff, we need to talk to the Colonel about my sisters," Zelda said.

"Yes, ma'am, we will. Let's get yer pa's story first. I intend to get Jupiter back also.

"Jupiter, sir?" she asked.

"Yes, ma'am'," the sheriff said. "My brother's horse."

The newlyweds strolled through the circus and bought ears of corn, sausages, and cold tea for their supper. John told Zelda about his fight with the Colonel and the missing tooth, and she laughed till she cried. They thought about slipping into the Big Top to see if the big man would make an appearance but knew they wouldn't be welcome. "Besides," John said, "shouldn't we go back to the hotel and *constipate* our marriage again?"

34

"Have you two eaten?"

"No." They looked at each other and smiled.

"We slept in," Zelda said with a slight blush.

"Good," the sheriff said. "I haven't eaten since yesterday on the train. Lead us back to the café across from the telegraph office, John. I'll buy us some breakfast, and we can talk."

They settled into a table at the back of the café so they could watch the front door. Zelda ordered the fruit bowl, with a poached egg, juice, and hot tea. The men preferred the BISHOP'S SPECIAL of ham, eggs, flapjacks, fried potatoes, juice, and coffee. John added the ALL-YOU-CAN-EAT SAINT'S PORTION for an extra twenty-five cents. After his third serving, the cook came out of the kitchen and cast their table a nasty look before using a wet dish towel to wipe SAINT'S PORTION from the blackboard menu.

"Yer pa says he met with the Colonel and he wants to adopt your twin sisters. But he says he doesn't know where they are."

"Liars! They're both liars!"

"Zelda, not so loud," John pleaded then stood up to glare at the café's patrons.

"Does the Colonel look like a suitable parent to you?" she said in a venomous voice. "He sends his clowns into my house in the middle of the night to take my baby sisters, and now he wants to be their father? Who would believe that?"

"Your pa says the Colonel's lawyer told him that as the babies' legal guardian, he has the right to put them up for adoption on grounds that he already has eight other children who have no mother and he can't afford to keep them." The sheriff handed the paper he was reading to Zelda, who started to cry. "These are the notes I wrote while talking to him. He said the lawyer intends to file the paperwork at the Salt Lake County courthouse on Monday and mail copies to your pa in Spanish Fork. I have no idea how legal this all is. I suspect you'd need a lawyer to sort it out."

"Where are the twins?" she asked.

"I don't know. Your pa says he never saw them. I suspect that's not a lie."

"What about Jupiter?" John asked.

"He was at the stables when I brought the horses back. The keeper said he was standing at the barn door when he got there this morning."

"I guess he likes it there."

"I think it's the feed he likes," the sheriff said. "I asked Chatham about the horse, and he says he found him grazing by the road and rode him up here. Says he intends to return him to the same place."

John laughed. "Grazing by the road with a saddle on his back and wearing a bridle. I guess he just thought he'd borrow him for a few days."

"That's what he said." The sheriff motioned the waitress to come over. "My ma can identify my brother's murderer. I'm sorry, Zelda."

"Don't be, sheriff," she said. "I won't watch him die, but I won't miss him."

The sheriff paid the bill and left a generous tip. "Let's go talk to the Colonel."

The conversation went about as well as everyone expected, which was not very well.

"It was your father, missy, who approached me," the Colonel said, pointing his finger at Zelda. The sheriff, increasingly alert in his deputy's presence, lunged for him as John lunged for the Colonel's finger, barely able to restrain him. "Stop messin' with me, deputy," he said, glaring at John, still in the sheriff's bear hug. "I've killed far better men than you."

"You'll be my first, Buffalo Billy," Deputy John said in a guttural voice unrecognizable as his own.

"Finish your statement, Colonel," the sheriff said. "And it better end with the location of those babies."

"I don't know where they are, sheriff. My plan was to come back to get them if the adoption goes through as planned. Frankly, I regret ever getting involved in this matter."

"There ain't gonna be any adoption," the sheriff said. "I'm taking Chatham back to Spanish Fork tomorrow to face murder charges. But you, sir, can be sure of this: we're gonna find those babies, and if there's anything like your smell on them when we do, there'll be a warrant for your arrest and US Marshals on your trail."

"That'll never happen, sheriff," the Colonel said, then he turned and walked away.

"Sheriff, arrest him," Zelda cried. "He's lying. My sisters were stolen in the middle of the night. My pa was involved, I'm sure, but he's not smart enough to pull it off by himself. The Colonel tricked him. Nobody else could have done it."

"Zelda, I believe you, but there's no evidence." The sheriff took his hat off and spoke directly, "He's not telling the truth, but we can't prove it. Those girls are gone by now. If his plan was to put them in a sideshow, he knows by now he won't get away with it. But they're still worth somethin' to him. I got fifty dollars I'll give you two if you want to follow his circus to Boise, but I'm not convinced your sisters will be travelin' along. Me, your pa, and Jupiter will be on the train back to Spanish Fork tomorrow."

John and Zelda looked at each other, the confusion clear in their eyes. "We'll meet you at the train in the morning," Zelda said. "We'll tell you what we're doing then."

35

Winter 1871

"Well, they met me at the train the next mornin'. Said they were going to watch the circus train before it left then follow it to Boise and watch it there. Said they wanted to pick somebody from the crew to question, and if that didn't pan out, they'd come home. I gave them the fifty bucks and never saw or heard from them again." Sheriff Becker cast his eyes to the floor, pulled out his handkerchief, and blew his nose. "They were so crazy in love with each other. Zelda was determined to find her twin sisters, and John would do anything just to be close enough to look at her." The sheriff looked up to see the twins crying; Doc and Jean were staring at him. "Last thing I did was give John my Colt .45. Took that relic of a pistol he was using back to Spanish Fork and put it in a drawer. Yeah, they were good kids. I still think about 'em." He blew his nose again. "I wrote to the sheriff in Boise, and he wrote back. Said he didn't know anything about John and Zelda or the twins. He did say one of the P&S circus clowns got beat up pretty bad by a young woman with a broomstick. He questioned her, but the clown wouldn't press charges, and he had to let her go. He didn't get names.

"Anyhow, I still had sheriffin' to do. I got Chatham and my brother's horse back to Spanish Fork, only to find my ma had fell and broke her hip. She was in so much pain that Doc Jones had her drugged up with laudanum, and she didn't even recognize me. So there went my murder witness. Now all's I got locked up is a horse thief, and he claims he's never seen the horse before. Judge

105

Widowmaker says I needed the stable keeper in Salt Lake to testify he saw Chatham ride Jupiter into his stable. So I wire Sheriff Jenkins about my problem, and he wires me back that the guy's gone. Took off with the circus when it left town. What a derned mess!"

"What did you do with our pa?" the twins asked.

"I kept him in jail for a week, then the judge said I had to let him go. Before that, I went out to have a meeting with yer brothers and sisters and told them everything. When he showed up at the farm, yer brothers ran him off, told him never to come back. Far as I know, he never did."

"What happened to your mother?" Jean asked.

"She lived about two weeks. Never was good though."

"That's a shame," she said.

"Yeah, I should have moved her into town a long time before. She worked her life away on that patch of red dirt we called a farm and never got any joy from it. She deserved better," he said, shaking his head. "I should have taken better care of her."

"We killed our ma," the twins said.

"No," Jean replied. "Your mother died giving you life. It was a sacrifice, but I'm sure she made it willingly."

The room was quiet.

"I think we should get some sleep," Doc said.

"Where's that boy?" the sheriff asked.

"He's across the…" Doc started.

"Oh yeah, I remember," the sheriff interrupted. "I'm gonna go check on him. Lock the door behind me." He reached into his pocket and pulled out a key. "This must be the store key."

"I believe it is," Doc said. "And this is the key to the new lock on this front door."

The sheriff reached over to Doc's desk and picked it up. "I'll be back in a little while."

The little hospital settled into its peaceful self as Sheriff Walter Becker eased out the door.

36

Summer 1849

"I think we should split up," Zelda said, climbing on top of him in the well of the bed's middle.

"What?" John said, visibly alarmed.

"One of us should take the morning train to Boise ahead of the circus. The other should take the next train, which leaves tomorrow. I checked the schedule. One can watch them load on this end, and one will be in Boise to see them unload there."

"Geez, Darlin', I don't know. If the Colonel thinks we're watching him, he'll be watching for us. What if you get caught?

"What if *you* get caught?" she said, not used to not getting her way.

"What if I do? Either way we're in trouble. He'll kill us both if he gets the chance."

"Let's ask the sheriff and see what he thinks," she offered.

"All right," John said, smiling. "But could we *compromise* our marriage one more time before we go?"

They entered the train station to see Sheriff Becker buying two tickets to Spanish Fork. Zelda saw her father tied to a post in a corner of the room and walked over to slap his face. "This is all your fault, you hateful man. You will hang for your sins, and no one will grieve for your soul when you get to hell."

"You little whore," he snarled. The comment brought John to Zelda's side and his hand to Chatham's throat. "Go ahead and hit me, deputy. I'm tied up."

"John!"

"Don't worry, sheriff. Zelda's right. His time will come, and I'll be there to see it." He pulled his hand away and wiped it on his pants.

"I ain't gonna hang. I ain't done nothin'. I ain't killed the sheriff's brother, and I ain't stole his horse. I ain't sold them babies either, but I'll tell you this much: they's mine. I'm they's pa, and they's mine." He looked over at the sheriff, who was watching and listening, then he spit on the floor. "The Colonel set me up on ever thang. I been watchin' him and his show for four days, and I ain't seen shit. Them freaks ain't on that train. He took 'em, and they's gone." He spit on the floor again. "And if I ever get my hands on you, missy, we gonna finish up where we left off."

This time, Deputy John did hit him. "You ever touch her, I'll kill you."

Chatham wiped the blood from the corner of his mouth and said, "Ha, no need for me to worry 'bout that. The Colonel's gonna take carra you, boy. Someday he's gonna track you down and cut yer balls off." John cocked his arm, but Chatham never flinched. "I know'd men like him in the Army. He ain't gonna forget about you."

"Look for me the day you hang," John said, returning his stare. "I'll be standing right in front."

John and Zelda joined the sheriff where he was watching them, from a table across the room. She told him they were going to follow the train and spoke to him of her idea to split up in their search. "This is big country," he said, shaking his head. "You don't want to get separated. Keep each other in sight and have a rendezvous point for later. One on each side of the tracks, at each end of the train." He pulled out his wallet, counted out fifty dollars, and gave them to John. "Take the passenger train after the circus leaves. You'll probably pass it when they stop to unload freight on the way," he said. "Let me think a minute." He walked over to Chatham, checked his ropes, and walked back. "This might be an impossible task. They know what you look like, and you'll be easy to spot. The babies are small and will be easy to hide. One thing that might work for you is they're probably noisy."

"Yes, they are," Zelda said. "And whoever is taking care of them will be busy."

"Well, there. There are things you will notice that I wouldn't. But if you don't get any good clues after watching for a few days, you might better come home. Yer pa might be right. They're probly not on that train. I also think he's right about the Colonel being a dangerous man. I think yer pa is too."

"My pa is dishonest and lazy," she said, glancing his way. "He's also a coward. Don't trust him for a minute."

"I won't," the sheriff said. "He'll be in a jail cell tonight."

They stood, shook hands, and said goodbye.

John and Zelda walked along the tracks, passing a paneled flatcar loaded with cattle and one white horse with a pinkish hue. "Poor Jupiter," Zelda said. "He was an unwitting accomplice."

"Huh?" John grunted.

Zelda laughed. "He was the victim of a crime when he was stolen and an accessory to the crime when he helped his thief get away."

"I'll bet he's confused about that."

She reached back and grabbed him in the butt.

"Zelda," he whispered, "this is Mormon country."

"That's it," she said, slapping him on the shoulder. "You're a genius!"

"Nobody's ever said that to me before. What exactly do you mean?"

"It means we're getting new clothes."

"I got new clothes. And they ain't even paid for. And now I owe the sheriff fifty dollars."

"No, I owe the sheriff fifty dollars."

"But if we're married, ain't it the same thing?"

"Yes, in a way. But I'm going to give him the money. My sisters are my family's responsibility."

"But this is my job."

"I understand that, but this is beyond what your job calls for. If we weren't married, the sheriff would have told you to go back to Spanish Fork with him. The murderer and horse thief have been caught."

"This trip started out with me chasing a kidnapper. I'm still on that job."

"Yes, Darling, and I'm glad you are. I just don't think your boss believes there's much chance of success." She stood on her tiptoes and kissed him on the cheek. "Your plan for a disguise is brilliant."

"What?"

"Let's find those new clothes."

They left the tracks and wandered into the city. After asking directions and making several street crossings, they came to a building signed LATTER-DAY DRY GOODS and ventured inside.

It was clear that the transformation was most significant for Zelda. She came out of the dressing room in a full-length blue-and-gray flannel-aproned dress with her beautiful hair invisibly tucked into a bonnet with a cone-shaped front that hid her pretty face. The effect was akin to throwing a towel over a rose bush. John's wardrobe change was still dramatic despite his argument that plenty of Mormon cowboys wore clothes just like his.

"I understand that, sweetheart," Zelda said. "The point is, we're trying to make you less recognizable."

"I ain't wearing that underwear," he replied.

"Yes, dear." She smiled.

The deputy came out of the store wearing baggy wool pants hung by wide black suspenders, a collarless white shirt, and a hat that looked like an upside-down flowerpot with a short brim. They described themselves to the store owner as newly converted by missionaries they'd met on the train and anxious to spread this joyous news to family members on a potato farm in Twin Falls. He offered to dispose of their old clothes, but Zelda told him they hoped to sell them, as they would have little money after this purchase. The garments were wrapped in heavy brown paper, and a box was found for John's hat lest it be crushed. The man insisted they take a knitted shawl for her and a denim thigh-length coat for him on their journey north. He also offered undergarments at a discount, but they demurred, insisting he had done enough.

"You're still handsome as a statue," Zelda said. "I shall have to carry a rolling pin to defend you from all the sister wives I don't want."

"Sister wives?"

"Forget it, buster! You'll have your hands full with the one you've got."

They stopped at the hotel to change clothes and celebrate their three-day anniversary with a quick consummation. They spoke to a surprised desk clerk on their way out and told him to tell anyone who asked that they were on their way back to Spanish Fork.

37

Winter 1871

Sheriff Walter Becker eased out the door of Frank James's hospital and pulled it shut behind him. He stood quietly in the doorway and stared at the second-floor window of Yokum's Dry Goods across the street. He waved his hat at the moon's reflection in the glass hoping for a response and watched a cloud drift slowly across the orb, leaving only darkness. A piano accompanied several male voices in a melancholy song from a distant saloon, and he glanced that way with a vague recollection of the melody. It seemed to be an echo of the town's mood after losing the Blazing Star and the twins, its true blazing stars. Alamo would never be the same if they left, and he wondered if it would survive. The snow crunched beneath his boots as he crossed the street, and he shuddered at a singular breeze and the aroma of strong tobacco it carried. He drew his pistol and pressed his back against the store's facade, making another scan for movement or unusual shapes. A sense of urgency surged through him as he moved around the building behind the muzzle of his gun. He approached the store's back door, saw that it was open, and spoke out, his voice breaking, "There better not be anything done to that boy." A deep and unsettling laugh came from the darkness behind him, and he turned and fired a wild shot into the night. He entered, raced up the stairs toward the window, and tripped over something in the middle of the floor. The cocked revolver fired again when he landed, and in the flash of light, he saw it was the boy lying next to him. He crawled to the table by the window, groped for the lantern, and lit it. The soft light filled the room with shadows and illuminated the boy's body, his head in a pool of blood, his severed ear nearby. Walter opened the window and fired the pistol again and again until it clicked empty. He called for Doc, for Delbert, and for the sweet God in heaven to help him in this, his life's most panicked moment.

Soon the room was filled with citizens. Doc James took charge of getting Samuel to the hospital, while the sheriff ordered Delbert to round up a posse for an immediate pursuit. Delbert, with a better grasp of the situation, organized the men to make sure Samuel was safely carried across the street.

"Jeanie," Doc said to his wife, pulling her aside. They both looked back at the bloody body part resting on the floor like a discarded apple core. "What do you think?

"We can try," she said. "That boy's body is already a mass of scar tissue. We can try."

"If it fails to take hold, we can always remove it later," he said. "We should get started immediately while he's still unconscious but have ether ready in case he wakes up. I don't like that lump on the back of his head. He probably has a concussion."

"Yes. The girls can assist," she said. "Frank, we've got to get Walter calmed down. We don't want him in our hair, and I doubt Delbert's going to want him in the posse either. I've never seen him so upset."

"Let me think about that. I might put something in his coffee. Where is he?"

"I don't know. He was just here pacing and fretting."

Jeanie sent Mr. Yokum into the store downstairs for a new clean towel and wrapped the ear carefully in its folds. She apologized for the mess they were leaving behind, but he brushed it off in his heavily accented English, "It is nothing. It is nothing. But, Mrs. James, what is this man who murders two of our people in his fire then attacks this boy?"

"I don't know, Mr. Yokum. I don't know."

The commotion traveled like a disjointed caterpillar to the hospital. The twins were inconsolable when the injured boy was brought in. Jeanie calmed them with a direct explanation of their night's mission. "Samuel needs our help. We're going to repair his torn ear. He needs both of you as much as he needs the doctor and me. We've never done anything like this before, but we owe it to him to try.

"We shall do it," Chastity said.

"Yes, Jeanie," Prudence added. "You can count on us. Where do we begin?"

"Soap and water," Jeanie said. "We must wash ourselves and Samuel and all our instruments."

Doc James took Delbert aside as the others carried the boy to the operating room. "Jeanie and I are going to try to r-reattach Samuel's ear, and we can't have any of you here, including W-Walter. It's going to take all n-night. I'd like to suggest that you b-boys try to get some rest before you take off after our villain. There isn't much you can do in the d-dark. Where is the sh-sheriff anyhow?"

"I don't know, Doc," Delbert said. "You better get inside."

"Holy J-Jesus, you don't think he's g-gone out by himself?" the doctor said, noticing now how violently he was shaking. "Find him and put him in a j-jail cell if you have to. Let me know w-when you've got him."

Delbert opened the door and half-carried the doctor inside.

"Th-there you are Walter," he said. "I thought you were out r-running around in the dark."

"I killed him, Doc. I killed that boy," the sheriff said, sobbing into his handkerchief, whiskey bottle in hand.

"W-Walter, the boy will be f-fine. Jeanie and I are g-going to sew his ear b-back on. Th-that was my idea to send him over there, n-not yours. Gimme some of that, p-please. D-Delbert, come join us."

The sheriff blew his nose and put the handkerchief in his pocket. He poured whiskey in a glass, stepped behind his friend, and braced his head. "All right, Doctor, now stick your tongue out and say aah." He smiled. "Here's your medicine."

He emptied the liquid into the man's mouth and said, "I always wanted to say that."

"Thank you, Walter," the doctor said. "I can't count on Jeanie to do th-that for me anymore. She doesn't think it helps me, but I feel much better and believe I'm already losing the st-stutter. Delbert's getting a posse together at first light."

"That's right," Delbert said, pouring himself a glass. "With no fresh snow, he'll be hard to track, but we better have a look."

The sheriff shook his head. "Doc, where's the boy? I need to talk to him."

"Well, Walter, he was across the street at Yokum's on lookout, was attacked, and got his ear cut off," the doctor said, standing on shaky legs. "You found him and probably saved him from bleeding to death. Jeanie and I, with the help of the twins, are going to sew his ear back on. I'll let you know how we do tomorrow."

Jeanie stuck her head in the room. "We're about ready, Frank. He's awake."

"I'll be right there."

"I want to talk to him, Doc," the sheriff repeated.

"Not tonight. I don't want him thinking too hard. We're going to put him back to sleep in a few minutes. Delbert…"

"We're goin', Doc."

The doctor shuffled into the room and went directly to the boy. "Samuel, how are you feeling?"

"I'm good," he replied.

"Okay, son, listen to me. You've been hurt, and we're gonna fix you up, but I need straight answers to a few questions before we get started. You're the bravest person I've ever met, but right now I need to know where you have pain."

"The back of my head and my ear."

"Which ear?"

"Um, my right ear."

"What's my name?"

"Doc."

"Yes, that's right. What's my wife's name?"

"Jeanie."

"Good. Do you know who these beautiful girls are?

"Prudence and Chastity."

"Very good. Girls, bring that lamp over here and move it slowly in front of Samuel's face, please." He watched the boy's eyes follow the movement and saw they did not remain dilated.

"Samuel," he said, "we're ready to begin. There's been damage to your ear, and there's a bruise on the back of your head. Jeanie's going to sew up your ear, and I'm going to be here to watch her do it. I would do it myself..." He held up two shaking hands in front of his patient. "But if I did, it might end up on your forehead." He smiled, and the women laughed quietly, tears held back.

38

Summer 1849

They assumed positions at opposite ends of the train, John idly grooming a yard with a rake he found leaning against a shed and Zelda pulling weeds in a poorly tended flower bed. The train appeared to be nearing the end of the loading process. Watching the traffic to and from the cars had been more confusing than helpful. Dozens of bundles and packages that were big enough to contain the babies had been loaded. Midway through their third hour of surveillance, John had had enough. It was obvious to him that theirs had been a wasted effort, and what he was thinking was obvious to Zelda when she saw him leaning against a lamppost watching her. She stood to brush off her hands on her apron then walked over to join him.

"I've got an idea," she said, bumping his hip with her own. "I'm going to find a cow, buy a bucket of milk, and take it to a woman I've been watching and offer it to her for free because I don't need it. When I see which train car she takes it to, it'll be our first clue to where the twins are."

John looked at her and smiled, still unable to comprehend the emotions she ignited inside him. He couldn't remember anything of significance from his life before her. Leaning forward, he kissed her then placed his hands on her shoulders and turned her to face the train. Together they watched a boy lead a goat with two kids up a ramp into carload of horses and camels. "I don't think they need the milk.

"No, I don't guess they do," she said, a tremor in her voice. "What are we going to do?"

"Maybe we should talk to someone?" he asked. "Doesn't seem like having Siamese twins on that train would be an easy secret to keep from the crew."

"No, it would be impossible," she said. "There, that woman must know. Right there going into that green coach. I have an idea." She turned, ran into a fabric shop, and emerged ten minutes later with a package wrapped in brown paper and a *Book of Mormon*. "I'm going to deliver these diapers and this ticket to heaven, then I'm going to ask her about the twins."

"Zelda, the train's fixin' to leave. I don't think there's time." But she was gone, off at a run to the green train car and up the steps to knock at the door. It opened, and Zelda extended the package with her beautiful smile and disappeared inside.

John, trying to be invisible, closed the distance to the train when he saw a familiar figure walking beside it carrying a worn suitcase. Keeping his face down, he walked up behind the stable keeper, pulled the sheriff's Colt from his belt, and stuck it up under the man's coat against his backbone. "What the hell?" the man said after his initial surprise. "I was hoping I'd seen the last of you."

"Watch your language, pardner. You're in the presence of a missionary for Jesus."

"And I'm the angel Gabriel. What do you want from me?"

The deputy walked the keeper between two coaches and stopped in the middle of the tracks. He put the gun back in his belt, pulled a ten-dollar bill from his pocket, and put it in the man's hand. "The Colonel kidnapped my wife's twin sisters—Siamese twins. You know what that means? They're stuck together. They're not freaks, they don't belong in a circus, they're babies. We want 'em back."

"He hired me to put new shoes on twenty-three horses and repair some tack," he said, looking around. "I'll be takin' a train back to Salt Lake when I'm done. I still don't know what you want from me."

"We're followin' the circus to Boise on the next train. I'll find you when we get there. You tell me where those babies are, and there'll be another ten dollars for you. We can't afford any more than that. That's all we want."

"Here's your money back, deputy. If I know anything by the time we get to Boise, I'll let you know."

"Thanks. Sorry I choked you," Deputy John said. "Them circus people had me riled up."

"I figured that part," the stable keeper said.

A long blast from the train's whistle accompanied an enormous plume of black smoke and steam as the engine roared to life. The train made a sudden jerk forward, and the coupler next to the men tested its strength and held. They stepped into the clear and looked up and down the train's length as the last of its passengers boarded. The stable keeper trotted off to the livery car, and John stepped into the open to locate the green coach. No Zelda anywhere.

The colorful cars and coaches picked up speed, and the rare chance to rest cast its spell over the circus's male population. Their hammering, lifting, and carrying chores over, the train's rocking motion overcame the noise and odors that would be normal only to a circus troupe, and they slept. The situation in the green coach with its female population was different. Their tasks of cooking, childcare, and costume creation and mending continued unabated whether the train was in motion or parked. John caught up to it, climbed aboard, and banged on the door. A short fat woman appeared, stuck her head out the door, looked both ways, and said, "What can I do for you?"

"Is my wife still here?

"Pretty girl with the diapers?"

"Yes," he said, stepping inside and looking beyond the woman to the coach's interior.

"No, but we took the diapers. We have three little ones here and can always use more," she said, taking a breath. "I invited her in for a cup of tea, but the train was moving, and she said she was aware of that and was in a hurry."

"Yes, so am I. Do you know where she went? I didn't see her get off."

"Well, funny thing—" The woman sneezed, pulled a handkerchief from her apron pocket, and blew her nose. "Please excuse me. I'm allergic to camels."

"Yes, do you know where she went?"

"Yes, as I was saying, she asked about Siamese twins. Said she heard we had a pair on board." She stopped, took a couple short breaths as if she would sneeze again, then gathered her strength. "Excuse me, where was I?"

"Siamese twins?"

"Oh, yes," she said. "I told her we had them for a couple days, but they're gone now. I told her I was surprised she knew about that because it was supposed to be a secret. But you know it's hard to keep a secret in a circus."

"Yes, I really am in a hurry. Where did she go?"

"Your wife?"

"Yes, please."

"I told her she'd have to talk to the Colonel about the twins. I don't know who else would know, but he would for sure. I told her he would be in his coach by now because I saw him walk in that direction a few minutes before."

"I was out there and didn't see him go by."

"He was on the east side of the tracks. She went in that direction," she said, pointing.

John was out the door and immediately tripped over the coach's wooden stairs that had been pulled up and laid on its rear platform. Barely missing a face-first plunge to earth, he staggered to his feet and gauged his jump, which would be complicated by the train's increasing speed. Hanging from the ladder, he hit the ground running—briefly amused by his effort. He guessed the speed to be that of a slow horse in a good run. Although he wouldn't have thought his luck to be good, Deputy John got in two footfalls before heading directly into a six-foot sagebrush, breaking his fall and breaking the plant in half. Temporarily dazed, he got to his feet in time to see the Colonel's coach passing, Zelda and the Colonel standing on its rear platform.

"He's taking me to the twins!" Zelda yelled.

The Colonel—standing next to her—lifted a wineglass in salute to him, put his arm around John's wife, and kissed her on the cheek as the train rounded a curve and disappeared.

39

Winter 1871

"It looks pretty good, Doctor," Jeanie said.

"Yes, it does, Doctor," Frank replied. "Couldn't have done a b-better job myself—ten years ago."

"The ear is red and swollen."

"A good sign, I think," he said. "That means there's b-blood getting to the tissue."

"Will he be able to hear out of it?"

"I hope so. We just reattached cartilage. The eardrum didn't appear to be affected."

"Poor kid. He looks like he's been in a battle with a grizzly bear."

"Yes, I've w-wondered about possible scarring on his soul."

"Well, he's a tough kid, stoic." Jeanie sighed. "He's in love with those girls, you know."

"Yes, I'm not surprised. My guess is there's a b-broken heart in his future there."

"They've asked me what I might know about a separation," she said. "They had a client recently from Chicago who told them about a doctor who separated Siamese twin babies."

"I know," he said, rolling over to face her. "I r-read about it in one of my journals. Twin boys joined at the head. Both d-died after a twelve-hour operation. Impossibly complicated. These girls would be much less so, but a d-difficult procedure nonetheless."

"They're going to ask you about it."

"It would be e-expensive."

"They have money. The possibility of a separation is why they got into the prostitution business to begin with."

"I'll t-talk to them," said the exhausted doctor. "Then I'll write a letter to the surgeon and f-find out what I can."

While the hospital slept, the sheriff, his deputy, and a ten-man posse searched for the source of the evil that had descended upon their town. The effort to track the predator was as futile as Delbert had predicted. The snow around Yokum's Dry Goods was thoroughly beaten down by the previous night's rescue effort. All tracks led to and from main street. Riders were sent out to circle the community looking for side trails and possible encampments, but nothing of note was discovered.

The sheriff and Delbert walked by the Jameses' hospital and looked in the window for movement. "They must still be asleep," Delbert said.

The sheriff pulled his watch out of his pocket, showed it to his deputy, and said, "It's almost noon. They must be around."

"They were working on the boy's ear all night, Walter. I'll bet they're still resting. We might better wait until we see they're up and about."

"Yeah, right. The boy's ear." The sheriff shook his head. "We need to talk to him."

"Yes, sir, we will. Let's go get some breakfast."

"All right. I want to stop at the jail and get my notes first."

Seated in the back, they had a clear view of what was left of the morning crowd at Mom's Café. There were no unfamiliar faces as they all eventually turned to look at the two men.

"Everyone in town's got the jitters, Walter," Delbert said. "I'll make another round and talk to them. Maybe someone's seen something by now."

"That's a good idea, Delbert," the sheriff said. "Tell me what happened last night."

"You'll do better talkin' to Doc and the boy about how things started out. I heard your shootin' around ten and ran over to see what was goin' on," Delbert said. "What were you shootin' at?"

"I dunno."

"Sheriff, let's back up a bit. I think whoever this guy is, brought his motive to this town with him. None of this makes any sense. Seems like it has to do with the twins, but if he wanted to kill 'em, he could have done that the night of the fire or the night he ran through Doc's place. But the boy. Why in the world would he cut off the boy's ear? You think it was to punish him for saving the girls from the fire?"

"Goddamn, Delbert, those are good questions," said the sheriff in a flustered voice. "Write those down," he said, pushing his papers across the table. "Add what you remember about last night and today. I gotta talk to Doc and get what he remembers too. I'm so fuckin' mixed up."

"Walter, you need to get some sleep. I'll keep an eye on things this afternoon."

They finished breakfast and walked back to the jail. Delbert put the old man on a cot in a cell and covered him with two blankets. He stepped back outside to get an armload of wood, stirred the embers in the stove, and rekindled the fire. The atmosphere of the little log building had changed since the Star burned. No longer was it a daily gathering spot for morning coffee and gossip. It was disorganized and dirty and symbolized to Delbert the tension that held the town in its grip. Alamo was rightfully scared, and considering the sheriff's failing state, he felt it was up to him to step forward to reassure its citizenry. He grabbed the broom and made a swift pass through the room while he fretted, ending up at the hole in the floor that served as a dirt receptacle. Using the broom handle, he stirred the hole's contents knowing the floorboards would need to be pulled and the cavity cleaned before spring this year. *I'll put the Grimes boys on that,* he thought as he sat down at the desk and its clutter of unopened mail, invoices, and messages. He removed the contents of the sheriff's envelope, spread out the pages, and studied their details. The sheriff had put forth a noble effort to forestall his confusion, but the record of events didn't point to anything. Delbert touched the pencil lead to his tongue and rewrote a few sentences then added questions about the bandit's motive. He stared at the pages when he was done and shook his head as he got up and away from the desk.

There was a knock on the door, and a head appeared. "Is Sheriff Becker here?"

"He's here. Come in."

A tall lean man took off his hat and slapped it on his thigh. He stomped his snow-covered boots and stepped inside. "Thank you. It's really starting to come down out there. Yer fire feels good," he said, walking over to stand by the woodstove.

"The sheriff's sleeping. I'm his deputy, Delbert Givens. What can I do for you?"

"Ha," the man said, extending his hand. "You got my old job. I'm John Walker, US Marshal."

"Well, I'll be go to hell," Delbert said. "I don't know what brought you here, Marshal, but I'm sure glad to see you. We got a big problem."

"Deputy Givens, if it can wait an hour, I've got to take care of my horse and get a room for myself. Maybe by then the sheriff will be awake, and we can talk." The marshal stepped forward to shake Delbert's hand and said, "I'm glad to make your acquaintance, sir." Then he walked out the door.

Delbert didn't know what to do. He was tempted to wake the sheriff, but knew he needed sleep. *Heck*, he thought, *everyone in town needs sleep after last night, even me*. He replaced the planks in the floor, walked back to the jail cells, and listened to the old man snore for half a minute. The sound, repetitive and disturbing at every level, made the deputy yawn; and lacking a better plan, he found an empty bunk and dozed off.

"Sheriff, you look good."

"Thanks, John," the sheriff said. "I feel pretty good, but my memory's gone to hell, and it's not a good time for it. I'd ask you what you've done these last many years, but I'd have to ask you again tomorrow, so maybe we'll skip it for now. I do want to hear it though."

"We'll do it, sir, and as many times as you want to hear it. I have been around a bit."

"Tell me this, John, whatever happened to your beautiful wife?"

"Zelda."

"Yes, Zelda."

"That'll be part of my story, sir."

"You know the twins are here, don't you?"

"Yes, sir. That news gets around," John Walker said.

"Delbert, see if that coffee's ready, and I'll get my notes. We'll go over what's happened in the last couple weeks and see if John can make any sense of it."

The three men sat around the sheriff's desk as he read from his list of events and discussed its history, then they went through it all again.

"I'd like to go see all these places, sheriff," Walker said. "Then we could go to your hospital and talk to your witnesses. Is there anyone with them now?"

The sheriff looked at his deputy. "No, sir," Delbert said. "So far all our trouble's been at night."

"Go find the Grimes boys, Delbert. Get them shotguns and put one in front and one in the back of Doc's. Tell them we'll be there to relieve them in a while then meet John and me at the Blazing Star."

"Yes, sir."

The sheriff put his pages in their envelope, tucked them in a desk drawer, then buckled on his gun belt. A surge of confidence flowed through him as he patted his former deputy on the shoulder then led him out the door in the wrong direction.

"Sheriff, where've you been?" Delbert asked.

"I, uh, took the long way to get here," the sheriff replied. "Wanted to show John the layout of the town."

"I talked to Doc, told him we were coming," Delbert said. "He gave me this picture. He thought the marshal would be interested in seeing it."

"Well, yeah, let's have a look," the sheriff said. "Did he tell you what it is?"

"It's the Star, sheriff. The Blazing Star."

The old man studied the photo then looked at the building's ruins. "Here, John, have a look."

The marshal's eyes met Delbert's briefly, then he held the picture in front of them—in front of the structure's foundation. "It must have been quite a place," he said. "Where would the twins have been?"

"Right here on the second floor." Delbert pointed to the balcony at the front of the building. "The door to their room was locked from the outside. The door to the adjoining room had a chair jammed against the doorknob so the only direction they could go was outside to the balcony. The boy ran in through the front door, up the stairs, and let them out. The ceiling collapsed on them coming down the stairs, but he got them up and out through the front door."

"That's Samuel?"

"Yessir."

"He's the one who got his ear cut off?"

"Yessir. The boy's got the heart of a buffalo."

"Let's go meet him."

40

Summer 1849

John watched aghast as the train disappeared around the curve and ran forward until he could see it fade into the horizon. He was at once furious and heartsick and at a loss for what to do.

"Zelda! Zelda!" he yelled as he stood in the smoke and stench of the great machine. A residue of ash and dust settled on and around him. He threw his hat between the rails and stomped it until its felt was stretched and torn. Three boys watched him in silence, their dogs barking a response for the group.

"I'll kill him. I'll kill him. I'll kill him," he mumbled as he walked down the tracks back through the city. He wanted to run after the train, he wanted to steal a horse and chase it down, he wanted to talk to Sheriff Becker. What could he do? When would the next train go north?

Back at the hotel, he stopped at the front desk to speak to the clerk, the only person left in Salt Lake he knew. He was out of breath and distracted. "When does the next train leave north?"

"Tomorrow at 9:10," said the clerk.

"I'll be checking out in the morning," John said. "Is there a way I can leave my wife's bags here until we come back through?"

"Certainly. She won't be traveling with you?"

"No, she left with the circus."

"Oh."

"Yeah. Change of plans."

"Just bring them down, sir. I'll put them in a storeroom and tag them with her name."

"Thanks, we'll appreciate that," John said and laid a quarter on the desktop.

In their room, he fell on the bed and stared at the ceiling. He closed his eyes and imagined Zelda on top of him. Things happened in this bed that he'd never imagined were possible, intimate moments with his new wife he'd never forget. But the images and memories of her faded, and the sight of the Colonel with his arm around her, grinning at him, took him to a different place. He stood and stripped off the strange missionary clothing she'd bought him and smiled at her cleverness and enthusiasm. Finally redressed and comfortable in his own clothes, he packed her things carefully in her bags and carried them down to the lobby.

"I don't know how long before we're back. This trip isn't going the way we thought it would," he said to the clerk.

"That's fine, sir. These bags will be safe here. I assume you'll be leaving in the morning then."

"Yeah, I will," John said. "You don't happen to have a train schedule with stops on the way to Boise, do you?"

"We do, sir, right here." The clerk opened a printed copy of the Mid-Northern Flyer's departures and arrivals between Salt Lake City and Boise. "There are quite a few stops as you can see."

"Yeah, looks like it'll take days," John said.

"It's not as bad as it looks," the clerk said. "You have to remember the train runs all night. You should arrive at noon on the second day."

"Do you know how long the circus train takes?"

"No, but it would be longer. They don't stop as often, but they must stop at night to tend the animals. They will surely stop in Twin Falls. Perhaps you could catch up to Mrs. Walker there. Unless it was your plan to meet in Boise."

John looked at the clerk and didn't know what to say. *If only we'd had a plan.*

"Thanks, you've been a big help," he said. "What's your name?"

"Benjamin, sir."

"Thanks, Benjamin."

The walk to the fairgrounds was familiar by now, and Deputy Walker hoped it would be his last. It was a pleasant evening, and he was at a loss for anything to do. The dueling emotions of anger and heartbreak still consumed him, so he stepped into a saloon for a little consolation.

"I'll have a whiskey and a beer, please," he said, looking the place over. It was a nicely put out establishment, well suited for the business district in the blocks that surrounded it.

"Yes, sir, I'll be right back."

The barman returned set a frothy mug in front of him and a shot glass of amber liquid in front of the stool next to him. "That'll be two bits," he said.

John reached into his pocket and laid a quarter down. "What's this?" he said, nodding at the separated glasses.

"It's a little game we have to play for the saints," the man replied. "City hall says one drink per customer. They want to shut us down completely, so we cheat on their rules while we can. They'll win soon enough." He smiled and continued, "The guy sitting next to you is out back having a piss."

John smiled and reached over to the shot glass, poured it down, then took a long swallow of beer. The relief to his tortured brain was swift. He opened his coat, revealing his badge, and said, "Your secret is safe with me."

The barman reached under the bar to bring up a different whiskey bottle and refilled the tiny glass. "This is the good stuff, deputy. No charge."

"Thanks," John said. "You don't happen to know who runs the livery over by the tracks, do you?"

"That'd be Lloyd Clark. He's a regular. Great fellow."

Feeling better, Deputy Walker continued his journey to the fairgrounds with an improved outlook and a spinning head. Chewing on a salted pretzel and a pickled sausage, he arrived at the site to see a small army of workers loading wagons with circus garbage and piles and piles of shit. He stood near the tracks and relived his afternoon's experience. *The short fat woman in the green railcar.* "I'll be go to hell!"

he said aloud. What did she say? *"We had them for a couple days, but they're gone now."* In all the days since they'd been kidnapped, it was the first time he'd heard anyone say they'd seen the twins. If they'd been taken from the train in the city, they were probably still here. Hiding Siamese twin babies in a big city could be the perfect solution to the Colonel's problem—at least temporarily. But now the jackass had another problem: what to do with Zelda. *And me,* John thought.

41

The more he pondered his situation, the more complicated finding his wife was likely to be. Since the train was making half a dozen stops en route to Boise, there was no obvious place to look for her. The Colonel might have enjoyed making a fool of John by stealing his wife, but he would have his hands full when Zelda realized he'd lied to her. Looking out the train's window, he believed his only option was to travel to Boise and look for her on the way. He would search every train station and get off when they caught up to the circus train. The Colonel would be waiting for him.

Having yet to learn that all trains arrive late, the Flyer surprised John by pulling into Twin Falls around midnight—four hours late. It was busy in the terminal even at this late hour. Passengers going in both directions stacked luggage, rejoiced in greetings, and cried their goodbyes. The moonless night provided him the cover to exit opposite the platform and cross the tracks in front of the engine. He entered the station from its rear and found a vantage point behind boxes of freight. John was expecting trouble, and he saw it before it found him. Standing in the shadows at each end of the platform were two of the clowns he'd fought with in Salt Lake—the circus was here. The men were armed with handguns and watched exiting passengers before meeting in the middle of the commotion. After a brief conversation, the taller of the two entered the last coach at its end and walked forward through the train while the other watched from the platform. After this final flushing action, they went through the station one more time then walked off toward the circus train. John followed at a distance with his bag strapped across his back and his hand on his pistol. A guard with a shotgun emerged from the darkness and took their report before dismissing the men for the night. The guard entered the Colonel's car, emerged five minutes later, then followed the tracks north until he disappeared. *Zelda must still be here*, John thought, *why else would they be so worried about me?* But it was the middle of the night, and there was little to do while the circus slept. He crept forward through the darkness past the train to a small grove of cottonwoods and tall grass and lay down to sleep.

At first light, a rooster crowed somewhere, followed by the sound of a hammer striking metal. John raised his head slowly to see that his cover was good, but he was cold and had to piss. He walked further into the trees to relieve himself then turned to watch an already active scene at the train. It seemed there was movement everywhere. Smoke was drifting skyward from the locomotive's smokestack, animals were being fed, and several men were pitching hay from a horse-drawn wagon into a sided open railcar. Two other wagons were in line to be unloaded, so John knew the train would not be leaving soon. Another line was forming at the green railcar, and he watched members of the troupe walk away with coffee, bread, and something hot in a bowl. His own stomach growled, reminding him he hadn't eaten since yesterday.

A familiar figure walked his way along the tracks carrying a tray stacked high with covered dishes. The short fat woman he'd spoken to on the green railcar was delivering breakfast to the Colonel's car, and he was either starving or there were others inside.

"The Colonel must be hungry," John said, catching up to her on her return trip. Surprised at how rapidly her short legs moved, he quickened his step to keep up. "Do you remember me?"

"Yes, I do. You changed your clothes."

"Yes, ma'am, I did. But my mission is the same. I'm looking for my wife. I saw her at the back of the Colonel's caboose after I saw you in Salt Lake, and she yelled to me that the Colonel was taking her to her Siamese twin sisters." He stepped in front of her. "Was he lying to her?"

"Yes, he was. But your wife is no fool and figured that out. They had a fight, and she broke a wine bottle over his head. I sewed him up," she said then moved to step around him. "I could lose my job if he knew I was talking to you."

"Where is my wife?" John said, easily blocking her.

"She got off in Ogden. I assumed she was going back to you."

"Where are her twin sisters?"

"I don't know. I told you before. They were taken off this train in Salt Lake."

"Those babies were kidnapped, and you're involved whether you like it or not." He opened his coat to show her his badge. "Do you think my wife—their sister—and me are going to let this stand?"

The woman looked up at the same time Deputy Walker felt the pressure of a gun barrel on his back. His pistol was pulled from its holster, and a voice said, "Don't move, asshole. Let's go talk to the man."

"I'm done fuckin' with you and your sassy wife deputy," the Colonel said. "She's not here. There are no Siamese twins here. And you're not going to be here much longer either."

John looked at the Colonel and laughed. "Looks like she got you pretty good. Maybe a dentist can use the new hole in your head to get into your mouth and give you a new front tooth."

The Colonel nodded to the man standing behind him, who brought the barrel of John's gun down hard on the back of his head. When he woke up, his hands were tied behind his back, and his ankles tied to his hands. The train was moving, and he appeared to be alone in the Colonel's coach. He struggled against the ropes, but the movement made his head throb and temporarily blinded him. A convulsion spewed bile from his empty stomach, and he gagged until he could barely breathe. His gasps turned into a long low groan, and he waited for a response, but there was none. No one else there. By rocking against his right hip, he could tell his pocketknife was gone; but turning his ankle, he could still feel the stiffness of the knife in his boot. Their body search hadn't found it. Rolling onto his stomach, he was able to elevate his feet over his back, untuck his pants with his fingers, and shake the knife free. The rest of the process made him think of wrestling a pig. He moved back and forth to keep pressure on the blade while sawing and stretching the rope. When he finished, his fingers ached and were cut and bleeding, but he was free. Desperately thirsty, he found a small water barrel and dipper and gulped down enough to stop the spinning in his head. His gun was gone, but he stuck his knife back in his boot, strapped his bag over his shoulder, and left through the back door.

From the Colonel's caboose, he climbed the ladder to the roof and started to move forward. It was impossible to know where they were, except that the train was somewhere in Idaho traveling west to Boise. Once it was discovered that he'd cut himself loose, the train would be searched, including the roofs. He watched the ground race past and knew he could not jump. If only he'd stayed in Salt Lake, he might be having breakfast with his wife right now after a long night of consummation.

"Lloyd, Lloyd, is that you?" After traveling over seven rooftops, John cracked open the door to the tack car. Inside was the hardware of the circus—miles of rope, stakes, tools, cables, saddles, and tack.

"What? Who is that?"

"Lloyd, it's John Walker from Salt Lake." Pushing on the door from the outside, it wouldn't budge. "Lloyd, let me in."

"What the heck are you doing here?" The farrier pried open the door with an elbow then moved back to his workbench, dragging the set of reins that hung from his neck. He stretched a harness breast strap in front of him then picked up an awl with heavy thread and began to stitch it. "Tell me," he said.

"Is anybody else in here?" John said. Looking around, he dragged what must have been elephant harness up against the door then added a box of steel tent posts.

"Not now, but that could change," Lloyd said, leaning over to spit on the floor.

"I took the Flyer to Twin Falls and got off when I saw the circus train to look for my wife. Then I found out from a cook that she got off in Ogden. Then the clowns hit me on the head and tied me up in the Colonel's caboose. I got loose and don't know if they know it yet."

"Sounds like you're in a pickle."

"Yeah, maybe," John said, bending over to pick up an apple that was rolling across the floor. "You gonna eat this?"

"Not if you do," Lloyd said, looking up from his work. "What're you gonna do?"

John polished the apple on his shirt then took a bite. "Try not to get hit in the head anymore." He chewed for a minute and said, "I still got problems. I ain't found the babies yet, and my wife's still missing. I owe that Colonel a good ass whoopin', but I'm a little outnumbered."

"Well, I'd like to help, but I don't know how. They're probly gonna find you before we get to Boise, and if it's in here, I'm likely to get my head busted too. These crackers are kind of a rough bunch."

"Do you think the train will stop before Boise?"

"I doubt it. Probly only fifty or sixty miles to go. And we're going too fast to jump," he said and looked up at John. "But there's no tellin' what you might do."

"Yeah, I already thought about that. Are there any guns in here?"

"I don't know. I don't have one."

Footsteps of more than one man scraped across the roof above them, going front to back. "I better go, Lloyd," John said then stacked a few more things against the rear door. Before he finished, the yelling began.

"Open the door. Open this goddamned door!"

John picked his way through piles of gear to get to the front door of the coach. He turned his head and waved at his new friend as the voices and pounding behind him got louder. He opened the door in front of him and stepped into the hands of four men.

42

Winter 1871

"Doc, this is Walter's deputy from Spanish Fork, US Marshal John Walker," Delbert said.

"Well, I'll be a bl-blue-nosed go-gopher," the doctor exclaimed. Stepping forward, he held his right hand steady with his left and extended them both to take John's hand. "I've heard a lot about you, Ja-John. I di-didn't know you we-were a marshal though."

"It's an honor, sir," John said. "Except to send some money I owed him, I haven't communicated with the sheriff much in twenty years. I've moved around a bit."

"How long have you been in town, John?" the sheriff asked.

"Just a few hours, sir," he replied. "I'm on my way to Helena and heard my wife's sisters were here, and I wanted to see them first. I've never met them."

"What was your wife's name again?" the sheriff asked.

"Zelda, sir."

"That's right," the sheriff said. "And where is Zelda?"

"I wish I knew," John said, looking around at the small group with a grim smile. "I've never found her."

"Well, Marshal, m-maybe it's time you met your s-sisters-in-law," Doc said. "First, this is my wife, Jean. Jean, this is John."

"Jean, it's an honor," John said, stepping forward to shake her hand.

She stepped past his hand and into his arms to give him a teary hug. "Walter has told us about you and Zelda and your time in Salt

137

Lake when you were looking for the girls. They'll be thrilled to see you."

"If you all don't mind, I'd like to t-take charge of this gathering," Doc said. "There's so m-much to do, and it's a dangerous time. Jean, where are the g-girls?"

"In the kitchen," she replied.

"Good. Take J-John back to meet them, then we'll go t-talk to Samuel."

John disappeared with Jean for twenty minutes then returned to the doctor's office to meet a young man with a heavily bandaged head.

"Marshal, S-Samuel here's been at the heart of this episode right from the start," Doc began. "He's been its h-hero and its v-victim. We haven't had a chance to talk to him about last n-night yet, so you'll be hearing from him for the first time just like we will. Jean and I r-reattached his ear, and since we've never done anything like th-this before, we don't know how it'll take. We'll have a l-look at it soon."

"I'm glad to meet you, Samuel," John said. "I just met the twins for the first time, and they think the world of you, son. I've talked to the sheriff, Delbert, and the doctor about what's been goin' on here. Can you tell us about what happened last night?"

"I ain't got much to tell," he began, staring at the marshal. "I was sittin' in a chair, watchin' the street and Doc's place, and next thing I know, I'm over here."

Doc put a shaky hand on his shoulder. "That's fine, s-son. You g-got hit on the head, and the sheriff found you. Half the town showed up to g-get you here."

"Samuel, you don't remember a voice? Nobody talked to you?" John asked.

"No, sir. I didn't hear anything."

"Sheriff, I'd like to go to the store across the street to see where Samuel was last night. Will you walk me over there?" John asked. "Doctor, we'll be back in a little while."

The two men entered the store, spoke to Mr. Yokum, and followed him to the stairway in back. Upstairs, the mess from last night had been cleaned up, and there was a clear path through the boxes and racks of clothes to the window over main street. The table and chair where the boy sat were still in place.

"There's a good view from here. The hospital and up and down the street," John said.

"Yeah, I feel terrible about that boy." The sheriff shook his head then sat in the chair. "It shoulda been me over here."

"It was a good plan. With the store locked up, the boy shoulda been safe up here. Maybe he dozed off." John stood with his back to the wall and crossed his arms. "Sheriff, did Zelda ever come back to Spanish Fork after you left us in Salt Lake?"

The sheriff looked up at him and smiled. "I still have some memories that old. Did I tell you it's the new stuff I'm having the most trouble with?"

"Yes, sir, you mentioned that."

"What did you ask me?"

"Have you seen my wife, Zelda, in the last twenty years?"

"No, I don't think so," the sheriff said, scratching his whiskers. "I stayed in Spanish Fork about a year, I think, after I last saw you. My ma and brother were gone. I didn't have any reason to stay. I couldn't sell the ranch, so I came up here to the gold strike. Turns out they needed a sheriff more than they needed another gold digger, so I got the job. I won't have it much longer though. My brain's dying."

John nodded then stepped back to the window and spoke over his shoulder. "Whatever happened to Chatham?"

"Well, I got him back to Spanish Fork, but my ma was sick and couldn't identify him. The stable keeper from Salt Lake took off with the circus, so I couldn't get him to identify my brother's horse. I kept Chatham in jail for a week, but the judge said that without any witness or evidence, I had to turn him loose. So I did. His family wouldn't have him back."

The sheriff took off his hat and laid it on the table. He leaned forward, set his elbows on his knees, and rubbed his temples with his fingertips. "I got these headaches that don't let up much anymore."

"Does Dr. James know about that?"

"No, I ain't told nobody. It's not a good time."

"Maybe there's something he could do."

"I've got a plan for it after we catch this bandit."

"What do you mean by that?"

The sheriff sat up, reached out for his hat, and said, "Oh, nothin'. What did you want to know about Chatham?"

"I think Chatham is here," John said. "I asked the twins if they knew him, and they said no, but they weren't telling the truth. I asked them if they knew Zelda, and they said yes, but they didn't know where she was."

"Why wouldn't they tell you the truth?"

"I don't know, but I aim to find out."

43

Summer 1849

"Let's try this again, deputy," the Colonel said. "I'm sure you've noticed that the rope that's been used to bind your hands and feet now also goes around your neck. You'll be fine if you don't relax your arms and legs and let yourself get strangled. It's a little trick we used when I was an Indian fighter in the cavalry. We called it the death knot." He laughed, enjoying himself. "I'll put your boot knife here in this drawer with your pocketknife and pistol. A much better gun than you were using a few days ago, I see. Oh, and let's not forget the thirty dollars from your sock."

The Colonel walked to open a cabinet door and removed a whiskey bottle. "Let's toast the capture of our stowaway, boys." He poured himself a shot then gave the bottle to his men, who passed it around. "Don't forget our new farrier. Join us, Mr. Clark."

"No, thanks," Lloyd said. "I've got work to do. I need to get back to Salt Lake."

"Mr. Clark, have you provided assistance to the deputy here?"

"I have not," the stable keeper said. "Last time I saw him, he had his hands around my throat."

"Ha ha," the Colonel laughed. "That sounds like our boy."

"Do you know what we do with stowaways, deputy?" the Colonel continued.

John glared at him, but tightly gagged, he could not answer.

"We throw them off the train," he said. "And now's your time."

The Colonel knelt on John's back, and he leaned down to whisper in his ear, "Your wife and I have been having a big time together. I especially love the little screams she lets out before she blossoms." He pulled the deputy's head up by his hair then slammed it down onto the floor, breaking his nose. "If I ever see you again, I'll kill you."

He stood, retrieved John's pistol from the drawer, and stuck it in the farrier's ear. "Lloyd," he said, "take the deputy out the back door and throw him off the train."

"I won't," Lloyd said, looking at John on the floor.

"Maybe you'd like to go with him?"

"You need me to finish my work. Your horses' feet are in bad shape. Do you want to run a circus or hang for murder?"

"You sound pretty tough considering your situation, Mr. Clark. Let's go back to the beginning," the Colonel said. "You take the deputy out that door and throw him to the tracks, or you get thrown out with him. I'll take my chances with the law." He hit Lloyd hard on the head with the gun barrel. "Do it now."

Lloyd fell to the floor next to the pool of blood surrounding John's head. He got himself to his hands and knees and struggled to stand.

"Help him, boys," the Colonel said. "I've got things to do."

The circus men descended on the two men on the floor, untied the rope around the deputy's neck so he could stand, and shoved them out the door to the platform. They wrapped them together with rope then pushed them off the train toward the rough terrain of the high desert.

"Jasper, find three or four farriers when we get to Boise and put 'em to work on the horses," the Colonel said when they reentered the car. "You boys can leave now."

"Yessir," the group mumbled incoherently.

The Colonel walked to the front room of his coach, tapped on the door, and went inside. "Zelda honey, the babies are still asleep. I'll have them brought back so you can see them later," he said in a soft voice. "We've got some time before we get to Boise, sweetheart. Let me help you get out of your clothes."

44

Winter 1871

"Samuel, I'm afraid our effort to reattach your ear wasn't successful," Jean said. "The arteries and veins that bring blood to your ear and recirculate it back to your heart are so small that we couldn't connect them properly. We're going to have to take the ear back off. I'm so sorry."

"You're j-just going to have to grow your hair l-long enough to cover it." Doc smiled. "Let's go g-get it done, son."

The twins walked with him to the surgery/dining room and held his hand as he lay down on its blanketed surface.

"I hope there aren't any dirty dishes under there," Prudence said.

"Oh dear." Chastity giggled. "We are missing a fork."

Samuel offered a small smile and closed his eyes when they kissed him. "Call me Sam after I wake up," he said. "There's not much of Samuel left to recognize." There were tears all around as they prepared for the procedure.

Two hours later, young Sam was freshly bandaged and awake in the bed he'd occupied for so much of the last month. His head throbbed with an aching pain that kept him from sleep and would continue to do so for longer than anyone would know. At midnight, he got dressed in the silent building then checked to be sure his pistol was loaded before opening the door and stepping outside. Across the street at Yokum's, Marshal Walker noted the activity from his station at the window. Sam looked in that direction and gave the smallest wave from a gloved hand. He walked slowly from shadow to shadow, stopping to watch and listen to the cold stillness of the winter night. A crescent moon broke through a scattered cloud cover to illuminate the wreckage of the Blazing Star as he passed. Much of the debris had been removed, but his memories of that night remained. He would never forget his vision of the twins trapped on the balcony and the horrors of the bodies inside. Almost on cue, another memory was triggered when he detected the pungent smell of strong tobacco. Firmly pressed against the inside corner of a feed store, he turned his head slowly to look for movement and test the air for direction. With a firm grasp on the pistol, he pulled it clear of his coat and held it before his face when he turned into a narrow alley. The darkness now complete, he felt his way to the rear of the buildings, the odor stronger as he traveled. A disorganized lot of shadows and silhouettes occupied the area behind main street. Storage sheds, corrals, haystacks, cords of firewood, and outhouses supported business owners in a disjointed pattern. The boy stood silent and still in the shadows, his senses alert and searching.

A match flared from behind a buggy, behind a barn fifty yards away. The brief flash of light was barely noticeable from his angle, and he watched for movement. Five minutes then ten minutes passed before a human shape emerged from the opposite side of the barn. Stealthy as a cat, Sam eased out of his cover and crept forward building to building until he saw a dark shape approach the hospital's back door thirty feet away. Pressed into a doorway, he watched the figure bend down to face the door's new lock and insert something into it. Holding and aiming his pistol with both hands, Sam pulled back the hammer, the action clicking loudly in the silence. The man jerked up at the sound, drew a knife from his belt, and threw it at the boy. The blade cut through the darkness and quivered in the doorjamb inches from Sam's face as he squeezed the trigger. The flash of the explosion temporarily blinded him, but he moved forward slowly to stand over the motionless body.

Gunshots in the middle of the night weren't unheard of in Alamo, Montana, but considering the tension the town's residents went to bed with of late, this one caused many to cover their heads and hope they remembered to lock the door. The nearness of the explosion not only awakened the small population of the Jameses' hospital but also prompted screams from the young women inside. Its older occupants' initial reaction was confusion as they made the transition from dream to reality to response. For John Walker across the street, the shot was a call to action.

"You all right?" The marshal was standing at Sam's side. He reached down and held his fingers against the man's neck.

"He threw a knife at me," Sam said, still staring at the body in front of him.

"Where were you?"

"I was standing in the doorway over there." The boy pointed at the building behind him.

Marshal Walker walked to the spot, saw the knife still stuck in the wood, and returned without touching it. "Did you see anybody else?"

"No, there's just him."

"Is there a lantern in that barn?"

"Yeah, I'm sure there is."

"Go get it, would you?"

The marshal knelt before the door and saw a small file and a piece of wire protruding from the door lock above the knob. There were voices on the other side of the door and a rattling of the doorknob.

"Don't open the door," he said in a firm voice. "Dr. James?"

"Marshal, is that you?"

"Yes, it's John Walker. Can you come out here, sir? Go through the front door and walk around."

"I will. Let me get dressed," the doctor said. "I'll bring the sheriff."

"Good," the marshal yelled back.

The boy arrived with the light and passed it to the older man.

"You all right, son? You want to go inside and warm up?"

"No, sir. I'm good."

"Good. Let's roll him over."

Together they turned the man on his back, uncovering a large patch of blood-soaked snow. The marshal stood, turned a circle, and took in as much of the terrain as the light would reveal. Looking back to the body, he asked, "Do you know this man?"

"No, sir, I don't."

Brushing snow off the whiskered face, the marshal held the lantern close as the doctor and sheriff arrived.

"Walter, do you recognize this man?" John Walker asked.

"Well, yeah," he said, scratching his chin. "That's Chatham, isn't it?"

"Yes, sir," Marshal Walker replied. "I believe it is."

"Who is he?" Sam asked.

"He's the twins' pa," the sheriff said.

45

Summer 1849

The two men bound together face-to-face exited the train into the Southern Idaho desert, going around forty-five miles per hour. They were fortunate to land in a small percentage of the hostile environment that wasn't the skin-tearing, bone-crushing terrain the Colonel had anticipated.

Prior to laying railroad ties and spiking rails to the ties, a bed of raised earth would be set to level the perpetual unevenness of the natural topography. Where streams and rivers were encountered, bridges and trestles were built to allow flowage beneath the tracks. Intermittent streams often went unrecognized or were ignored. John and Lloyd had the good fortune to land virtually unhurt north of the tracks in a marsh or pond, where the track bed blocked the natural passage of a sometime stream. Their water landing's immediate benefit was soon forgotten when they were faced with the possibility of drowning. John, five inches taller than Lloyd, seemingly had the advantage when landing on top in the three-foot-deep water. Bound, gagged, and with a blood-packed nose, he was unable to gain a decent breath when he raised his head above the surface. Lloyd's panicked response from the bottom of the pool overpowered the larger man when he spun to the top for air and took a glance at their situation. His hands having never been tied, Lloyd was able to twist and wrestle them to a position where both their heads were above water. He pulled John's gag down and out of his mouth and received a face full of gore for his trouble as John coughed and choked to clear an air passage. Lloyd, undaunted, unwrapped the rope that bound them together and pushed it over their heads before untying John.

"That coulda been worse," he said, taking a few steps away from the cattails and willows.

John, still coughing, gasped, "I'm gonna kill that son of a bitch."

"Yeah, that's what he said to you," Lloyd said. "Looks to me like he's holdin' all the good cards. Are you hurt?"

"No. Are you?"

"I been better. Nothing's broken. Yer lucky they cut that rope around yer neck. I expect you'd be dead otherwise," Lloyd said. "Look at me."

John turned to face him.

"Yer nose is crooked. Lie down here. I'll fix it."

John walked a short distance from the water and lay down on his back. "You know what yer doin'?"

"I saw it done a couple times. You ain't gonna like it, but I think I can straighten it some."

Lloyd knelt in front of John's head and pressed his knees tightly against his ears. He placed the heel of his right hand against the straight side of the nose and the heel of his left against the bent side. "Let me know when you're ready." Not waiting for a response, Lloyd pressed his palms together hard and fast, extracting a scream from the deputy as he sat upright to spit, choke, and cough.

"Aw!" groaned John. "I'm gonna kill him!"

"Yeah, you keep sayin' that. Here, let me take a look," Lloyd said. "Man, yer a mess. You got blood everywhere. Wash yer head here in this pond. I wouldn't drink it though."

They knelt in the water together and rinsed off. Lloyd continued, "I'm surprised the Colonel didn't have his boys take our boots off. He coulda made this a lot more unpleasant if he wanted to. He musta been in a hurry."

"Thanks for not throwing me off the train when the Colonel told you to."

"Yeah, that was real smart of me. You got throwed off anyhow, and now I'm here too. I got near three days' work done for that circus that I'll never get paid for."

"I'll owe it to ya," John said.

"Well, that's nice. I suppose you're well set up with cash."

"No, I'm not," John said, looking down at his bloodstained shirt. "I owe Sheriff Becker a month's pay plus fifty dollars for this trip. And I owe a dry goods store in Spanish Fork twenty dollars for these clothes."

Lloyd laughed, "Ha, maybe you can go back to that store and tell 'em the clothes didn't hold up and you don't think you should have to pay full price. You shouldn't have any problem comin' up with another thirty dollars for me." They walked away from the tracks toward higher ground to the north. "You kill the Colonel, you'll get hanged anyhow. I wouldn't worry about yer finances. There's gotta be a road goin' east and west someplace out here," Lloyd said, turning a full circle. "I can't figure if it'd be above or below them tracks. Which way you goin' anyhow?"

"I don't know, I can't figure it." John said. "That short fat cook in the green coach told me Zelda got off in Ogden and the twins got left in Salt Lake. I might ought to go to Boise and earn some money for a train ticket. I ain't walkin' back there."

"You say a short fat cook told you that?"

"Yeah, I talked to her twice."

"Don't know if I'd put much stock in her. She's the Colonel's wife," Lloyd said. "Near as I can tell, she's as full of shit as he is."

"Well, that's great news," John said, sitting down on a rock. "Now I got nothin' to go on and no idea what the hell to do. Did you ever talk to anyone on the train who might know somethin' and would tell the truth about it?"

"Can't say. I wasn't there very long and was workin' all the time. I wouldn't go near that circus if I were you," Lloyd said. "I got money for two train tickets. Let's walk."

46

Winter 1871

"S-Samuel."

"It's Sam, Doc."

"Sam, you get inside. You don't need to be out in this cold after that surgery."

"I cain't sleep, sir."

"I d-don't care. I don't want you going into shock. Get in b-bed and stay awake if you have to," Doc said. "I'll give you something for the p-pain when I get inside."

"Sam, don't say anything to the twins on who this is," the sheriff added. "We'll talk to them in the mornin'."

"Yessir."

"What should we do with him tonight?" Marshal Walker asked.

"Well," the sheriff said, "we can't take him in here. How 'bout we wrap him in a tarp and put him in the barn?"

"I'll get Delbert, and we'll take care of it," the marshal said. "You both get inside and get some sleep. I'll be by first thing in the mornin'."

"Good. Thanks, John," the sheriff said. "Cover his eyes so the magpies don't get 'em."

No one slept well that night. The doctor and sheriff told the women a man had been killed trying to break into the hospital and assured them that Alamo and its population were finally safe. The marshal went to the jail and rousted Delbert for his help to move the body. When they were done, he walked on to his hotel.

The lobby of Alamo's Last Stand was vacant when he entered. A low vibrant snore came from behind the desk, the soles of well-polished shoes visible on its surface. Climbing the stairs to his room in the dim lamplight, John couldn't shake or understand the depression he felt. Nothing in Chatham's demise could cause him to feel this way, could it? He had seen him twice in the two decades he'd searched for his wife. Both times, he almost spoke to him, considering the possibility that he knew something of Zelda. He guessed that Chatham had dogged the Colonel over the years, not willing to give up on a payday for the use of his daughters. No doubt the Colonel wouldn't have put up with that kind of harassment for long. But Chatham was like a snake laying in the weeds, looking for an advantage, waiting to strike. John suspected he'd come to Alamo with a similar mindset to harm or harass the twins.

Sitting on the edge of the bed, he pulled off his boots and rubbed his numb toes, one foot then the other. He walked to the dresser, pulled out his whiskey bottle, and set it on top. His heavy wool socks were next, and he put them on while standing there. A grimace covered his face, and the desperate loneliness that consumed him for so long tore at his heart. He pulled the cork and tipped the bottle to the ceiling for two long swallows. The warm swell in his chest soothed him as he lay in the bed and pulled the quilts up to his chin. He closed his eyes and drifted into the dream he suffered every night—the memory of his too-short time with Zelda and the desperate hope he carried everywhere, every day, that he would find her again.

John and Delbert retrieved Chatham's body from the barn at first light and delivered it to Evan Grove's Mortuary. They stopped at Mom's Café for coffee, and John described his early history with the dead man, going back to Spanish Fork and Salt Lake City. "He started the whole mess," John said. "Changed a lot of lives and killed a few. I shoulda shot him the first day I saw him." He finished his coffee, put a dime on the table, and stood up. "I shoulda done lots of things different."

The two men entered the Jameses' hospital to the wonderous smells of eggs, ham, and flapjacks. Neither having eaten much the previous day, they ate this morning until everything was gone then tried not to be noticed as they looked around for more. Sheriff Walter Becker and Dr. Frank James sat in a corner, the doctor explaining to the sheriff what had happened the previous night while the sheriff poured small amounts of coffee in the doctor's mouth. John and Delbert excused themselves to go outside with Sam to watch and listen to his description of his encounter with Chatham. Then they returned in time to see Jean and the twins return to the operating room from the kitchen.

The sheriff began, "Chastity and Prudence, your pa was picking the lock at the back door last night when Sam shot him. He threw a knife at Sam that missed his head by only a couple inches." He stopped there for a full minute so the young women could absorb the news. They looked at each other, then they embraced, and Chastity started to cry.

"We're pretty damn sure it was him that burned down the Star, came crashin' through here that one night, and cut off Sam's ear at Yokum's. But there's a lot we don't know," the sheriff said. He looked at Doc and asked, "What else?"

"The h-horse," Doc answered.

"Oh yeah," the sheriff continued. "He was on horseback when Sam saw him the first time, and we don't know where the horse is. And we don't know where he's been stayin'. Here's his wallet and gun, but he must have a poke somewhere."

"We d-don't know why the h-hell he's even h-here." Doc shook his head.

"We know," Prudence said, leaning over to kiss her sister on the cheek. "He was after us."

"We figured it was him all along," Chastity added. "We didn't say anything because it didn't seem like it would help."

"How do you know him?" John asked.

The girls looked at each other then said together, "He was a customer."

"He came to us five times before he told us who he was," Prudence said. "I slapped him and said, 'You better be lyin'.' Then he slapped me back and laughed and said, 'You're just a couple of whores. You woulda fucked me anyhow.' He said he wanted five hundred dollars. He said we caused him a passel of trouble and we owed him for it," she paused and hugged her sister again, and they both cried. No one else in the room breathed.

Chastity raised her head, coughed, and spoke in a guttural voice, "He said if we didn't pay him, he'd kill one of us. He laughed and asked how we'd like that. He asked which one of us wanted to get stabbed and which one wanted to watch. He said, 'How you bitches think that's gonna end?'" Then they leaned forward, still clutching each other, and vomited on the floor.

Jeanie hurried over to hold their foreheads and spoke out in a calm voice, "Someone bring towels and water, please."

Sam and Delbert jumped to the task and disappeared into the kitchen. John moved forward to kneel next to Chastity and wiped her mouth with a napkin. Jeanie stepped back to hold Prudence, and working together, they cleaned the twins. Doc and the sheriff stared at the women then looked at each other, collectively grinding their teeth, trying to comprehend what they'd just heard.

"That's a g-grim story, girls," Doc said. "I'm sorry you h-had to go through that." He shook his head and reached out to pat Sam's shoulder. "Your pa was an evil m-man, and Sam did us a f-favor. Now we don't have to h-hang him. I'm s-sorry you had to hear those things h-he said to you. But I'm s-sure you understand the c-consequences you would face if something h-happened to just one of you," he said.

"Um, excuse me, Doc." Delbert stood and addressed the group. "I've got something I should be doing."

"Is that you, Delbert?" the sheriff asked.

"Actually," John Walker added, "I think I'll be going too. Y'all don't need me here for this conversation. I do want to talk to you both, Prudence and Chastity, but I can come back later. I'll probly be leaving tomorrow."

"Excuse me again..." It was Delbert, back in the room and wearing a confused look on his face. He held his hat in his hands and looked directly at John. "There's a young man here, and he wants to see you, Marshal. Says his name is John Walker. And, sir, he looks just like you."

47

Summer 1849

John and Lloyd found the road barely a mile north of the tracks. It was rutted and narrow and clearly had seen lots of use. They followed it west for two hours then caught a ride with a Basque sheepherder and his dog on their way from Ketchum to Boise. They sat side by side on the too narrow seat of his camp wagon and listened to his barely understandable pidgin English as he rambled on and on about building a house and starting a family. The man himself carried the combined stench of human sweat, human shit, human piss, wet wool, woodsmoke, blood, and the overwhelming smell of everything sheep. His dog, who moved from lap to lap, didn't smell any better. They refused the dried mutton he offered and tactfully turned away from the wine he'd made himself and carried in a sheepskin bota. It was more than the two men could stand, and after a couple of miles, they thanked the man and announced they had arrived at their destination.

Lloyd held up both hands to the man, signing him to stay stopped while he walked forward to examine the two worn-out mules. John wandered off to piss with the dog in tow. Lloyd called the sheepherder down to unhitch the team so he could use his pocketknife to perform first aid on the overgrown and badly split hooves. The man continued to drink from the bota while he watched and nodded in appreciation when Lloyd finished. He smiled, removed a small shiny object from his pocket, and held it out to Lloyd in a filthy clenched fist. Short fat fingers with long broken nails relaxed and allowed the thing to roll onto the farrier's palm.

Lloyd examined it, bowed, and asked, "What's your name?"

"Jakome," the sheepherder said with a toothless grin.

And your dog?"

"Chooga."

The farrier advised the man that the animals would not last another ten miles without rest and proper hoof care. But Jakome just laughed, climbed to his seat, and waved for them to join him.

"No, thanks," Lloyd said, then he made a striking motion with his fingers and cupped his hands around an imaginary flame. "Can you spare some matches?"

The man nodded, climbed back into the wagon, and reemerged with a finger-sized piece of flint. He passed it down as John rejoined them.

"That'll do," Lloyd said. "Thank you, sir. Good travels. And take care of those mules."

"Graci Jesus, graci Jesus!" Jakome declared, looked down at the men, then slapped the reins on the backs of his team. Chooga, in an acrobatic maneuver, ran ahead of the mules then spun around to run and jump into the sheepherder's arms. The three men laughed while the shaggy dog licked the old man's face and got a piece of mutton for his effort.

"We'll pass them tomorrow even if we're still walking," Lloyd said, and they watched the wagon pull away at a slow but steady pace.

"You think his wife will be glad to see him?" John asked.

"He said he was going to start a family, not see his wife," Lloyd said. "His wives are still back in the mountains. Did you see the sheep piss and shit stains on the front of his pants?"

"Ha! You mean...?" John made a forward and back motion with his groin while holding the hips of an imaginary ewe.

"That's exactly what I mean." Lloyd grimaced. "That guy lives in two worlds. At least he'll be warm tonight. No shortage of wool in that wagon. I hope he unhitches and turns out those mules."

"What's the stone for?"

"It's flint. We got nothin' to eat, no coats, and no hats. But at least we can build a fire and not freeze to death."

"Yeah, no matches," John said, patting his pockets. He turned in a circle, saw the sheepherder disappear around a curve in the road, and flashed back to the last time he saw his wife.

"Let's find a place to camp," Lloyd said.

They climbed a sage-covered ridge to the north and took possession of a grove of quaking aspen and ponderosa pine by a small creek.

"This'll do," Lloyd said. "We wouldn't want to get caught in the open where we could be robbed by bandits."

"Yeah." John laughed again. "They'd sure be disappointed in what I've got."

Lloyd gathered the makings for a fire, while John collected pine boughs for a shelter. They washed and drank from the stream then split up to forage for something to eat. Half an hour later, they met back at camp, John with a shirt full of huckleberries and Lloyd with a fat blue grouse he'd killed with a rock.

"This cocky bird was all puffed up and strutting for a couple of hens," he said. "He was showin' off so much he never even saw me. I hit him with my third rock and ran up and grabbed him before he knew what was happenin'. Why don't you build us a spit, and I'll go to the creek and clean him?"

They finished eating and sat close to the fire as the sky darkened. "Half a grouse and some berries ain't much for supper," Lloyd said.

"Best I ever ate," John replied. "We should look for more in the mornin'."

"We will. I ain't got nothin' planned for early."

A couple of gunshot echoes reached them from the distant west. They looked toward the afterglow of the sunset, and John asked, "You suppose that's our sheep-lovin' friend shootin' his supper?"

"No, I don't," Lloyd said. "That man was so drunk he couldn't sneak up on his own shadow. I reckon we'll find out tomorrow, but he might coulda run into some trouble."

"Trouble with gunshots? Trouble with bandits?"

"I did some shoein' for another sheepherder once," Lloyd began. "He'd been up in the Ruby Mountains in Nevada with a flock just like our friend. Ya know what he did all day while his sheep ate grass?"

"No, what?"

"He panned for gold. He paid me in gold. Even had his own scale," Lloyd spoke in the golden glow of the fire. "Measured me out my fee at twenty dollars per ounce. Kept his nuggets in a pouch one of his rams used to keep his balls in. And I think he had more'n the one pouch I saw. I took it to the bank and traded it for dollars at twenty-three dollars per ounce."

"And you think our guy had gold in that stinkin' wagon?"

"There was a gold pan under that seat we were sittin' on. I saw it. Nothin' like a little stink to keep a robber away. Problem is, it ain't no secret sheepherders pan for gold. Most probably don't have any luck," he said, pulling the nugget from his pocket. "But some do."

John studied the nugget and let it roll around in his palm. "It's heavy," he said, handing it back. "I never seen any before."

"It's generous payment for the little work I did."

They talked well into the night. Lloyd described a series of family tragedies, including the early deaths of three babies and the recent passing of his wife of eighteen years to consumption. "We never would have made it past the children except for help from the church. But after Sarah, I couldn't hardly take it. I started drinking, and I ain't quit. Guess I must not want to."

They lay down on beds of pine needles and took turns feeding the fire. The sky was ablaze with shooting stars, and together they counted thirty-one. The nocturnal movement of creatures around their camp added to their discomfort, but the cold was the bane of their night. They agreed that had they not had the good fortune to fall in with old Jakome, they surely would have frozen to death.

The morning was frosty, and they had a hard time leaving the fire. They did harvest more huckleberries, but the grouse hunt ended poorly. John found a dead pack rat in the fork of an aspen tree not far from where they'd slept, pointed it out to Lloyd, and asked, "How hungry are you?"

"I ain't never seen pack rat on a menu before, and I won't be addin' it today," he growled. "I am pretty hungry though. Let's mosey."

They scattered and buried the fire then walked back to the road. The sky was clear, and John turned to walk backward occasionally to balance the small amount of warmth the early sun offered. The trail gradually steepened to a long grade to the northwest, which warmed them in turn.

"This would have been tough on the sheepherder's mules," Lloyd said. They both focused on a narrow column of smoke that rose from the other side of the wide ridge before them.

"You suppose that's Jakome's fire?" John asked.

"I'll bet so. But he wouldn't build anything that would smoke like that," Lloyd said. "Let's get off this road and take a look."

They hiked north again, paralleling the ridgeline, picking their way through sagebrush and cedars. After half a mile, they climbed the slope cautiously, crawling to the crest to view the valley below.

"Holy Jesus," John whispered. "I don't see Jakome."

"You might not want to see him."

"Looks like he got a couple of 'em."

"If they got into his wine, they could just be dead drunk."

If the destruction of one man and his possessions could be called a massacre, the scene before them would be it. Since it was more than a mile away, it was hard to determine what had happened and what was left. Half a dozen Indians were visible, though only two were moving. The remains of Jakome's wagon were smoldering, and the contents scattered. The old man was not visible; his mules were tied to a tree.

"What should we do?" John asked.

"Well, we could attack, but I think we'd end up with Jacome, wherever he is. And I suspect it's not a good place," Lloyd said. "They'll be getting outta here soon. They won't want to be there when someone comes along. Not including us, of course." Then he added, "It's a long way away, but try to remember what they look like."

The two Indians began to sort through the debris, stopping to kick and yell at three of their band, who woke up and began to vomit. One did not get kicked and did not move. The mules were brought over and loaded with fleece, various tarps, ropes, and several bags of dried mutton. Six horses were retrieved from a grove of aspens, and the motionless Indian was tied to the back of one of them. The two in charge made a final pass through the sheepherder's possessions, but nothing else appeared to interest them. The three with hangovers managed to get on their ponies but were beaten by the two leaders with the bows and quivers they'd left behind. When the band left, only the two had rifles.

Lloyd and John watched the Indians until they were out of sight then descended from their ridgetop and approached the sheepherder's camp. As they grew closer, it became clear that the horror they'd expected had been exceeded. The wagon had become a torture pyre. Old Jakome had been stretched across its frame, his limbs tied to the four wheels and roasted. John dropped to his hands and knees and wretched. Lloyd looked over his shoulder in the direction of the Indian's departure while clenching and unclenching his fists. They circled the devastation, stopping at a patchy, bloody animal hide next to scattered bones and a firepit.

"Looks like they ate Chooga." Lloyd choked. "I'm gonna find those savages someday."

The two men spent the morning removing the charred body and digging a grave with a handleless shovel. They interred the remains of the man and his dog together. At the grave, each spoke with gratitude of their brief friendship and understood that they might have met a similar fate had they not left him. They talked about the gunshots and decided that old Jakome had gone down fighting.

"They must not have known about the gold," Lloyd said. "They were so bent on torture they probably never searched him. Whatever he had in his pockets is buried with him now, but he wouldn't have carried his whole stash in his pockets. There must be more hidden here someplace."

The search took most of an hour. The center of the wagon was destroyed. Boxes on the frame had been emptied and burned, the wheels were scorched, and the iron rims detached and warped from the heat. It was John who found it. Under the heavy oak tongue in front of the first axel, a cavity had been carved out and nailed over with a piece of sheep horn. They pried the horn off with a bent nail, and a tin box fell to the ground with a thud. Tied shut with leather thongs, they carefully opened it to see Jakome's treasure. Gold nuggets padded in wool and several small pouches of gold dust were packed firmly in the container.

"Dang," John exclaimed. "What do we do now?"

"We move on down the road. We're done here," Lloyd said. "Let's find something to carry this in and talk while we walk."

They found an odd-shaped piece of soft leather, made a strap from a length of harness, and walked off with a satchel of unknown worth.

The teller at the Wells Fargo Bank in Boise stepped back in shock when the two men entered and asked to open a joint account. Their torn and bloody clothing, sunburned faces, and foul smell caused him to nod to the armed guard at the door who was soon at their side. A glance at the contents of Jakome's tin box soon had them in the bank manager's office where they were greeted with a respectful smile.

During the long trek to the city, they'd discussed their recent discovery and Jakome and wondered about their obligation to him. Their brief encounter had left them with little information except for his plans to build a house and start a family. It seemed the money was theirs to keep. They decided they would hold out enough cash to outfit themselves with new clothes, weapons, and enough to travel comfortably and eat well. Upon their arrival in Salt Lake, they would recover their halves of the balance from the Wells Fargo Bank branch either together or alone. If in a year's time there was money left in the account, it could be withdrawn by the survivor. Their treasure totaled $5,250.

Several hours later, they emerged from the Gem State Hotel having bathed, dressed in new clothes, and eaten. In a nearby hardware store, they armed themselves with new Colt revolvers, holsters, and sheathed knives. The next time they encountered the Colonel or any of his clowns, they'd be ready to deal with them. Feeling better, they walked out of the hardware store and looked across the street and smiled at the same time.

"The GOLD NUGGET SALOON," John read aloud. "Perfect!"

"I'm buyin'," Lloyd said with a smile.

They sat at the bar and toasted their change of fortune with whiskey and beer. John ate pickled hard-boiled eggs, sausages, and pretzels, there seeming to be no end to his hunger.

"What are you going to do now?" he asked.

"Well, I plan to go to the circus and get my tools," Lloyd said. "They were my dad's before they were mine."

"I'll cover your back."

"Then I guess I'll take the train back to Salt Lake," Lloyd added, swallowing a large gulp of beer. "What about you?"

"I'm going to get the Colonel to tell me where my wife is."

"I was afraid you were going to say that," Lloyd said. "I'll go with you. Maybe we should bring the sheriff along."

"Might could." They paused to raise their shot glasses. "Let's go over to the tracks and watch for a bit," John said. "Which way to the circus?" he asked the bartender.

"Circus left yesterday," he replied, pocketing the five-dollar tip with a smile. He pulled a rolled-up poster from beneath the bar and spread it out. His finger drifted to the dates near the bottom. "Last show was the third. Today's the fifth."

The men sat back down and stared at the multicolored paper. John held up his hand and checked off his fingers against the days in his memory. "How in the hell…"

Lloyd elbowed him in the side and pointed at the brightly colored boxed print at the top: new attraction: beautiful siamese twin baby girls!

"Did you see this?" John asked the barman.

"Yessir, I did," he replied. "I had to stand in line for half an hour and pay two bits to get in."

"How did you know they were girls?" John asked.

"Oh, they were girls all right," he said excitedly. "The mother was there and pulled back their blanket for every ticket holder, and they wasn't wearing a stitch of clothes underneath."

"What did the mother look like?"

"Short fat gal." He laughed. "Cain't say she looked much like the babies."

48

"You don't look so good," Lloyd said.

"Ah, I been better," John groaned. "Couple days on a train and I'll be fine."

"I ain't so sure 'bout that," Lloyd said, hoisting his new duffel bag from the floor. "I'm afraid you'll do something stupid when you get to Reno. You should know I won't be touching your half of our money for at least five years. I guess by then I'll figure if it's still there, you're dead."

"Or else in jail." John swung his feet to the floor. "They don't still hang people in Nevada, do they?"

"Oh, I think they do. Especially the stupid ones."

"Well, that's not good news. I don't seem to have any control over stupid."

"Take care of yerself, pardner." Lloyd held out his hand. "And don't drink so much."

John shook the hand and said, "I'll look you up next time I'm in Salt Lake."

After Lloyd left, John cradled his head in his hands and groaned. His pain was intense, but at least he had a direction.

The train ride to Reno was brutal. It was uncomfortable and dusty, and the motion kept his stomach in turmoil. His frequent trips to the water closet alarmed his fellow passengers so that they leaned away when they saw him coming. He wondered at the sign over the door. There was a water barrel and dipper inside next to a box with a hole in the top and the blur of passing railroad ties beneath. As soon as the train would stop, the conductor appeared to latch the door and stand nearby to ensure that no one went in to use the commode while the train was stopped. *Surely this setup can't continue*, he thought.

The train arrived in Reno in the middle of the night on the third day. John climbed from the platform, considered his history with trains and train travel, and determined that he would buy a horse and ride to his next destination. He walked into the station and gawked at the circus poster on the wall. The new performance dates indicated tomorrow would be the last day. The twins were not listed as an attraction.

He walked the short distance to the Silver Lady Hotel, booked a room, and slept until ten. After a big breakfast, he took a hot bath and dressed in his change of clothes, feeling better than he had in days. Admiring himself in the mirror, he pulled his hat down then gave it a rakish tilt, certain he would be unrecognized.

The circus was set up five blocks from the hotel. The distance was not great, but with the press of midday pedestrian traffic, John stepped into a barbershop for a shave and a haircut. Half a dozen men, not counting the two in barber chairs, sat together drinking coffee in relaxed conversation. They greeted him with glances and nods, never losing connection with their peers or the subject at hand. It was several minutes before one of the elders focused on him, with the remainder turning like roosters to a new hen.

"What brings you to town, son?"

"Came to see the circus."

"Where from?"

"Came on the train from Boise."

"That's a long way to come for a circus. Wasn't it just there?"

"Yeah, I missed it. Have you been?"

This was the cue for the group to join in. From the response, it appeared they all had been to the Phantasmagoric Circus & Sideshow's "Greatest Show in the West!" The conversation took off as if it was the next item on an agenda, an agenda where John wasn't scheduled to speak. It was hard for him to imagine that the topic hadn't already been broached since the circus had been in town for three days, but it suited him since he had no desire to ask or answer awkward questions. Few of them had ever seen a tiger, elephant, or a camel; and they agreed that the skill of the trapeze artists and horsemanship of the riders was exceptional. Their description of the show and events matched what he'd seen except that it failed to mention the Colonel or the twins. *How is that possible?* he thought.

John managed to get in and out of the barber chair and out the door with a small bottle of Samson's Pomade without further notice. The boardwalk traffic had thinned so that he traveled the remaining distance to the fairgrounds in minutes, slowing for his final approach. He drifted away from the road to circle the large tents and smaller exhibit sheds and made his way to the railroad tracks beyond. His original plan had been to locate the green railcar and watch it until he spotted the short fat woman. If he could isolate her, he hoped to bribe her to answer his questions with one, two, or three of the double eagle twenty-dollar gold coins in his pockets. But now that he had walked the length of the train and seen that the Colonel's caboose was missing, this interview could be more complicated. What if she'd gone with him?

The vantage point he selected provided good cover, a view of the circus railcars, and the heavily traveled road to the city. Traffic in and out of the green car was steady, but he'd yet to see the unmistakable face and shape he was looking for. Several of the women looked familiar, but he couldn't be sure. He remembered a couple of the men who passed by. If he had to question one of them, he'd have a decision to make—the bribe or the barrel of his gun down the man's throat.

Then there she was, walking toward him on the road from the fairgrounds, a younger woman in tow, both carrying large baskets. He watched them pass then emerged from concealment and followed them down the busy thoroughfare into the city. They chatted while they walked, stopping at a fabric store where the short fat woman produced a piece of paper from her pocket and handed it to the younger woman. They examined it together then separated, the younger woman taking the paper and continuing down the boardwalk into a general store. John followed her inside, smiled, and tipped his hat when she looked his way. Not an attractive girl, she blushed and concentrated on her list.

"Excuse me, ma'am'," he said, removing his hat. "I believe you dropped this." Taking her hand, he pressed a three-dollar gold piece in it.

Visibly flustered, she looked at the coin then pressed her other hand against the pocket of her apron. She removed a small purse, opened it, and looked inside.

"No, sir, this is not mine," she said, extending her hand with the coin to him.

"You and I are the only people in this aisle, and I'm sure it's not mine," he said, holding up both hands. "Say, didn't I see you at the circus this morning?"

"Maybe. I was there." She smiled, still holding the coin between her fingers.

"Can I ask you a question?"

"Yes," she said, flattered by the attention.

"I'm a medical student on my way to Boise to visit my parents and was told on the train from San Francisco that there were Siamese twin babies in this circus."

"Yes, sir." She smiled. "They were with us, but you missed them. They're on their way to San Francisco in the Colonel's special railcar."

"Dern, I was hoping I'd get a chance to see them and meet their mother. My professors would want to know if there are other twins in their family."

"Their mother died when they were born," she said with a sad smile. "At least that's what their sister said."

"Is she on the train with them?"

"Yes. Her name's Zelda."

"And the Colonel too?"

"Oh yes," she said.

John reached into his pocket and pulled out one of the twenty-dollar gold coins and pressed it into her hand. "Here, darlin'. You dropped this too."

He walked out, his heart racing, then he turned and went back inside.

166

"One more thing," he said to the dumbfounded girl, still staring at the coins. "What will they be doing in San Francisco? Maybe I can see them there when I get back."

"Oh, I wouldn't know that, sir," she said, putting the coins between her ample breasts, making sure he watched her do it.

Stumbling backward, he gave the girl a wink and was back on the street. He took a few steps and leaned his back into the store's façade. *Zelda must have been on the train all along. She may have been in the Colonel's railcar when Lloyd and me got beat up and thrown off. Could I have been that close?* He pushed off the building and turned back toward the fabric store. The short fat woman was coming out and never saw him when he grabbed her elbow and guided her between buildings to the back of the lot. When they stopped beneath a large oak, she recognized him and stiffened in surprise.

"You thought I was dead," John said, standing close. He held a gold coin in front of her face. "Where's my wife?" She grabbed the coin, but he held her clenched fist-tight.

"She's in Ogden. I already told you." She winced. "That hurts."

"Believe me, your pain is nothing compared to what I've been through because of your lies. Where is she, and where are the twins?" he hissed. "Tell me the truth, and you can keep this coin, or I'll strangle you right here."

"They're all on a train to San Francisco. The babies have been sold and are going to China. Your whore will be there and working on her fucking back to support her opium habit."

John pushed her back against the tree and held her there by her throat. He pulled the pomade out of his pocket, pulled the cork out with his teeth, and emptied it over her head. Letting go of her hand, he smashed the bottle into the ground, stepped back, and said, "You let the Colonel know you saw me and that he should keep looking over his shoulder. I'll be there soon."

49

John was on the train again the next day with only one thought: locate the Colonel's railcar and watch it until he saw him. Unless he'd gotten a wire from the short fat woman, John would have a surprise advantage. If she had been lying to him as usual, he could be walking into another trap or find nothing at all.

He'd been fortunate to sit next to a former teacher on the second day of the trip who was going home after visiting his sister in Boise. The elderly man was fascinated by John's story and answered his most basic questions, anxious to help him reunite with his wife and nieces. Focusing on John's most recent conversation with the short fat woman, he not only narrowed the younger man's general idea of where China was but also informed him of the existence of Chinatown, which he considered a possibility. The man explained the effects and dangers of opium, having had some experience with it himself as a young man. He told John an overwhelming number of prostitutes in the bordellos of San Francisco were addicted to opium and, in fact, were slaves to it. John angrily assured the man that Zelda was a headstrong, intelligent woman who would not tolerate addiction. He told the man they had been married less than a month and she could never be a prostitute. Standing over the man with clenched fists, he told him he intended to find her and bring her home. He stopped himself from punching the man in the stomach and picked up his bag and moved to another seat.

The man's name was Joseph Box. He was not a former teacher, but he fancied his appearance fit that mold and often introduced himself as such. Joseph and his younger brother, Cecil, owned several businesses in the Bay Area. He was certain from hearing John's story that he knew what was happening to the wife and nieces. The demand for American girls and young women in Asian cities, such as Shanghai and Hong Kong, was enormous. The twin babies, as they were described to him, could be priceless. Joseph had no idea who this Colonel was, but he was quite sure he knew what he was up to. He also knew his family could put John to work immediately in a capacity where his age and temperament would be assets.

The train pulled into the Oakland Long Wharf in a driving rain. As John looked out the window, it was apparent that he would know little about this place until the weather changed. "Please contact me, John," the older man said, handing him a business card on his way out of the train. "I didn't mean to upset you. I can help you find your wife and her sisters."

John, still in his seat, looked at the card then looked up at Joseph Box. "I'll think about it," he said.

"I can offer you a place to stay also. I have several bedrooms in my house," he offered, pulling his watch from his pocket. "My carriage will be here shortly. You're welcome to join me." He offered his hand, and John shook it.

At a loss for what to do, John exited the train and entered yet another train station. He walked the length and width of the building, looking through every window at a blurry vision of railcars and engines. In this weather and this late in the day, starting a search for the Colonel's coach would be a miserable waste of time. He thought maybe he should take Joseph Box's offer, at least for tonight. He could come back to the tracks tomorrow.

"Mr. Box," John called out, catching up to the man, "your card says you live in Oakland."

"Yes, it does," he answered. "I have several houses. I have invited you to stay with me in my Oakland house tonight. I will be taking the ferry to San Francisco in a day or two. You will be welcome there also."

"Ferry?" John asked.

"Yes," Mr. Box responded. "We are in Oakland. San Francisco is across the bay. The ferry is a boat that will take us there."

"A boat?" John asked. "I don't know. I've never been on a boat before."

"I assure you, John. It's quite safe," Mr. Box said. "It's the only way to get there."

"But the Colonel's railcar would be here, wouldn't it?"

"Yes, you're right. You can come back here to look for it." Mr. Box smiled. "Please join me."

The ride across the city was a miserable event even in the enclosed carriage. John lifted the canvas flap at the front of their compartment several times to check on the driver and two-horse team, knowing their lot was a hundred times worse than his. Mr. Box, apparently used to this sort of weather, sat across from him snoring rhythmically. John had no watch, but he guessed it took most of an hour before they pulled into a barn and came to a stop. The doors were immediately opened, and they were greeted in a language that sounded like a mixture of birdsong and squeaky wheels to John. Mr. Box responded to the chatter in kind to two small men who bowed enthusiastically.

"Let me give the driver a hand putting the horses up," John said, fighting the efforts of one of the men to take his bag.

"No, no," Mr. Box said. "You'd only slow things down. Come with me."

John followed the trio beneath a covered walkway to a house larger than many hotels he had seen. Their small procession continued through a passageway into a living area that was at once welcoming and warm. Aromas from a nearby kitchen stirred a response from John's empty stomach, and he was immediately happy not to be holed up in the train station for the night. He removed his hat as Mr. Box turned to him at the bottom of a staircase and said, "Li Song will take you to your room, where you can get ready for dinner. I'll meet you back down here in fifteen minutes."

They sat at the end of a long table under the soft glow of gaslights while being served courses of delicate, delicious food by two Chinese men dressed in white. Wineglasses were refilled and plates and bowls replaced with such efficiency that John never noticed it happen.

"Mr. Box, I've never eaten like this before," John said. "And your house is beautiful. Where I come from, teachers don't live like this."

"Please call me Joseph." He smiled. "I'm sorry. I purposely misled you. Not just you actually. I say that to most people I meet when I travel. It seems to put them at ease and allows for more relaxed conversations. Like when I met you. I think your journey is fascinating, and I'd love to help you. I'm getting old, and my business bores me. It's profitable but doesn't interest me anymore. I let my brother do most of the work, and he enjoys it. So..." He waved his hands in the air, drank some wine, and stuffed a large prawn in his mouth.

"On my way to Boise, my friend and me met a sheepherder who was drinking wine he made himself. He was drunk and got killed by Indians," John said, looking at his glass.

"I'd love to hear more about that sometime, but now I must go to bed," Joseph said, pushing his chair away from the table. "Li Song will show you back to your room. Good evening."

The rain stopped sometime in the night and was replaced by dense fog. Looking out the window the next morning, John's measure of the day's light was the same as the previous afternoon, only the texture was different. He followed his nose to the kitchen, where he was greeted in broken English by two Chinese women. They served him dark, rich coffee and a fruit-filled pastry that was delicious beyond his experience.

"Good morning, young John," said Joseph Box in a booming voice. "How did you sleep?"

"Good morning, sir. I slept pretty good," John replied. "If I hadn't looked out the window, I'd still think it was last night. Does the sun ever shine in this place?"

"Ha, yes, of course, it does. And it's really quite beautiful. You'll see."

"Yes, sir. I'll look forward to that. What would be the best way for me to get back to the rail yard?"

"Anxious to get started, aren't you?" Joseph said. "I understand. Have breakfast with me, then I'll have one of my boys take you. It's really no trouble. I have nothing for them to do this morning."

They ate, and John added to his story, describing Zelda and the twins as he understood them. He also added a description of the Colonel and his railcar, regretting he didn't know his name.

"Thank you very much for your hospitality, Mr. Box. I don't know what I'd have done last night if it wasn't for you," John said, holding his coat, hat, and bag. "If I don't see you again, I'll write you a letter to let you know what I found. I still have your card."

"John, you must come back here tonight. Give me a chance to help your search," Joseph said. "My sources in the city are impeccable. As I said, if your wife and her sisters are here, I can find them. Especially the babies. They will be a secret that's impossible to keep. Leave your bag and come back here tonight. This may take longer than a day. Go to the railroad and see what you can. Tomorrow we'll go to the city and meet with my brother and connect with his agents."

"I hate to trouble you further."

"Believe me, young man," Mr. Box said, catching his breath, "this interests me more than anything I've done in a long time."

By the time John arrived at the rail yard, the fog had lifted but blocked the sun to maintain the gray damp dreariness that soaked into his bones. Hands in his pockets, he walked through the expanse of engines and cars to search for the Colonel's coach. Half an hour later, he found himself staring at the relatively nondescript vehicle on a rail siding away from any traffic. Doors at both ends were locked, but he hadn't come this far to be denied access by padlocks. Standing at the rear door, he used his knife and a discarded railroad spike to lever and pry loose the heel of the lock's hasp and removed it. Closing the door behind him, he stood still for a time and took in the garish trappings, reliving his previous visits. Traces of his blood still stained the floor where the Colonel had broken his nose, and he brought his hand up to touch its crooked set. He rested his hand on the Colt in its holster and walked slowly through the coach. The place was a mess. The well-built and tastefully furnished car was littered with dirty dishes, clothing, newspapers, food scraps, bottles, and other indescribable garbage. It smelled stale and musty and got progressively worse as he moved forward. Opening the door to the front compartment, John stepped back in disgust. An unmade bed with leather straps fixed at

172

the corners dominated the room, but his nose directed his eyes to two wooden buckets in a corner filled with cloth diapers and human waste. He stepped back to take a breath then moved inside and lifted them by their rope handles. He considered dumping the buckets on the Colonel's bed as he passed but continued through the rear door and threw them into the San Francisco Bay.

John opened windows as he walked through the car on his way back to the front compartment. He stood for a time and tried to absorb his wife's presence and the horrors she must have endured. The leather straps on the bed had blood on their padded loop ends. She'd fought her restraints and no doubt plotted an escape, at least until the twins arrived. There was a makeshift bed on the floor of the closet where they must have slept. Zelda would have found joy in them at least. Innocent babes who were indirectly responsible for so much pain. In a drawer at a bedside dresser, he found several empty small glass bottles. He removed the cork from one and winced at the sour, bitter smell then put it in his pocket. A larger bottle contained a few white pills, and he pocketed that as well. The dresser on the other side of the bed held clean diapers and towels. On the floor between that dresser and the wall were a large number of the pills, intact with scarred surfaces. *This had been in her mouth, and she spit it out,* he thought, holding one in his fingers. Feeling her closeness and her pain, he put it in his mouth and swallowed it. Then he lay on the bed, his head on the pillow where hers had been, and inhaled her smell. The magical fragrance was missing, but he closed his eyes and let his memory take him back to those few nights they'd shared.

It was dark when he woke up. Voices and light drifted in through the open window next to the bed, followed by a rattling of the lock at the rear door. John quietly left the bed and squeezed into the corner of the closet opposite where the babies had slept. He cocked the Colt, held it against his chest, and watched the light get brighter as it was carried forward through the coach. A lantern entered the room and moved through the small space searching for the intruder.

"Nobody here," a voice said loudly, leaving the room.

John left the closet and crept to the doorway, his dreamy feeling interrupted by a reality he didn't understand. The conversation in the

back of the car continued in low tones, in voices he couldn't identify. Drawers and cabinet doors were being opened and closed. He
guessed something was being searched for and removed. The commotion confused him, and he turned to the bed in the darkness and
heard Zelda call his name. He moved toward her and heard a crash
then another, followed by the slam of the back door and intense
pounding against it from the outside. A flickering orange glow came
to him from the passageway, followed by the smell of burning kero-
sene. He turned from the bed and stepped into the light of a growing
fire as it climbed from the floor up the walls on both sides. Back in
the bedroom, he grabbed quilts and rushed out to bat at the flames,
but his action only fanned the fire, and it grew. Throwing the blankets on the floor, he ran across them to the back door to turn its
latch, then he kicked at it and rammed it with his shoulder, realizing
it had been nailed shut.

"Zelda!" he screamed and ran up to the quilts, only to stop as
the dancing flames consumed them. "Zelda, I can't save you," he
cried and backed away into the Colonel's cabin. He lifted a heavy
chair from its place at a desk and carried it to smash the glass from a
window he had partially opened. But as the chair passed in front of
that window, the glass shattered, the chair splintered, and a bullet ric-
ocheted off it, creasing his skull above his ear. Stunned, he picked up
a pillow and held it before the window to see it explode in feathers,
followed by the blast of another gunshot.

John fell to his knees to escape the smoke and crawled forward
to a closed door on his right. He reached up to open it, slid inside,
and gulped the clean air. The reprieve from the smoke was refresh-
ing, but he knew it would be temporary. The door behind him was
already too hot to lean against. A thin stream of orange light from a
tiny window near the ceiling lit the small space, which he thought
must be a closet.

"This is a closet all right. It's a water closet," he said aloud. Of
course, the Colonel would have one. He went to the water barrel next
to the sink, lifted the lid, and drank two dippers full. He took one
step to the commode where he lifted its lid and tore off the seat. The
box resisted, but he ripped and kicked it with such force it soon fell

away. In the darkness of the hole below, he could see the shadows of railroad ties and rails and wondered briefly if he'd be dropping into a pile of the Colonel's shit.

On the tracks, he scrambled to take cover behind the rear wheels. Watching for muzzle flashes, he low-crawled away from the searing heat behind him to the next car on the line and stopped for a breath. The Colonel's coach was totally consumed by now, and two men stood from a position behind a stack of ties a hundred feet from the inferno to watch it burn. John crossed parallel tracks to come up behind them and said with a cough, "Don't move."

The taller of the two spun around, perhaps reflexively as his rifle was pointed at the ground, and John shot a hole in his chest. The second man lifted his hands immediately and dropped a shotgun which discharged as it hit the ground, taking off his right foot. John moved to the man, reached in to remove his belt, and looped it below his knee. Using the shotgun to twist the belt into a tourniquet, he handed its stock to the screaming arsonist and told him to shut up.

"If you hold on to your shotgun tight enough, you might not bleed to death," he said. "Before I leave, I want to know a couple things, or I'm going to throw that gun in the bay."

"Yeah, yeah. What do you want?" the man gasped.

"Where is my wife, Zelda, and her twin sisters?"

"She's with the Colonel at the Occidental Hotel."

"What were you doing here in his railcar?"

"We were picking up the opium he kept in it."

"Do you know who I am?"

"Oh God…yeah! We threw you and the farrier off the train in Idaho. He wants you dead more than anything."

"Even at the loss of his coach?"

"Oh yeah."

"Here comes help, asshole," John said. "You mention my name and I'll hunt you down and shoot off your other foot. You got that?"

"Ah, I got it."

John reached into his pocket and pulled out the bottle of pills from the coach. He removed the cork and shook out two. "Here, swallow these. You're gonna need 'em. You owe me a favor."

50

"John, where have you been?"

"I'll tell you, first I gotta' sit down."

"Li Song, bring water," Mr. Box said. "You've been in a fire. These blisters. I'll call a doctor."

"I'll be fine," John said. "I just need to rest a bit."

John woke up twelve hours later, bandaged and in pain. A Chinese man sat near the bed and jumped up, speaking rapidly, "You stay, John. You stay." Then he ran from the room. John got out of bed, walked to the water closet, and pissed in the bucket.

"Ah, there you are. How do you feel?" Mr. Box asked.

"Um, I'm not sure. I feel hot," John said in a weak voice, and he walked back to sit on the edge of the bed. "What are these bandages?"

"You've got second-degree burns," Mr. Box said. "The doctor said you'll be fine. But there will be pain for a couple days. The wounds must be kept clean. You were given a morphine injection last night, and there are pills, besides the ones that were in your pocket if you need them. I think you know you must be careful with these things."

"Yes."

"Where did you find the pills and the laudanum bottles?"

"They were in the room where Zelda was kept in the Colonel's coach," John answered with a mixture of anger and heartache. "The pills were on the floor in a corner. She spit them out. I took one and fell asleep."

"Your nemesis may have used them to try to control her," Mr. Box said.

"You don't know her," John said angrily, resenting this suggestion as he had on the train.

"Yes, you're right. I don't know her," Mr. Box said. "I do know about opium addiction. It's a very serious thing."

"I have to go to San Francisco."

"Yes, I know," Mr. Box said. "I'll go with you. We'll take the two o'clock ferry this afternoon."

"Where are my clothes?"

"They were torn and burned. They've been thrown away. There are new clothes in the wardrobe." Mr. Box waved his hand in that direction. "Ah, here is your food. Eat, then you must tell me everything."

John ate with enthusiasm then described the incident at the Colonel's coach as he remembered it.

"You didn't see the Colonel?"

"No. He wasn't there."

"Did you recognize the two men who started the fire?"

"I didn't get a good look at the man I shot. I may have seen the other man before. He said he knew who I was. I told him I'd find him and shoot off his other foot if he said anything."

"Yes, indeed," Mr. Box said. "Burning the Colonel's coach would be a serious matter if he didn't authorize it. I suspect he valued it a great deal. If those two men wanted to kill you, they could have just waited for you to emerge as they did. He may have been there."

John stared at Mr. Box and said nothing.

"There are several issues here that are problematic, and a couple where we may have an advantage," he said. "As for the man with one foot, he may not look forward to seeing you again, but I suspect the Colonel has the wherewithal to protect him. The Colonel may be a big man in his world, but he's in mine now. I think we can both venture to guess that his plans for your wife and her sisters are twofold. He wants to make money selling them, and he wants to punish you. Kidnapping is a crime. However, as you have told me, she initially came to him willingly even though under false pretenses. The babies were taken under the design of their father. You broke into the coach and were trespassing. As an aside, possessing and distributing opium is not illegal, though I suspect someday it will be.

"These are the legal issues as I see them. My connections with the law locally and in the state of California are not positive, so I suggest we resolve these matters without their involvement. Did you speak to anyone on your way here yesterday?"

"Yes, several people, asking directions."

"And you used my name?"

"No, just the street name."

"Well, you definitely looked and smelled like you'd been in a fire," Mr. Box said thoughtfully. "The man you shot and the man who shot himself in the foot will get the police involved. Unfortunately, they may already be looking for you. We better get out of here."

They watched the first policeman arrive at the departure dock from a porthole in the cargo hold. The crossing was uneventful, and their disembarkment, each leading a haltered horse in the fog, was unremarkable. A San Francisco policeman scrutinized the departing passengers but never noticed them.

"There is no shortage of crime on this side of the bay. Local police will be less interested in solving Oakland's problems," Mr. Box said. "My carriage is this way."

They arrived at the Box brother's house on Bay Street at suppertime. This second house was no less grand than the first, and the food no less delicious than the meals that had been served on the other side of the bay. Joseph described John Walker's situation while they ate, with brother Cecil apparently just as interested. "I'll send Hop Sing over to find out if they're at the Occidental. What's this Colonel's name?"

"I don't know," John said. "I never heard him called anything but Colonel. I heard him refer to the cavalry a couple times, but I don't know. When can we go?"

"After we get some information. We don't want to be surprised. We want to surprise him. What does he look like?"

"Lots of hair. Owns a circus that's headed this way from Reno. He's loud and a showoff."

Cecil's eyebrows shot up when Joseph described Zelda and her twin sisters and that they would be included.

"Fascinating!" he exclaimed. Cecil rang a bell, and another in an unending supply of Chinese men arrived and listened to his instructions. Hop Sing's eyes also brightened as he got his instructions, then he bowed and dashed from the room. "I understand your impatience, Mr. Walker, but I assure you, this is the best course," Cecil said. "After we finish eating, I'll outfit you with a less obvious weapon than the large caliber Colt on your belt. I have a smaller revolver that can be carried in a shoulder holster under your coat that isn't noticeable. I assure you it's very effective."

"Yes, sir."

"John is a deputy sheriff in Spanish Fork, Utah, where he's from," Joseph said.

"Oh my," Cecil replied. "Far from your jurisdiction."

"Yes, sir. It's been a long trail."

They moved into a large wood-paneled room and sat near a fireplace with a roaring flame that sucked humidity from the space. The brothers smoked long black cigars and discussed business. They all sipped aged brandy that was poured from a heavy glass bottle with a Box Brothers label.

"This is the best whiskey I ever drank," John said.

Both brothers smiled. "Actually, John, this is brandy. It's distilled from grapes. We have several vineyards north of here," Joseph said. "You're correct. It is very good."

About two hours after he left, Hop Sing appeared in the doorway and nodded to his employer.

"I'll be right back," Cecil said and left the room.

John left his chair and walked to the window, glad to see that it wasn't raining. He arched his back and stretched, trying to get used to the holster under his arm. The new clothes Joseph had bought for him were nothing like anything he had worn before. The fit was perfect, but the vest and tie were more than he could tolerate and were left in Oakland. He knew Zelda would like to see these things, and he was nervous to think it could happen soon.

"He has dinner reservations in the Occidental at nine p.m.," Cecil said. Are you ready, John?"

"Yes, sir."

"Good. The carriage is waiting."

Sitting abreast in the outside front seat, three Chinese men in black suits drove the carriage behind two bay geldings through the city's orange glow of gaslights. Traffic, both pedestrian and horse-drawn, was constant from John's view at the rear seat window. The brothers, sitting across from him, maintained a low-tone conversation, ignoring his presence as he tried to relax. But his heart was racing when the doors on both sides opened and he stepped out to gaze up at the impressive eight-story Occidental Hotel.

One of the black suits stayed with the carriage, while the other two led the Boxes and John inside. The lobby of the hotel was palatial, with high ornately decorated ceilings, fine furnishings, and thick oriental rugs. A few patrons sat in overstuffed chairs reading or talking to one another. Waiters moved around the room taking orders and delivering drinks. Cecil spoke to one of his men, who walked to the dining room, spoke to the maître d', and disappeared inside. He reappeared minutes later, nodded to the group, and they moved forward to join him. Standing together, they scanned the room then turned to look at John.

There she was, sitting alone in an alcove, looking at a menu with a glass of wine in one hand. She looked elegant in a blue satin gown, auburn hair touching her bare shoulders in long curls, her face lightly made up to accentuate perfect red lips. He walked toward her without the sensation of movement, unaware that his companions had stayed back to give him this moment. She looked up from the menu and gasped. Her eyes welled as she stood, slowly walked around the table, and threw her arms around his neck.

"I thought I'd never see you again," she cried, tears flowing freely into his shirt.

"Zelda," he said, his face in her hair. "Zelda, Zelda."

She pulled away briefly, opened his coat and looked at the gun, then pulled his face to hers and kissed him.

"You fucking ham bone," a guttural voice behind him groaned. "You're hard to kill."

John turned, reaching out as he did to grab the Colonel by the hair and drive his forehead into the man's nose. He reached around with his other hand to strike out with his fist when his gun roared at his side. The face before him grimaced before he could hit it, and he looked down to see blood emerge from a hole at the Colonel's groin. John turned and saw the rage in Zelda's eyes and the blood on her mouth as she bit into her lip. He fought her for the gun, and she stepped around him to growl over her captor, "You'll never rape me again!" Then to her husband, "Kill him. Kill him."

John later remembered nothing from those mad moments. The pistol was in the Colonel's mouth when he was pulled off, and the shot he fired tore into the bloody floor.

"John, c'mon. We've got to get out of here," Cecil said, pulling him up by the arm.

"Get the girl," Joseph ordered his men.

In a close group, they walked out of the hotel as if nothing had happened. Cecil spoke to his driver, then they loaded and were gone. In the carriage, Joseph covered Zelda with his coat and wrapped her in a lap blanket, but nothing could tame the violence of the rigors that shook her. She sobbed uncontrollably and clutched John as if these men would rip him from her arms.

"We were certainly recognized," Cecil said. "We'll go to the warehouse tonight. There's an apartment there. We'll be comfortable enough."

"What will we do? We can't stay there forever," John asked.

"Be patient, my friend. We'll know more soon enough," Joseph said. "We need to take care of your wife tonight."

By midmorning, the sun was shining on the city, slowly evaporating exposed raindrops and puddles everywhere. John came out of the small room he and Zelda had shared, looked through a curtained window, and smiled at the sight. The Box brothers were seated around a large wooden crate drinking coffee and waved him over.

"Good morning, young John," Joseph said. "How is Zelda?"

"Finally asleep," he said. "She talked all night. It's been a rough time for her. Who's that?"

"That's Wing Lee. He was with us last night."

"I don't remember him," John said.

Cecil laughed. "Yes, change their clothes and they're hard to tell apart. And I see them every day."

"Mmm, this is good," John said, sipping hot black coffee. "What news is there?"

"Well, it's not good," Cecil began. "Wing has been to the hotel. He has a cousin who works there. Your adversary is alive and in the hospital. The police are looking for all of us. You are the only one they haven't identified and the one they want the most. They believe you are the shooter."

"Yeah, good. It has to be me."

"We can hide you, but we'll have to talk to the police soon," Joseph said. "There'll be no hiding for us. We need to have a story."

"Not much chance of using the truth is there?" John said, shaking his head.

"I don't know," Joseph said. "Yours is a complicated saga. Once you commit to it, there'll be no turning back. Would a jury believe you? You know the Colonel will deny everything and have a tale of his own. What has Zelda said?"

"She's confused and upset. He's been forcing opium into her all along. She's spit it out when she could, but knows it's been in her food," John said. "What will happen to her now?"

"Her body will go into withdrawal," Joseph said with a grimace. "It's a painful process. I've been through it. Where are her twin sisters?"

"In a whorehouse. She thinks they take her to see them every day. But she's confused about that too."

"We can take care of her. Our people have experience with this," Cecil said. "If the twins are at Madam Ah Toy's, as your informant said, we will find them. I know Ah Toy well."

"Back to you," Joseph said. "I don't see how you can claim self-defense. We've been told the Colonel was unarmed. You could be charged with attempted murder right now. If he dies, you could hang."

Cecil looked at his brother then at John. "You're going to have to run."

There was panic in John's eyes. He walked to the window, lifted the curtain, and again looked out at the beautiful day. Looking back at his friends, he leaned his back against the wall and slid to the floor. He covered his face in his hands and groaned, "But I just got my wife back a few hours ago."

A loud banging on the door brought them all to their feet.

"Check the windows and doors," Cecil said in a firm but low voice.

Wing Lee raced around the building while the pounding continued. "All police," he said on his return. He held up both hands with fingers spread—twice.

"Twenty?" Joseph asked.

"More," Wing Lee replied.

"John, follow me," Cecil said.

51

Winter 1871

John Walker walked to the front room of the Jameses' hospital and confronted a figure that could have been him twenty years ago. The young man stood before him with his hat in one hand and a worn-out pair of wool gloves in the other, nervously shifting his weight from one foot to the other. His slicker and leather chaps were wet from melting snow, as if affected by the heat of the older man's stare.

"She sent me to find you," the young man said.

The elder John Walker sat down behind the desk and tried to comprehend what was happening. How could he not know about this boy? He'd come to Alamo looking for answers, certain the twins would give him direction, some idea of where to look next. Instead the mystery of his life was becoming more bizarre.

"Where is she?"

"Spanish Fork. I'll take you."

"Spanish Fork?"

"She's hidin' out there waitin' for you."

"How long have you been looking for me?"

"About four months. I heard the twins were here and thought they might have seen you. I got lucky."

Marshal Walker felt the rest of the group standing behind him without having to turn to look. They were as enthralled as he was by his son's presence, shamelessly listening to this life-changing conversation. He turned and introduced them without getting up: Doc and Jean, Sheriff Walter Becker, and the sheriff's deputy, Delbert.

Prudence and Chastity came forward to embrace young John, crying as they did.

"What's happening?" the sheriff asked.

"This is the marshal's son, W-Walter," Doc said.

"He's not a marshal. That's my deputy, John," the sheriff said, looking at the young man near the front door.

"No, no, Walter. I mean…" Doc started.

"He's right, Doc," John said. "There is no marshal here. I lied about that. I was in Helena and heard about the trouble in Alamo. I also heard the twins were down here and guessed the trouble had to do with them. I figured it was one of two men behind it. Both killers. I been lookin' for 'em on my way to find my wife. Chatham was one, and Sam took care of him."

"You're not a m-marshal?"

"No, I'm not," John Walker said. "I told Delbert that, and no one ever asked to see a badge. I didn't figure anybody would. You all needed help, and the sheriff an' me have history."

"Wait a minute," the sheriff said. "Who are you?"

"I'm John Walker, sheriff, your old deputy. That young man over there is my son. His name is John Walker too."

"I didn't know you had a son."

"I didn't either until a few minutes ago."

"M-Marshal, I m-mean, John, who is this other killer? M-might he be here?" Doc said.

"I don't think so, Doc, but I don't know where he is," John said. "His name is Kasper Cobb—former Army captain, circus owner, and original kidnapper of these twins. Calls himself Colonel. He was shot in San Francisco, and I was charged with the crime. I was on the run for a while, got caught, and have been in San Quentin until two months ago."

"You think this c-colonel might show up h-here?"

"I don't know, Doc," John said. "If he does, I reckon I'll be gone to Spanish Fork."

"We won't be here either," the twins said together.

"Wait, wait!" the sheriff said. "I ain't followin' this.

"I better be goin'," Delbert said.

"H-hold on, Delbert," Doc said. "You're a part of this. L-Let's hear this out so we all know what's happening. Our lives are changing, and I w-want to talk about it n-now. John, s-say that so the sh-sheriff can hear it again."

"Sheriff, Zelda and me had a son," John began. "That's him right there. I just met him. He tells me Zelda is in Spanish Fork waitin' for me. I ain't seen her in twenty years, and I'm goin' to her, and I ain't never gonna leave her."

"Take me with ya," the sheriff said. "I wanna be buried with the rest of the Beckers in the red-dirt cemetery up on the hill. I gotta see it first and pick my spot."

"W-well, Walter, now you've got all the women crying. Even J-Jeannie," Doc said, clearing his throat.

"Look, Doc," the sheriff said, "you know what's happening to me. I ain't gettin' better, and I wanna leave while I can remember my friends' names. It's time for me to go home. John, will you take me?"

"Yes, sir."

"G-girls? You started to say something."

"Doctor," Prudence said, "we're going to Chicago, and we want to take you and Jeannie with us."

"We've wanted to talk to you about the possibility of being separated," Chastity added. "I mean, we will always want to be together but maybe not connected."

"Jean m-mentioned that to me," Doc said. "I wrote to a Dr. Hunt, who p-performed such an operation on conjoined t-twins a year ago—unsuccessfully, I m-must add. I read about it in one of m-my journals, a complicated but n-necessary procedure on infants joined at the h-head. He responded to my l-letter and said he'd m-meet you. I'll give you the letter to take. As far as me j-joining you, I'm afraid my health w-would prevent it. Jean could go though."

"I won't be going for the same reason as yours, dear," Jean said.

"Oh my," Prudence said. "We were counting on you, Doctor. You see…Chastity is pregnant."

"Hmm," Doc responded, while the rest of the men cleared their throats and looked at the floor.

"It's yours, Sam." Chastity smiled, looking directly at him.

"How long?" Doc asked.

"Well, I've missed six moons," Chastity replied. The men were clearly getting more uncomfortable.

"Y-Yes, well, that will be a f-factor," Doc said. "If this is th-the path you've chosen, y-you should probably leave immediately. Sam, you m-must go with them."

"Delbert, nobody's mentioned you yet," the sheriff said, looking at his deputy. "Before I forget what I just heard, you're the new sheriff. You've got experience, and you know everybody in town. Congratulations!"

The sheriff walked over to Delbert, who was pressed against the wall, and brought him to the middle of the room. He took the badge off his shirt and poked Delbert with the pin while attaching it to his. Delbert jumped, and the group laughed and clapped, to the new sheriff's embarrassment.

---⭐---

52

Summer 1871

The John Walkers sat beside each other as the train rocked gently, rolling south out of Idaho. Walter snored loudly in the seat behind them, no other passengers willing to sit next to him. John Sr. turned to look at the old sheriff and wondered at his decision to leave Alamo and the only friends he had. It had been a difficult departure for Doc and Jeanie, both so shaken by the goodbye that they could not say it. When asked by John this morning if he regretted leaving his two best friends, Walter had no memory of leaving or of them. He asked John who he was and where they were going and was told that he, Walter, had asked to go back to Spanish Fork so he could be buried with his family. The fifty-five-year-old man patted John on the shoulder and nodded and smiled. Dr. Frank James would die a month later, and Jean would continue to run their little hospital with no medical education, except for thirty years of on-the-job experience.

The twins cried hard and promised everyone they would be back, so sure that with the horrors behind them, a new life awaited them all. They would leave in a week, having dresses and a coat to finish before their departure. Delbert was stoic as usual, proud to be the new sheriff and determined not to let his town down. Sam, never really having had a childhood, was off on another adventure. He was going to Chicago with two beautiful women, having impregnated one of them, and he couldn't think of anything he'd rather be doing.

"I saw the Colonel once," young John said.

"Where?" John Sr. asked.

"It was a long time ago. In San Francisco before we left, before Joseph died. It was at Cecil's house. The Colonel came with four men. One of them only had one foot, I remember," he said. "I didn't hear 'em talk, but Ma told me later. She said the Colonel knew she had a baby boy, and he told Cecil he'd come for his son. He said since mom shot off his dick and he'd never have any more kids, he was gonna take me. But as soon as he saw me, he knew I wasn't his. He was really mad, and said if he ever saw Ma again, he'd kill her. He called her a whore. He said if he couldn't have me, he'd take the twins. Cecil told him to get the hell out and if he ever came back, he'd be the one who got killed."

"Why didn't Cecil tell me about you?"

"Ma told both the brothers not to say anything about me. She said she knew she'd see you again and wanted me to be a surprise. She wanted me to be your wedding present. She calls me Johnny."

"All right, Johnny. How come your ma never came to see me?"

"Cecil told her the guards should never know that you were married. He told Ma they would rape her. He told her they would make her do whatever they wanted against threats they'd hurt you. She cried every night."

"We've been married more than twenty years and have only spent five nights together. Those nights are all I've had to hold on to," John said. "I missed out on raising my son."

They traveled through the night and disembarked in Salt Lake City in the afternoon. John led the way—as he remembered it—to the Depot Hotel. The city had changed so much that he passed by it the first time, had to backtrack, and choose it from four others in the same block.

"I see you've changed your name," he said to the young woman at the front desk.

"I beg your pardon?" she replied.

"This hotel," John said. "The last time I was here, it was called the Depot."

"Yes, sir," she said. "It's been the Paradise Inn since before I was born."

"Yeah." John contemplated. "Do you have two adjoining rooms?"

"I do have those rooms," she said. "If you'll sign the register right here."

"Is Benjamin still here?" John said as he wrote.

"Yes, he's the owner."

"Could I speak to him?"

"Yes, sir. Who should I say you are?"

"My name is John Walker. He wouldn't remember me."

"I'll be right back."

A bald, rotund man limped out from the hotel office and stopped short of the desk to stare at John. "Deputy Walker?" he said.

"I'll be dogged," John said, smiling and holding out his hand. "Benjamin, you remember me."

"Of course, I do. I still have your wife's bags."

"That's good news. I'll pick them up in the morning when we check out," John said.

"So she's not here. I'm sorry to hear that," Benjamin said. "I gather this is your son."

"Yes, this is Johnny. And this is Sheriff Becker, late of Alamo, Montana, formerly of Spanish Fork. I don't believe you met him when we were last here." Both men stepped forward to shake the innkeeper's hand.

"Will you be here in the morning, Benjamin?"

"Yes, sir. I'm always here," he said with a chuckle.

Upstairs in the rooms, they separated, giving the sheriff and his ferocious snore his own space. "Sheriff, we'll be right through this door," John said. "We'll have breakfast in the morning and be on the eleven o'clock train with time leftover. Let's go see if that café is still across from the telegraph office."

The café hadn't moved, and they feasted on home-cooked fare better than anything they'd eaten since they boarded the train in Dillon.

"You remember this place, sheriff?" John asked.

"Yes, I do," he replied. "We ate breakfast here."

"That's right," John said, tapping his son with the back of his hand. "That market across the street is where your mom and I got married. It was a telegraph office back then, and the operator was a justice of the peace."

"Sounds very romantic." Johnny smiled.

"Oh, it was that," his dad said, clearing his throat. "We'd only left Spanish Fork a couple days before. My head was spinning."

They ordered the ALL-YOU-CAN-EAT MEAT LOAF SPECIAL. After both John Walkers sent the waitress back for a third refill, a grizzled old cook emerged from the kitchen and stared at them, reliving a vague recollection of a long past memory. He shook his head with a grimace and erased the offering from the long-standing blackboard, still balanced on its ancient easel.

"I have an old friend to look up," John said. "You're both welcome to come along."

"Sure," Johnny said.

"I think I'd like to go bed." The sheriff patted his stomach and yawned.

"We'll walk you back to the hotel."

That chore accomplished, the Walkers followed the tracks toward the fairgrounds, stopping at Lloyd Clark's expanded livery on the way. Two additional barns, a series of corrals, holding pens, and loading chutes flanked the west side of the tracks. Two young men worked the walkway, pitching hay to a hundred-odd cattle and some forty horses.

"Lloyd around?" John called out over the milling hungry stock.

"He'd be at the Forester about now," the closest boy yelled back.

"Is that the same place he'd been drinkin' at twenty years ago?"

The boys looked at each other and shrugged. "I reckon," the near one hollered.

The older man waved and climbed down off the fence. "I only been to this place once," John said to his son. "Lemme see if I can find it again."

Like a homing pigeon returning from a long journey, John Walker shuffled through the door into an unchanged saloon that time and the growing city had passed by. "See that old man at the end of the bar?" he said to his son.

"Yessir."

"Go sit next to him and ask if you can buy him a drink," John said, handing his son a dollar.

"Yessir."

John followed his boy to sit on the other side of Lloyd Clark as the young man spoke to him. Much as he expected, Lloyd fell backward into his arms when he looked at the image of John as an impossibly young man.

"Lloyd, Lloyd," he said, spinning him around, "look at this face! This is the John Walker you'd expect. That's my boy."

"You son of a bitch. You almost killed this old man," Lloyd said, catching his breath. "You're still alive."

"I am, and you've got a new business," John said. "Did Jakome's money build that?"

"Yeah, pretty much." He laughed. "I see you spent your half."

"Yeah, I did, but I didn't build anything like you," John said, putting his arm around the older man. "Lloyd, this is my son, Johnny. I didn't know about him till 'bout a week ago. I was surprised as you are."

"Howdy, son," Lloyd said, shaking the boy's hand. "Let me buy you that drink." Then he looked at the boy's dad. "You didn't know about him? How is that possible?"

"It's a long, long story, and I'm gonna tell you the whole thing," his old friend said. "But not tonight. You look good."

"So do you. At least your son does." Lloyd shook his head. "It's amazing how much he looks like you. Where's your wife?"

"That's a big part of my story. I've only seen her for a few hours since I've seen you, and she didn't tell me she was pregnant then," John said. "I was trackin' her and chasing the Colonel until I got in trouble with the law. Then I was on the run till I got caught and spent some time in prison. I spent Jakome's money along the way."

"I'll be a catdog. He was just here, you know."

"What?"

"Yeah, couple weeks ago," Lloyd said. "He asked about you. Course I didn't have nothin' to tell him. I told him he still owed me fifty dollars and another fifty for my tools. He pulled five twenty-dollar gold pieces outta his purse and paid me."

"Was he alone?"

"Near as I could tell, but I don't know."

"I can't figure that guy. I still owe him a nightmare, and he knows it," John said. "I can't figure why he's dogging me. I still plan on huntin' him down, but I gotta go see Zelda first. Lloyd, what did he say? Did he say anything about what he was doin' here? Where he'd been? Where he was goin'? I need somethin' to go on."

"John, I ain't got nothin' for ya'," Lloyd said.

"Do you know somethin'?" John said to his son.

"You gotta talk to Ma," the young man said. "But I'll tell you this, she says the Colonel's lookin' for her. She says he's crazy."

"Goddammit! Where is she?"

"I'll take you," Johnny said. "She made me promise to never say it out loud."

53

Summer 1871

During the time the twins were finishing their wardrobe, Sam busied himself around Alamo working all manner of jobs to earn traveling money for the trip east. Doc busied him with repairs to his hospital, both needed and unnecessary. He called on patients to provide jobs for the boy and quietly insisted that he be overpaid. Exhausted at the end of every day, Sam slept well those nights.

It was difficult for Sam and the twins to say goodbye to Doc and Jeanie when the chores and the sewing were finished. The three of them had spent every night since the fire in the Jameses' hospital, and they had become a family. The girls promised to return, confident their dream would be realized and eager to show themselves off. But they were sobbing at the end, holding the couple, becoming a group formation in the gesture. Sam was stoic standing nearby, staring at Doc, knowing he'd never see him again.

"And the baby," Chastity exclaimed through her tears. "I'm going to name it Frank or Jeanie! Is that all right with you, Sam?"

"Yeah," he said. "That's what I been thinkin'."

"Of course you have," Chastity said, punching him on the shoulder.

Traveling with the twins was less than the flattering experience Sam expected. Having grown up in a whorehouse, Sam might have thought he knew *everything* about women, but this experience was new to him. He'd anticipated the attention they'd attract. The stares, the covered-mouth whispers, and the pointing and gawking children were there as expected. He was always on alert, prepared to defend their honor and guard their possessions. The clothes the twins had crafted for themselves were stunning and filled two large trunks that they accessed every evening for the following day's fresh look. They had booked passage on a Pullman car that was necessarily made over to suit them at the station by a conductor and two firemen. The finished sleeper was a close fit for the girls, who never stopped insisting that they would pay for a sleeping compartment for Sam. He continued to refuse to take money from them for anything and chose to sleep in his passenger seat until they arrived at a bank where he could get his own money from the account his mother had opened for him. The nights were uncomfortable, but in his life's experience, he had learned to tolerate pain and did not complain.

The morning sickness was the most difficult part of the trip for them all, for it was not only Chastity who suffered but Prudence as well. Sam assumed the bucket duty and made countless trips to the water closet, both for the delivery of fresh water and the disposal of all waste. Because of his effort, the twins rallied every day to present themselves as they knew was expected. After all, their performances were legendary even when it was only to be observed.

The trio arrived in Salt Lake City a fortnight after the Walkers and the sheriff had been there. Sam's attempts to withdraw money from the bank account his mother had established for him in St. Louis drew amused looks from bankers in Salt Lake, Denver, and Kansas City. He wondered at the solemnity his mother gave to the transaction and the confidence she and the banker held that he would be able to withdraw the money. The security he'd felt having money in the bank was gone. Maybe Chester could fix it.

It took a week for the train to roll in to St. Louis, with a hundred stops on the way. The early summer weather was brutal. Cold and rainy with the occasional blizzard, the passengers were always cold, and the conductor was busy hauling fuel to the wood-burning stoves in every coach. The twins had little patience for the discomforts of rail travel and looked forward to the scheduled overnight stops to take advantage of the hotels and their dining rooms. Though Sam slept on the floor, he did so with anticipation, knowing he would be called to the bed every evening for a bit of frolic with the girls.

On the last night of their journey, on the last of the day's trips to the water closet, Sam was stopped cold as he turned to face a poster on the inside of the door:

WANTED FOR MURDER

SAMUEL SHINES

$10,000 REWARD

COURTNEY FAMILY, ST. LOUIS, MISSOURI

The drawing on the printed bulletin was of a boyish face with a long scar going down his left cheek. After staring at it for a full minute, he caught his breath and noticed it actually kind of looked like him. He carefully removed it from the door, rolled it up, and stuck it in his shirt.

Sam set the clean water bucket in its corner and the waste bucket in its place. The twins smiled at him from under a patchwork quilt then said in unison, "What's the matter?"

"This," he said, handing them the poster.

"What is it?" asked Prudence.

"What does it mean? Is this you?" Chastity asked.

"Yeah, it's me," Sam replied. "I'm gonna go through the train and see if there are any more. This one was in the toilet, and it wasn't there last time I was. I'll tell you about it when I get back. Where's my hat?"

The passengers were settled in for the night, either wrapped in blankets in their seats or out of sight in compartments. Sam walked slowly through the cars, hat pulled down to his eyes, collar up, and looking for someone looking for him. He found one more poster in the water closet of passenger car number 1 and took it. Stopping at the woodstove in his car, he rolled the poster up and put it in the fire.

"So what is this?" Chastity asked, poster in hand.

"And don't say you'll tell us later," Prudence added. "Did you find any others?"

"I did," he replied. "Three. I burned 'em. I didn't know anything about this before today."

"Where did this come from? Did you murder someone?"

"Yeah, I did. I killed the man who killed my ma," he said. "Last time I saw him, he was on his way to hell."

"This was when you lived in St. Louis?" asked Prudence.

"Yeah."

"Where we'll be tomorrow," added Chastity. "Where there'll be posters like this all over the place."

"Maybe," Sam said.

"We've got to cover those scars," Prudence said.

"With makeup?" Chastity asked.

"Or a hat," Prudence said. "A hat with earflaps."

"Is it cold enough for that?" Sam asked.

"Or we could dress you up to be an idiot," Chastity said.

"Well, that wouldn't be hard," Sam said.

"You're not an idiot," Prudence said. "What do you have to do there?"

"I have to see Chester and go to the bank to get my money," Sam said. "And I'd like to go to my ma's grave."

"We'll see what we can do with makeup tomorrow. Come to bed," Chastity cooed.

They arrived in St. Louis around noon. A porter at the loading dock looking for fares to the Missouri Hotel helped Sam load their baggage on his cart. The walk to the hotel was short, and the appearance of the twins distracted gawkers from noticing Sam—or anyone else in the vicinity. The twins had done what they could to cover the scars with powder and rouge and insisted they could do better after a stop at a pharmacy. Sam kept his hat pulled down and his collar up until he got to their room, where he spent the rest of the day.

The twins returned to the room at suppertime with fried chicken, bread, cheese, bean soup, and beers. They described their afternoon's adventure while they ate then spent half an hour applying neutral colors of makeup to Sam's face.

"What was your name, sir?" Prudence asked.

"I think the beard helps," Chastity added.

"Yeah, it may be a while before I can grow anything like this," Sam said. "Where did you find it?"

"A costume shop," Prudence said. "This city has everything."

"I'll be leaving soon as it gets dark," he said. "Might be late when I get back."

"Be careful," they said together.

54

"Mr. Maxwell, it's me, Sam."

"What? Who?"

"Samuel. Penny's son."

"I'll be darned," Chester said then stuck his head out the door and looked in all directions. He reached out with both hands and lifted the boy off his feet to get him inside. "I got your letter but didn't know if you'd make it or not. You grew a beard, but I don't think you gained any weight."

"No, sir," Sam said, pulling the beard off his face. "I ain't ready to grow a beard yet either."

"I think I know why you're wearin' that. What're you doin' here?"

"I'm on my way to Chicago with Siamese twins. One of 'em's carryin' my baby."

"Come in here and sit down," Chester said. He walked across the room to the staircase and yelled at his son, "Billy, come down here!"

The boys greeted each other with big smiles, but when Billy extended his hand to shake, Sam grabbed his wrist and turned it over to look at his palm. They both laughed and fell into the hearty hugs of old friends. Chester poured them glasses of water from a pitcher at the sink and added a glass of whiskey for himself from a bottle in the cupboard. He opened a bureau drawer and pulled out one of Sam's wanted posters. "I guess you might have one of these. These things started showing up just after you left," Chester began. "Courtney's brother was behind it, and that pissant's so broke he musta borrowed the money to have 'em made. He heard about your ma dyin', and you disappearin's all it took. It was a big deal for a while with that much reward money, but pretty soon the word's out it ain't real, and most everyone's forgot about it. The sheriff's still pissed off about the posters, but he does want to talk to you. He asked me if I knew where you were."

"I found four on the train," Sam said.

"Yeah, I see 'em still," Chester said. "I always tear 'em down. That disguise's a good idea. Tell us what you've been doing for the last year. Start with this other scar on your face."

"I'll get to that, but it'll make more sense if I start at the beginning."

Sam began at the riverboat trip up the Missouri and finished an hour later, with his arrival at the St Louis train station.

"You mean to tell me the Siamese twins are here at a hotel?"

"Yessir. I sleep with 'em every night," Sam said, glancing at Billy.

"You suppose we could meet them?" Billy asked.

"Sure. I'll want to get my money and get outta town pretty quick," Sam said. "I tried at a few banks on the way here, but the bankers weren't havin' it."

"I still got yer ma's letter. I read it after you left," Chester said. "I haven't stopped thinkin' about what it means.

"Yessir. I know what it means."

Chester walked back to the bureau, opened the same drawer the poster was in, and removed a folded piece of paper.

"She had you sign your name Samuel Maxwell," Chester said. "Not the name on the posters."

"Yessir."

"Ya know, I was seeing your ma long enough before you were born to be yer pa, but I gotta wonder how she could know it was me," Chester said. "I mean, if she sees a dozen men a day, how could she know?"

"Maybe she wanted it to be you."

"Well, yeah, I thought of that too," Chester said. "After Billy's ma died, I was so heartbroke I couldn't stand to be alone. Your ma got me through that, and eventually I fell in love with her. What a thing, huh?

"I pondered it a lot," he said, looking at Billy. "And I don't know if it makes me a bad man or what, but I loved 'em both. I'd like to see where you buried her."

"We could go tomorrow after the bank," Sam said. "Then we could go see the twins. They're amazing."

55

Summer 1871

The twins' earliest memories were of life with the Box brothers in Oakland. They lived in a carriage house behind a barn near the big house with their nephew, John, and sister, Zelda. Zelda worked for Joseph, first at cooking and housekeeping but soon moved to bookkeeping and business management, as he tired of those things. She was meticulous and keen and soon became indispensable to the brothers. The children were taught by tutors, but the twins were not sheltered. They often traveled across the bay to San Francisco and were exposed to the arts and theater at an early age.

Curious about everything, they easily adapted to the curiosity they evoked wherever they went. Gracious and solicitous to the crowds they attracted, they became well-known. In their teens, they attended the Mission High School in San Francisco and became the first girls to complete the four-year program. Both were ambitious but held far different ideas on where their careers should take them. Chastity fancied herself in the medical field as a doctor, while Prudence wanted to be a gambler—impossible dreams for Siamese twins to share. They would need to be separated, and that would take money. It was in high school that they decided to become prostitutes.

"What if something happens to me when the baby's born?" Chastity said.

"Nothing's going to happen. You're fit, and you'll be in a hospital."

"We will be in a hospital!"

"That's right. I'll be right there with you," Prudence confirmed. "Look, we haven't talked about this much, but this separation is as much about the end of our lives as living our lives. You know that," she said. "We need to find out what our options are."

"Staying together would probably be our safest choice," Chastity said.

"Yes, that's no doubt true. I still want to know what other possibilities we have. Don't you?"

"Yes, I guess so."

"Good. We'll talk to the best doctors we can find and make our best decision."

56

The business at the bank went well. Sam didn't wear his beard, which looked less authentic in daylight, but the girls did a believable job of covering his scars with makeup. Sam was nervous when he wrote down his account number and signed his name on the withdrawal slip. The teller scrutinized the document, compared it to the original, then smiled at Mr. Maxwell's stern expression as he counted out the cash. The boost to Sam's confidence was immediate, and he insisted on buying lunch for the group back at the hotel. The twins looked exceptional coming down the stairs, and Sam could not hold back a smile when he saw the shocked look on Billy's face. They were charming as they were wont to be and effusive in their praise of Sam as they described his heroism when he rescued them from the Blazing Star. Father and son Maxwell put down their forks and stared at him when the girls threw in the story of Sam shooting Chatham.

"He was our pa, and he was breaking into Doc and Jeanie's hospital in the middle of the night," Chastity exclaimed. "He was coming to kill us."

"He was the devil!" Prudence confirmed.

"He threw his knife at Sam's head."

"The same knife he cut Sam's face with."

"Dang, son," Chester said. "How old are you?"

"Sixteen."

"And how many men have you killed?"

"Two," Sam answered. "Two murderers."

"Hmm. I ain't never killed nobody," Chester said. "And there was a couple I shoulda."

"I got in a fight at school once and got a black eye," Billy said.

"Almost the same," Sam responded.

They all laughed then ordered apple pie for dessert. The mood of the table was festive, and the conversation turned to the beautiful afternoon and what the travelers would do on their last day in St. Louis. The girls wanted to go back to the room, freshen up, and go shopping. Sam would go to the cemetery. Chester decided he and Billy should go home to clean the house and prepare the evening's supper, where they would all meet again.

"Mr. Maxwell," Sam said, taking him aside outside the dining room, "have you ever seen that guy behind me sitting by the window, reading the paper?"

Chester sidestepped Sam to look casually over his shoulder. "No, I don't think so," he said.

"I'm pretty sure he was on the train, and I saw him across the street from the bank this morning. Now he's here," Sam said. "I'm gonna get my pistol and see if he shows up at the cemetery."

In their room, Sam asked the girls if they would carry his money for him.

"Yes. We have pockets in secret places where we keep ours," Chastity said. "It will be safe."

"Yes, from anybody except you." Prudence laughed.

"Yeah." Sam smiled. "I'll look for it later."

He waited for them to leave (which took forever) then stuck the .44 Colt in the back of his pants and pulled his coat down over the grip. Sam didn't bother with the beard since the hotel staff had seen him without it and would now draw their attention. The man with the paper was gone when he walked through the lobby and nowhere in sight when he stopped to look around outside. He walked toward the river, stopping several times to check his back, but saw nothing. A small procession was leaving the graveyard as he approached, and he removed his hat and stepped under a tree to watch them pass. The parade walked through the gate, and light banter erupted as a bottle was opened and passed around.

Sam's mother's grave was much as he had left it. The wooden marker he'd made was a kilter, so he dug it out with his knife and reset it deeper in the soil. Tiny yellow buttercups and small white daisies pushed up through the early green grasses around the markers and tombstones, and he picked a handful to lay among the white river rocks. He sat next to the grave and remembered the times he came here with her. It was apparent to him that whores didn't have a long life expectancy, and he watched her as she tended their graves. He wished he had a picture.

"You got balls comin' back here, boy."

Sam stood up and turned around to face the man who'd been following him. He was short and skinny and struggled to keep the double-barreled shotgun pointed at Sam's chest.

"Who're you?"

"Name's Calvin Courtney. You killed my brother."

"Your brother deserved to die, but I didn't kill him," Sam said. He looked over the little man's shoulder and gave a wave. Calvin turned around to look, and Sam rushed forward, pushed the barrel of the shotgun aside, and stuck his pistol in Calvin's nose.

"Ugh," Calvin cried out.

"Shut up, you fuckin' idiot. I ain't even close to bein' done with you. Let's take a walk." Sam took the shotgun, broke it open to make sure it was loaded, and put his gun back in his belt. He pushed Calvin downhill through the cemetery to the river then turned downstream. They walked along a path familiar to him from many trips in search of the white rocks. It was after high water receded that he most often found them, scattered along the shore beneath an old grove of cottonwoods. His mother told him they were eggs that some ancient animal or bird buried in the riverbank and were loosened by high water every year. Sam had broken a couple open, but they just crumbled into white dust, offering no clue to what they might have become. Today there were no eggs, and he wished this chore could be so simple.

"What'd you think you were gonna do with me anyhow?" Sam asked. "Turn me in and collect the reward?"

"Ha! Everybody in St. Louis was lookin' fer you," he laughed. "I been ridin' trains back and forth from Kansas City for more than a year hangin' posters. I knew you'd come back. I figured sooner or later, someone would bring you around lookin' for the reward. I don't need no money. Me and my brothers are gonna hang you."

"So you've seen the women I'm traveling with," Sam said.

"Ha! They're pretty good-lookin' for freaks!"

Sam swung the shotgun like an axe at a tree, hitting Calvin in the ribs. He groaned as the air left his lungs, and he struggled to stand.

"You fucking idiot! Those girls' lives depend on me getting them to a doctor in Chicago. Don't think I'm gonna let anything happen to them or to me," Sam snarled, kneeling on his chest with both knees. "It's you or us, Calvin."

57

Summer 1849

After the incident at the Occidental, the Box brothers decided to provide this unusual family with shelter and security. Neither had ever married or had children, so this responsibility filled a void they'd never known. The twins and young John were well-mannered and entertaining, and with Zelda's contribution to their business, they considered the little family an asset. Zelda recovered from her opium addiction months before John was born with help from the brothers and the determination that was her core strength. She had no memory of the incident at the Occidental or of the hours she spent with her husband afterward. Joseph told her John took the blame after she shot the Colonel and that there were no witnesses who could dispute his claim.

Zelda decided to stay with the Box brothers in the Bay Area because she had no other reasonable options. She damn sure wasn't going on tour with the circus. The news that she'd maimed the Colonel pleased her, but it put John on the run and destroyed their family. Her heart was broken, but if she were to see her husband again, it would probably be near this place. She and the children were safe, and she would wait here for a sign.

58

Summer 1849 and Autumn 1865

The Boxes liked and respected John Walker, especially knowing he was innocent of the crime for which he was hunted. They were able to keep him hidden for a time, but his pursuit by San Francisco Police Chief Virgil Ducker was relentless. The corrupt police chief had been outfoxed by the Boxes in too many smuggling ventures, and he was always looking for retribution. John's association with the Boxes made him a target.

The Colonel's injury not only emasculated him but also removed a sizable chunk of his left buttock. The wound proved to be a slow healer and kept him away from his circus, which languished in Oakland. His financial backers in Denver grew tired of the delays, and the circus was disassembled and sold for parts. Performers were dismissed, animals sold, and train cars repainted and offered for commercial use. A few of his henchmen with no marketable skills waited for his recovery.

The Colonel and his little gang stayed in San Francisco for several years working for Chief Ducker in his black-market businesses. They prospered as enforcers and hijackers, but the Colonel tired of the work and left for his home, Virginia, when he heard rumors of the South's secession. He had grown up with slavery and would fight to save it. It was at war's end that Lieutenant Kasper Cobb met William Cane in a Richmond hospital, where they recovered from battle injuries.

When the devastation was over, soldiers from both armies, but primarily Union veterans, brought home an invisible wound—an addiction to painkillers derived from opium. Soldiers at Confederate hospitals—where at the end, medications were virtually nonexistent—were more fortunate to have not been exposed to "God's own medicine," simply because it was not available.

Cane and Cobb were discharged with a memory of their pain-free experience and realized its business potential. They took advantage of the postwar chaos to travel north to cities and towns less ravaged by the battle to burglarize pharmacies of their opium supplies and cash. Making the occasional sale along the way, they eventually made it to New York and to Chinatown, where they found a legitimate opium connection. The city was the perfect source for everything needed for the production of Colonel Phantastic's Cure-All Elixir. They bought bottles, corks, wooden cases, and had labels printed. Their recipe included mineral oil, sugar, elderberry extract, camphor, alcohol, and of course, opium powder. They measured and tested until they had a product that suited their own need, set a suitable supply of it aside, then diluted the balance for maximum profit. Their ingenuity and hard work convinced their Chinese suppliers to finance the purchase of a three-ton ice wagon that was painted and refurbished to make it suitable for travel behind a team of sturdy, medium-sized draft horses. Though not part of the original plan, Cane and Cobb agreed to transport an aged grandparent to San Francisco for further passage to China. Neither of them had any intention of carrying the old man farther than the New York state line, but he proved to be incredibly useful. In constant motion at the beginning and end of every day, he tended the horses and tack, built the fire, and cooked and served breakfast and supper. While riding in the back of the wagon, in the first two days, he made each of them a new shirt. His name was Ho Hum, and he seldom spoke, except to bow and thank them for taking him along—several times a day.

The trio traveled steadily westward, stopping in towns and villages to put on their little show, often in the shadow of snake oil salesmen who'd previously passed through, offering a similar though usually useless product. Met with skepticism and often hostility, they were eager to separate themselves and their tonic from the competition. Sellers of snake oil liniments and elixirs were known to send a shill into the crowd whom they would call on to come forward to sample then praise the product. The Colonel would smile at these stories and offer a different kind of proof of effectiveness.

"Ladies and gentlemen, who here has pain?" he would ask. "Which of you brave veterans have difficulty sleeping at night because of battle injuries?" Invariably, several hands would raise, and the Colonel would look down at the volunteers to gauge their fitness. "You, sir, what is your name?"

"Cleeves, Beezy Cleeves."

"Thank you, sir," the Colonel said, looking around the audience. "Have you ever seen me before? Do you know my product?"

"No, I ain't seen you before, but I know you're a reb."

"Yessir, you are correct," the Colonel announced to groans and boos from the group. He raised his hands and continued, "Lieutenant Kasper Cobb, late of the Twenty-Seventh Virginia Infantry, also known as the Bloody Twenty-Seventh. I was one of the sixty-two wounded at Chancellorsville and recuperated at the Chimborazo Hospital in Richmond next to Sergeant Cane here, who travels with me today."

"What about the Chinaman?" a voice called out. "Was he at Chancellorsville too?"

There were guffaws and hoots and a smile from the Colonel. "No, but he was at Chimborazo, and he's why the sergeant and I are still alive. This man carries with him an ancient family recipe that saved our lives and can change yours. I hold in my hand the answer to your prayers. Who among you is in pain right now? Who will test this miraculous potion? I ask you, who is willing to give up your pain?"

The Colonel held up a bottle of Colonel Phantastic's Cure-All Elixir, poured a shot glass full, and drank it down. "Who will join me and give up your pain?"

First one hand went up then two, as the veterans formed a line. They drank their shots, and some found shade to rest in while their broken bodies absorbed the relief. Soon, there was a new line at the rear of the wagon where Sergeant Cane exchanged their dollars for "the cure."

The early results were impressive. Cane's initial inventory indicated they would likely have to go back into production by the time they got to Chicago. They still had labels, but stocks of everything else would have to be replaced, a much simpler task having already done it once.

The Colonel recommended no more than two shots of elixir each day, but he knew the concoction was addictive and that many of his customers would disregard these instructions. It was just a matter of time before they'd be pursued. They moved slowly and would be easy to track, so they decided to move on after every stop when their transactions were completed.

59

"I'm gonna need a few more bottles of yer fancy syrup," a voice said as Ho Hum was cleaning up after breakfast. Silhouetted against the rising sun, it was hard to see their visitor. The Colonel stood up and casually walked to the rider's side for a better view. The man was seated on a bay mare and dressed in the uniform of a Union cavalry officer. A pistol was holstered on his hip, and the stock of a shotgun protruded from a saddle scabbard.

"Well, sir," the Colonel responded, standing up and glancing over his shoulder to see Cane disappear behind the wagon, "you are in luck. Another hour and we'd be down the trail. How many bottles do you need?"

"I'll take 'em all," he said, pulling out the shotgun and laying it across his lap.

"Indeed," the Colonel said, walking to the officer's side. "And how will you be transporting that much of our inventory?"

"Oh, yeah," the man said, turning the mare so the sun was not in his eyes. "I guess I'll be needing your wagon and horses too."

"We can't let that happen," the Colonel said.

"My brother was killed at Chancellorsville…"

"Everyone lost someone in the war," the Colonel interrupted and glanced over his shoulder. "It's over, and it don't mean you can steal from me. Sergeant Cane has a rifle pointed at your heart right now. I'll leave you a few bottles of tonic under that big tree behind us, and we'll be on our way. If you follow us, I'll kill you."

One day into their third week, Ho Hum alerted the veterans to a rider approaching steadily from the rear. They pulled over to a shady park by a stream to water and rest the horses then watched the small dust cloud arrive. A young man, a boy really, came slowly to them riding bareback on an old broke-down mule.

"Colonel," the boy said, raising his hand to salute against a holey wreck of felt that was once a hat. He swayed as if he were drunk, fell forward against the mule's neck, then managed to push himself upright. "I need a bottle of your medicine."

"Slow down there, boy," Cane said. "Let's water your mule and stand him in the shade a bit." He watched a slow but steady drip of blood pool on the mule's other side and walked around to see a red rag wrapped around the stump of the boy's leg. "Let's get you down, boy, and wash yer wound in the stream."

"Naw, I cain't," he gasped. "I ain't never will git back up here."

"We'll get you back on," Cane said, reaching up to pull the boy down. He carried him to the water and set him down next to it. "Ho Hum, come over and look at this," he said. "Colonel, lead that mule down here to drink and get him a scoop of grain."

Both men moved to their tasks, and Cane watched Ho Hum unwrap the leg. He grumbled in his high-pitched chatter of a voice and indicated that Cane should hold on to the boy lest he fall into the water and drown. Ho Hum returned with water to drink, a piece of clean cloth, and a jar of salve. He brushed off a colony of maggots and proceeded to wash the leg as the boy screamed and passed out. Cane held him close while Ho Hum cut black crust from the stump with scissors. He stepped over the rail-thin body to lift Cane's hand and set it on the boy's forehead. "Hot! Hot!" he said.

"He's on fire," Cane murmured. "Colonel?"

Cane saw his partner pull the grain bucket away from the emaciated mule's mouth and watched the kernels fall from the old animal's lips to the ground. He walked over as Cane washed the boy's face with a clean rag and saw him open his eyes and smile. "Thought I'd never catch you guys."

"Where'd you come from, son?"

"Aaaa, Allendale."

"Allendale? That must be twenty miles back," the Colonel said. "I don't remember seeing you there."

"Yessir, I missed it," he gasped, closed his eyes, then came back. "I got bad pain," he said. "But I got a dollar. I got a dollar right here." He reached for his pocket, got his hand inside, and pulled out a crushed and torn piece of newspaper and held it up.

"Yeah, boy," Cane said, taking it. "You got it covered. Ho Hum, get me a bottle of number 1."

The old man returned with the bottle, and propping him up, they slowly poured a little in the boy's mouth. He sipped and choked and started to cry.

"Slow, boy, slow," Ho Hum said.

The boy drank until he passed out. Ho Hum pulled his pant leg up, and they looked at the enflamed red stripe that ran from the wound up the inside of his leg to his groin.

"Goddamn," Cane said. "This boy's dying."

"Wake him up and give him more," the Colonel said. "This can't go on."

The boy came back, and they poured the potent liquid into him until he fell asleep, then they woke him up and did it three more times. Finally, he stopped breathing, and they gently laid him on the ground.

"This ain't right," Cane said.

The Colonel walked to the wagon and came back with a rifle and a blanket. "No, it ain't right," he said, tossing the blanket on the ground. "Dig a hole over there by those flowers." He picked up the bottle, wiped off the rim, and took a long pull. "I'll take this mule for a walk."

60

They ran out of elixir well before they arrived in Chicago. William Cane's sister lived in the city and, having not seen him in more than five years, warmly welcomed him and his partners into her home. The siblings stayed up late that first night reliving childhood memories and the joys and regrets of their relatives. Sarah gave Will a small packet of letters she'd accumulated over the years, and they read and talked about each one.

"I saved this one for last. It mentions you," she said. "It came a week ago. Do you remember cousin Cyrus?"

"From Kalamazoo?"

"Yes."

"Yeah, sure."

"Well, he's a city councilman in San Francisco, and he has a job for you," she said.

"Yeah, what?"

"He wants to hire you to be a policeman," she said, handing him an envelope. "Here, read this."

The Colonel was up at dawn, walking through Sarah's neighborhood, impressed by the display of ornately trimmed houses and their immaculately landscaped yards. He came upon a bustling café and maneuvered through tables to the only vacant one in the back by the kitchen. A pleasant waitress brought him coffee, a slice of bread with strawberry preserves, and a copy of the morning's *Tribune*. Sitting back in his chair, he scanned the crowd, certain none of the patrons were aware of his presence. A bulletin board on a nearby wall caught his eye, and he walked to it to inspect the small pieces of paper it had accumulated. Seeing one that interested him, he unpinned it and took it back to his table.

FOR RENT

THREE-BEDROOM HOUSE

FENCED YARD, BARN, AND CORRAL

$20/month

28 Locust Avenue

When the waitress returned with his check, he asked for directions to Locust Avenue then set off to find it.

"Kasper, I need to talk to you," Will Cane said, sitting on his sister's front porch.

"Good, Will," the Colonel responded. "I have some things to discuss with you."

The two men sat on the stoop and revealed to each other the details of their recently formulated plans.

"I'll take Ho Hum with me," Will said, glancing the old man's way as he pulled weeds from a flower bed. "We'll travel by train as far as it goes and by wagon after that. I'll stay here a week and help you put together a new batch of elixir."

"I'll appreciate that," the Colonel said. "Yours sounds like a reasonable plan. You think you'll like being a policeman?"

"Yes, I do," Cane said. "Regular, honest work will suit me. I'll find a pretty girl to marry, and we'll buy a house like this in a neighborhood with streetlights."

"And you should do well," the Colonel said. "We made a good profit on this adventure, and your share will be more than enough for your trip West with Ho. Come with me to see the house I intend to rent. Ho Hum, come with us."

The three men walked the short distance to the house, and the Colonel described his idea to build another traveling show that might include animal acts and magic and other unusual talents. "I believe I can put it together right here in this city."

"Yes, sir. A city this size must have many talented people," Cane said. "As you travel, you'll no doubt find more."

"I figure that's right," the Colonel said. "If that doesn't happen, I'll sell elixir for a while then head West."

61

Summer 1871

Chester rented a team and buggy for the night and sent Billy to the hotel to pick up Sam and the twins. Chastity and Prudence were totally charmed by father and son Maxwell and impressed by their cozy and comfortable little house. They were served split pea soup, fresh baked bread with honey, and a pumpkin pie for dessert.

"Chester, this is delicious!" Prudence exclaimed. "Will you marry me?"

"Absolutely," Chester replied. "But I have to be honest, I didn't make the bread or the pie. Mrs. Marks across the street rescued me on those."

"Well, you're very resourceful. There are details that would have to be worked out on the other matter," she said, laughing. "I may not be the marrying kind, so don't talk to the preacher yet."

The evening was a great success for everyone but Sam. He smiled and responded when spoken to but never offered to liven up the conversation with his dry wit. The girls insisted on doing the dishes, and they all sipped whiskey around the dining room table afterward. The ride back to the hotel was relatively quiet, as the girls snuggled under the buffalo robe Chester sent along and wondered at the city's beauty under its gaslit streets.

There were two policemen at the entrance of the hotel when they arrived, and Sam slipped away before the carriage stopped. Billy was helping the twins out of the narrow back opening when he was flanked by the lawmen, and the three of them were escorted inside. They took Billy aside, removed his hat, and studied him in the light.

"Where's the scar-faced boy?" one of them asked.

"I don't know," Billy responded.

"Ladies?"

"We don't know either."

"He was seen leaving with you both a few hours ago."

"He said something about finding a friend."

"Will he be back tonight?"

"Maybe," they said together. "We'll tell him you were looking for him."

"Yeah, I bet you will."

"I'll walk you to your room," Billy said.

They climbed the stairs, and Billy walked up and down the hallway looking for anything unusual before going inside. He pulled a chair up to the bed, where the twins sat and spoke in a low voice. "He stopped wearing his disguise and got noticed. There's probly nobody in this city who hasn't seen those posters."

"Oh dear, he's got to get out of here," Chastity said. "Our train leaves tomorrow."

"The police will be watching you. I'll help you get to the station," he said. "Sam will probly come to our house. I'll take the buggy back to the livery tonight and make sure I'm not followed home. We'll make a plan, and I'll be here in the morning to let you know what it is."

"Oh, thank you, Billy," the twins said.

Sam and Chester were sitting at the kitchen table in the dark sipping whiskey when Billy came through the back door. "Figured you'd be here," Billy said. "They asked us where you were. We said you were with a friend."

"The only friends I got in this town are right here," Sam replied.

"Sam killed another Courtney this afternoon," Chester said.

Billy looked at Sam and felt a little fear surge through his stomach. "What?"

"He was commencin' to take me home so his brothers could hang me. Now he's floatin' down the Missouri with his double-barrel shotgun through his belt and down his pant leg," Sam said. "It was him or me."

"That's three," Billy said. "Somebody's gonna write a song about you."

"If the sheriff don't know I know you, he could find out easy enough by askin' around at the Lewis & Clark," Chester said. "Billy and I are gonna walk around the block. If the police are watchin', that'll distract 'em. Take a blanket off my bed and make yer way to the graveyard for tonight. One of us will find you there tomorrow. The girls could wait for you to catch up in Edwardsville. It's only twenty-five miles, but I gotta think on it more."

"If I leave right now, I could be there before they are," Sam said.

"Well, yeah," Chester thought out loud.

"Send my poke with 'em. And the disguises too," Sam said, swallowing the last of his whiskey.

"Let me get you a canteen and a couple of biscuits," Billy added. "I wish I was goin' with ya. My life's a lazy day compared to yours."

Sam walked up to Billy, grabbed him by both shoulders, then shook his hand. "I'll bet you live longer 'n me. I'll write you a letter and let you know how this all works out. I probly won't be comin' back to this town ever."

"I'll come see you wherever you are," Billy said. "I just hope it's not in jail."

"I ain't goin' to jail," Sam said and reached behind his back to pull out the Colt. He checked the cylinder to make sure it was full. "Chastity and me are havin' a baby."

62

Chester and Billy stopped at the livery, rerented the buggy, and picked the twins up at the hotel. Sam's things were stuffed into one of the steamers, except for his disguises, which were carried in a handbag. At the train station, two policemen accosted them as they stopped and immediately pulled Billy aside, removed his hat, and studied his face for scars. The twins climbed out of the carriage, approached the policemen, and simultaneously slapped each in the face with a left and right hook.

"What have you done with our nephew?" they said in unison.

"The boy with the scar is your nephew?" the taller of the two asked.

"Yes, what have you done with him?" they yelled, raising their hands to strike another blow. "Our train for Detroit leaves this morning, and he's not here."

The officers quickly stepped back, out of range. "Ma'am...er, ma'ams, we don't have him. The sheriff wants to talk to him, and we're here to take him downtown."

"We'll be back in a month. You can talk to him then. Tell that to the sheriff!" Chastity said. "If you see Daniel, tell him we'll be waiting at the doctor's office."

Sam was waiting for them in Edwardsville. Standing behind a stack of boxes at the freight end of the platform, he casually waved as the train pulled into the station.

The twins hurried out of the car and nonchalantly walked to Sam's hiding place. Before he could say anything, they pushed him against the boxes and began attaching the beard and applying the necessary rouge to cover his scars. "How's your day so far, Sammy?" Chastity asked.

"Good, I guess. I can sleep while I'm walking, so I'm not tired," he said.

"Well, that's good news. We're tired because we don't sleep while you're walking," Prudence said.

"There's a policeman at the other end of the platform," he said. "He hasn't seen me, but that don't mean he's not looking for me."

"Well, he didn't ride here on the train. We would have seen him," Chastity said.

"This one's not wearing a uniform."

"Then how do you know he's a policeman?"

"I know," Sam said. "And he probly knows I'm traveling with you. We better split up if he gets on the train. I'll sit where I can watch him."

"You do that," they said. "We're going out back to pee."

"The potties here are one-seaters."

"Listen, honey," they said, "we've dealt with this situation before."

Sam smiled and looked over their shoulders to see the policeman he'd been watching was no longer visible. "Go out for another pee in Springfield," he said. "I'll talk to you then."

Disguised and feeling confident, Sam walked through the station to a food vendor standing next to a miniature replica of a Conestoga wagon. He bought a ring of bologna, a chunk of cheese, and three apples and carried his bounty visibly in his arms as he walked past the girls. They whistled and winked at him—in unison, of course—then walked out the door to find his grocery connection. Returning with three bottles of buttermilk and a bag of doughnuts, they sat across from him; and collectively, they ignored one another. Sam, in a window seat, lowered his head and looked through his fingers at the man in conversation with another on the platform. When the train began to rattle and jerk forward, the two remained behind, and Sam remained undiscovered. He smiled to himself, wondering if this was the end or if the search would continue as he traveled north.

The train was only half full when Sam traveled its length and looked at every face.

"Those men are gone," he said, pulling his knife from his pocket to carve the bologna and cheese.

"The policemen?" Chastity asked.

"Yeah, I should be good, unless they wired ahead."

"It's hard to believe the Chicago Police would be interested in chasing you down to send you three hundred miles back to St. Louis to be questioned," Prudence said. "Surely, they have their own priorities."

"Yeah. But maybe those guys were Courtneys'," Sam replied.

"What are Courtneys?"

"They're brothers who are after me."

"Why are they after you?"

"They're brothers of the man who killed my ma."

"This conversation is longer than it needs to be," Chastity said. "Why don't you just tell us what's going on?"

Sam described his ma's death at the hands of Mr. Courtney, how he got the first scar on his face, how he beat Courtney to death with an iron pipe, and how Chester had gotten him out of the city on the Missouri riverboat. Then he told them of the incident yesterday when he was accosted by the small brother in the cemetery.

"The family wants to hang me."

"Of course they do," Prudence said. "For them it's a matter of self-defense."

"You'd be impossible to find in a city the size of Chicago, but we might not be," Chastity said. "What do you want to do? If the Courtneys find us in Chicago, they'll figure out who you are, beard or not."

"We'll be there tomorrow," Sam said. "I'll be watchin' for 'em."

63

They arrived in Chicago and hired a buggy to take them to a nearby hotel. They booked a room at the daily rate, knowing they would look for something else depending on the doctor's forecast for their time in the city. In the morning, they set off to see Dr. Hunt at St. Luke's Hospital, where they presented a desk nurse with his letter to Doc James.

"Dr. Hunt is in surgery today," she said. "He can see you tomorrow morning at nine."

"We'll be here," the twins said.

The early October afternoon was dazzling in the big city. A dry and warm southwest breeze brought up the rank smell of the Chicago River then carried it over their heads as they walked toward the great lake. Sam, who had never seen a body of water he couldn't see across, raced ahead and sat in the sand to remove his boots and socks.

"Come on. It's warm," he coaxed as he waded out to his knees.

"You're a joker," Chastity called out. "That water's cold as a snowball."

"I could stay here all day," he teased, sending a splash their way.

"Come out and buy us something to eat. We're hungry."

An old black man leading a swaybacked white horse pulled a food cart to the boardwalk and waved them over. He walked to the back of the colorful vehicle and started a fire under a small stove then poured water into two copper pots.

"Yo dinna be ready shortly," he called and waved again. "Tell yo friend to get out of dat wata befo his toes falls off."

"We tried," they said. "What are you cooking?"

"It's de special of da day," he said over his shoulder. "I garontee yo gonna lak it. It be ready in 'bout fifteen."

The twins sat next to Sam at the side of the wooden walkway and watched him pull dead skin away from an ankle.

"Does that hurt?" they asked.

"No, not much," he said with an unseen grimace. "It's been a long time."

"Yes, it has. It's still red and raw," Prudence said. "And there's blood on your sock."

"It's all right," he said. "Maybe I'll let it get some sun for a bit."

The twins pulled their skirts up to bare their legs. "Hmm, that feels good," they said.

"Your legs are as white as those sails," Sam commented, as four sailboats tacked across the water in front of them. "I'd like to do that someday. They'll go really fast in this wind."

"Yassir," their cook said, standing behind them. "It be this way all summa. Hardly been any rain atoll. It be dry, dry, dry, an da wind jus keep on blowin'."

They turned to look at him. "What's your name, sir?" the twins asked.

"I ain no, sir." He laughed. "I's jussa nigra slave move up here afta the war, hopin' not to get hanged. Jus' talkin' to yawl pretty wimin wid dem legs showin' be nuff to get a rope around my neck in Georgia."

They looked at each other, pulled their dresses down, then asked him again. "And your name?"

"Bacon."

"Bacon?"

"Dat's right," Bacon said and laughed again. "Pleeze pas da bacon. Dat's me. Da food be ready, I be settin' yo plates on dat table next to da wagon."

He held out an arm, and the girls smiled as they took hold and stood up. They walked away, and the man bent down to look at Sam's leg. "I got sometin' to hep wit dat," he said. "Salve for de burn, an tonic for yo pain. I wone say notin' to yo wibes."

226

Sam looked up at him and said, "Thanks, I'll appreciate that."

They sat at the man's little table and feasted on sausages with mustard and onions, buttermilk biscuits, ears of corn, dill pickles, caramel apples, and sarsaparilla.

"Thank you, Bacon. That was marvelous," the girls said when they were done. "Our young friend with the damaged ankle said he would treat us to our lunch this fine day."

"As I s'pected," he said. "Please folla me, young sir."

They walked to the wagon's tailgate, and the man rolled back a tarp to reveal shelves of condiments, jars of medicines, and bottles of liquids of unknown origins. He rifled through them until he found and removed a jar and a bottle.

"What is this stuff?" Sam asked.

"Dis jar, my granmammy made," the man said, holding it up to the sun. "Maht be a spider tail or a snail tongue in it. She like dat kinda ting. Hea, let's put som on yo leg."

"Whew," Sam said, slowly pulling on a sock. "That stinks."

"Yassir. Yo leg feel betta in da mornin'."

"What's this?" Sam asked, holding a bottle up to the sun.

"All da bottle labels fell off. Hea's one dat was in da box. Kin yawl read it?"

"Yeah, I can read it."

"Hea den," he said, handing it to Sam. "I gots a whole case a dis I foun' in da basemen weya I live. It take away yo pain shonuff."

"Colonel Phantastic's Cure-All Elixir," Sam read aloud from the label Bacon handed him. "There's a number 1 on the top of the cork."

"Ebery bottle gots dat," Bacon said.

"Where do you live in case I want more?"

"I live in Mrs. O'Leary's basemen'. My horse, Whitey, live in da barn wid her cow, Mollie, on Dekobin [De Koven] street."

"Good. Thanks," Sam said. "What do I owe you?"

"Dat be fo dollas, all toll."

"Thanks, Bacon," Sam said, extending his hand.

Bacon shook the hand and said, "Don be drinkin' too much a dat bottle at one time. It kick yo young ass."

64

"Good morning," Dr. hunt said, standing to greet them from behind a large desk. The third-floor view through the window behind him captured many tall buildings and a distant Lake Michigan.

"Good morning, Doctor," the twins said, reaching forward to shake his hand.

"Please sit down," he said and moved around the desk to guide them to a sofa. "I understand from Dr. James's letter that you wish to be separated."

"Yes, sir, that's correct," Chastity said. "We've thought and talked about it a lot, and it's what we want."

"All right, let's get started," he said then went to the door and opened it. "Mildred, bring in a couple of gowns, please. Mildred will get you anything you need. Go ahead and get undressed, and I'll be back when you're ready."

"You're pregnant?" the doctor said walking back into the room. "Hmm, whatever we do will have to wait until after the baby is born. When was your last menstrual cycle?"

Chastity looked at Prudence.

"February," Prudence said. "We always cycle at the same time."

"I'm not surprised," he said. "Have you always?"

They looked at each other and said, "Yes."

He looked at Prudence and asked, "Did your cycles stop as well?"

"Yes."

"Interesting. Please lie down on this bed," he said and led them across the room. "How did you get these scars?"

"We were in a building fire and lucky to get out," they said.

"Sam saved us," Chastity said. "He's in the waiting room. His burns are still bleeding."

"Hmm," he hummed. "Did Dr. James treat you for these burns?"

"Yes, he did, with his wife, Jeanie," Chastity said. "He has Parkinson's disease."

"Is she a doctor?"

"No, but Doc says she can do anything he can do," Prudence said. "They've been together for thirty-four years."

"Indeed."

Dr. Hunt examined them everywhere with finger pressure then went over them again with a stethoscope, especially in the conjoined area. He checked Chastity vaginally then studied her again with the stethoscope.

"As near as I can tell, your baby is properly positioned and has a normal heartbeat," he said. "You are near to term. I'd say three weeks, but anytime is possible."

He went to the door and poked his head out. "Mildred, go get Dr. Elliott. Also, ask Arlene to go to Gerome Dresser's office to see if he can come and bring his camera at once."

Turning back to the twins, he said, "We have an obstetrician on staff, and Mildred will see if he's available. Also, I'd like to have you photographed. We have an associated medical school, and this will be a teachable moment. I will need a team of resident students to assist in the procedure."

"Will you do it then?" they said. "Will you separate us?"

"Do you often do that?" he asked. "Talk in unison?"

They laughed and said, "Why, yes, we do. Will that stop if we are separated?"

"I don't know." He smiled. "There is no precedent for this that I know of."

"So will you do it?"

"I'll let you know before you leave," he said then went to his desk and began to write. The obstetrician arrived and examined

Chastity, then with Dr. Hunt at his side, they examined them both again, head to toe.

The photographer came and took pictures at the direction of the doctors, visibly shaken by what he saw. "I'll have prints tomorrow," he said.

"I'll want any proofs and copies you make. The negatives also," Dr. Hunt said. "You must give me your word on that. I'll want photos taken after the procedure as well."

"Yes, sir," Gerome Dresser replied.

The photographer left, and the doctors spoke to each other quietly at the desk. They went to a massive bookcase, pulled out several volumes, and carried them to the door.

"Dr. Elliott and I have some things to discuss. We'll be back," Dr. Hunt said. "Oh, where is your husband?"

"He's sitting in the waiting room," Chastity said. "Actually, we're not married."

"Oh?" Dr. Hunt said. "That will have to change. This is a Catholic hospital. You must be married. He should be here when we get back. I'll have Mildred bring him a clean gown. Have him put it on. I'll look at his bleeding burns. You two can get dressed."

They went to the waiting room, got Sam, and brought him back to the doctor's office.

"Here, Sam. The doctor said you should put this on," the girls giggled.

He held the gown up, turned it around, and said, "I ain't wearin' this."

"Sam honey, you don't have to walk down the street," Chastity said. "The doctor wants to see your scars. We told him your ankle is still bleeding. Also, we have to get married."

"What?"

"We thought that might take your mind off the gown," they said, laughing.

"I can't get married. I'm only sixteen. I ain't got a job, and the law's after me."

"You're old enough to get me pregnant. Around here that's old enough to get married," Chastity said. "We'll worry about that other stuff later. This is important to us."

The door opened, and both doctors walked in. Sam stood to shake their hands, and the girls introduced him.

"He won't wear the gown," they said.

"Where are you bleeding, young man?"

"My foot," Sam said. "I don't need to put on that dress for you to see it."

"Very well. Show me then."

Sam took off his boot and sock and rested his foot on a stool.

Both doctors examined it, then Dr. Hunt went to the door and asked Mildred to go see if Dr. Sholes was available.

"This wound is not going to heal on its own," Dr. Elliott said. "There is a doctor here doing remarkable work with skin grafts. It would be best for him to look at it. Before he arrives, I want to see your other scars."

Dr. Sholes arrived, and for a short time, Sam held the attention of the three. When they were done, they huddled at the desk then turned to their prospective patients.

Dr. Sholes looked at Sam and said, "Your wound needs a skin graft. This procedure involves taking healthy skin from your body and placing it over the injured area. He pulled a notebook from his pocket. Today is Wednesday, October 4, 1871. I could do this on Friday the 6th at nine a.m. I don't mean to alarm you, but this area on your ankle will eventually become infected, and you could lose your foot.

"We don't have much money," the twins said.

"As I mentioned earlier, we have a medical school affiliation," Dr. Hunt said. "These are unusual procedures, and we will use the opportunities you present to train student doctors. There will be no cost to you."

"This means you'll separate us?"

"Assuming everything goes well with the birth of your baby, yes," Dr. Hunt said. "You should know this is a dangerous procedure.

One or both of you could die. You are young and healthy and would be likely to share a long life joined together as you are."

"We know that."

"I'd like to see you again on Friday afternoon," Dr. Elliott said. "Your baby has a strong heartbeat, but the positioning is unclear to me. Your husband will still be a patient then. You can see me then visit with him. How about one o'clock?"

"Yes, we'll see you Friday."

"Sam," Dr. Sholes said, "I'll bandage that leg right now before you leave."

65

Sam hired a carriage at the hospital entrance from the few that were there for that purpose. They arrived back at the hotel, went to their room then to the dining room with much to discuss.

"I think it went well," Chastity began.

"Yes," Prudence said. "The baby's good, they're willing to do the separation, and Sam's leg can be fixed. All for free."

"What about getting married?" Sam asked. "I'm six years younger than you. And what about all the mess followin' me around?"

Chastity reached across the table and held his hand. "Don't you want to marry me, Sammy?"

"Sure I do," he said. "But what are we gonna eat?"

"We'll figure that out later," Chastity said. "You're a hard worker. You'll get a job. We're young. It'll be a great adventure! We'll have a baby who looks like us!"

"Like you, I hope," Sam said.

"Then it'll look like me too." Prudence laughed.

They ordered food and discussed logistics. Sam would look for a less expensive hotel or house to rent close to the hospital. The girls would research the wedding options, knowing a Catholic service would involve the necessary conversion, making it far too complicated. A judge or justice of the peace would be simplest. In anticipation of their new body types, they would modify two dresses into singles.

"How does your leg feel, Sam?"

"That doctor took off a bunch more skin, and it hurt bad until I took some of the tonic Bacon gave me. Now it feels better," he said.

"What was that?" they asked.

"I don't know. Something he found in his basement."

"You don't seem to be limping as much."

"Yeah, I feel better all over."

The next day, the girls began sewing; and Sam, fortified by another dose of the Colonel's elixir, climbed onto a horse-drawn trolley and rode it toward the hospital. After making three transfers, which included three conversations with three separate teamsters, the consensus recommendation was the Windy Sailor's Lighthouse. The building's facade showed its age, but the lobby was clean and had a fresh flower fragrance. At ten dollars a week and one block from the hospital, it was a pricey but positive solution to their housing issue.

Sam stayed on the first trolley on his return trip to follow the lakeshore back to the hotel. There was a storm over the water that morning, and white caps crashed into the rocks of a distant jetty, warning all boats to stay ashore. Up ahead, several mothers with children were strolling along the beach, and Bacon was at his place by the boardwalk serving lunch to passersby. Sam got off the trolley and walked forward to stand in line to place his order. The good smells awakened his forgotten hunger, and his stomach growled accordingly.

"Young sir, whea yo butiful wibes?"

"They're busy, and I'm hungry. What's the special today?"

"Same as yesserday, an same as da day befo," he said. "It depens on what's I kin fine."

"I need another bottle of your tonic too," Sam said. "Doctor's gonna cut on my leg tomorrow, so I may have some pain."

"Yassir, bess take two case it's bad," Bacon said. "I take it ever'day fo ma back an fo da pain in ma chest. Wast yo name, young sir?"

"My name's Sam."

"I gotta brotha name's Sam. Hea's yo food, Sam," Bacon said. "I'll give you da medicine when yo done."

Sam ate while the warm October breeze blew hard around him. Several seagulls swooped in, landing close by, and watched for an opportunity to snatch a scrap. A young woman pushing a pram passed by on the boardwalk, and a wind gust took her bonnet away like a kite toward the lake. Sam sprang up, chased it down, and returned it to the grateful maiden.

"Thank you, sir," she said. "I never could have left my mistress's baby to have done that myself."

"Yer welcome," he replied, turning to watch the gulls fighting over the last of his lunch, the newspaper wrapper sailing high into the airstream.

"Here, let me pay for your food," she said, struggling to free her purse.

"No, no, ma'am," Sam said. "I was done anyhow."

She blushed and stepped forward to touch one of the scars on his cheeks with a gloved hand. "This must have been painful," she said then leaned in to kiss the wound. "Thank you again. I'm here most days at this time."

Sam watched her walk away and smiled when she turned and gave him a little wave. When she was out of sight, he limped toward Bacon's wagon, feeling the blood swoosh between his toes in his boot.

"Mista Sam." Bacon smiled, showing his toothless grin. "I bleebe you kin hab as many wibes as you want. Lemme hab a look at yo foot."

He gently pulled the boot off then rolled the bloody sock into the grass. "Lordy, Lordy, I's glad da docta goin' to fix dis foot. It's a mess. Stay hea."

The old man went to his wagon and returned with water and clean rags. He washed the foot then rinsed out the boot and left both to dry in the sun. "I'll give you dis sock back afta I git it washed. We wrap yo foot in dis cloth when yawl leebe," he said then took the sock to his wagon and returned with a bottle of Colonel Phantastic's tonic. They each took a swallow, stretched out in the grass, and gazed at the lake.

"I don't know what this stuff is, but I like it," Sam said.

"Yassir, me too," he said with a worried look. "I don knows I could git by widout it."

66

On Friday, October 6, 1871, Dr. Sholes grafted skin from Sam's left thigh to his left ankle. He reported on a successful surgery to the waiting twins and that Sam would be a patient overnight for treatment and observation. They could visit him this afternoon.

Bellhops from the Windy Sailor's Lighthouse delivered their luggage that morning, and the twins returned to the room anxious to unpack. After lunch, they walked back to the hospital and sat with Sam for two hours, content to chat quietly and fuss over him when he was awake. The following day, he was discharged with a pair of crutches and told to return daily for a dressing change. Chastity was told to stay close by. The wedding license was purchased that same afternoon, and the ceremony scheduled for Sunday morning. Judge Junior Jackson, late of Memphis, Tennessee, would preside.

It was a small affair. The witnesses were the judge's wife, Georgia, and Prudence. Georgia went out to the courthouse lawn and picked a dozen mums for Chastity's bouquet. The girls had bought Sam new clothes, including a suit coat and tie, and they fawned over him until he blushed. He was nervous and fumbled and dropped the rings the girls had purchased at a secondhand store. Everybody laughed and cried, but they got through it, and there was a marriage. After the ceremony, the twins sang two of the most popular songs from their saloon dance collection, "Don't Kick That Dog" and "Yo Mama Was a Ho," and there was more laughter and dancing.

The morning's joy carried them into the afternoon as they rode through the city in their rented carriage enjoying the day and sharing it with anyone who noticed it in their smiling faces. They drove along the lakeshore, taking in the beautiful day, the wind strong against the girls' bonnets. Sam kept his hat on the floor under his good foot. When they got to Bacon's food wagon, he was buttoning things up.

"Bacon, Bacon," the twins exclaimed, "we got married!"

"Lode hab mercy!" he exclaimed. "What a joyful day! I wanna make yawl sumpin to eat, but I's all sold out. Mista Sam, how long you got dat buggy?"

"All day," Sam said. "I can take it back tomorrow. There's a barn behind the hotel for the horse."

"Wea den, lemme make sumpin special fo yo suppa. Yawl come by ma house tonight an git it den take it to yo room an eat it dare."

Sam looked at the girls, and they nodded excitedly.

"Hea," Bacon said. "I kin write it."

He found a piece of newspaper and a pencil and wrote De Koven in the margin.

"I lib on Dekobin Street. Yawl will see dis wagon in da back."

"I'll be there before dark," Sam said.

They went back to their room in the afternoon to consummate the marriage. For them it was the high point of the special relationship they'd created and planned to carry forward in a new direction. In this final sexual experience the twins would share with this man, Sam coupled with Prudence while she reached over to bring Chastity along with practiced fingers. Chastity cried out as Prudence and Sam climaxed in a rapture that was separate but united. Sam, a step behind in his understanding of the significance of the event, followed dutifully, his instinct to protect always strong.

Dr. Sholes had provided Sam with a bottle of pills for his pain and told him to take no more than one every six hours. He shook one out before leaving the hotel room, washed it down with a glass of water, and received multiple kisses from the girls on his way out the door. The stable boy in the barn helped him harness the horse and held the crutches while Sam clambered aboard. The boy didn't know exactly where De Koven Street was but pointed Sam in a southwest direction and assured him he could get directions on the way. Several miles later, Sam drove up to a ramshackle house on a street where prosperity was a memory and dreams were for sale. Bacon's wagon was parked in the back, and his horse, Whitey, was chomping hay next to an old cow in the shade of a decrepit barn.

"Mista Sam," Bacon's voice called out. "Yawl found me. Come down to ma house. It cool down dare."

Bacon stood by an open cellar door then took Sam's arm and guided him down the stairs. A single lantern cast an orange glow across the small space. The dirt floor had been recently swept, and heavenly smells wafted from a wood cookstove. Kitchen utensils hung from the ceiling nearby, and carpentry tools lined a wall next to a table with two chairs. A cot covered with quilts and a handmade chest of drawers occupied a near corner.

"Someday a tonado gonna come down dis street and blow all deez crappy houses away. Ha ha!" he laughed. "An I be de onliest one left. Unlest all de foks come down hea wid me first. Ha ha!"

"I like this place, Bacon," Sam said. "You should be proud of it."

"Yeah? I ain been proud of nutton fo long time," he said and placed his hands against his lower back and leaned into a stretch. "It's free though. All I gots do is take care a Mrs. O'Leary. Gib her sompin ta eat ever'day and open de hole in her flo above my stove so she stay warm in da winter. Milk her cow an feed her chickens."

"Does your back hurt today, Bacon?" Sam asked.

"Yassa, it do," he said. "Not bad as da pain in ma chest dough. It be bad today. I bes be takin a swallow ole numba 1 hea now. You want some for yo foot?"

"No, Bacon," Sam said. "The doctor gave me some pills to take, and they make the foot feel better."

"Yassir. Hea be yo suppa in dis box hea," Bacon said. "I's gonna take it up to yo buggy."

The old man shuffled back to the cot, pulled out a wooden box, and removed two bottles. He pulled the cork out of one, took a long swallow, recorked it, and put it back in the box.

"Hea's a bottle a numba 1 for you to take wid you." He grinned. "May be da las time you see me, never know."

"No, Bacon," Sam said. "I got to take this buggy back tomorrow. I'll come by and say hello."

Bacon smiled and patted his shoulder. "Hea," he said. "Carry dis lantern fo me. I gotta feed deez critters den I's goin' to bed."

Sam hobbled up the stairs, managing the lantern in one hand and two crutches under his other arm. Bacon set the box in the buggy then turned, and they shook hands. Sam handed the old man the lantern, watched him disappear into the barn, then drove away.

67

Sam got back to the hotel a little before 10:00 p.m. He unharnessed and brushed down the horse, fed him, watered him, and put him in a stall. When he got to the room, he tapped on the door, got no answer, and fumbled through his pockets to find his key. He made a quick survey of the space, ending where he started. Looking down at the tabletop, he saw a note: Gone to the hospital. IT'S BABY TIME!

"No shit!" Sam said and stumbled out the door. The hotel lobby was a mass of confusion since he'd been there ten minutes earlier, with hotel guests and employees moving haphazardly in all directions. Not wanting to get trampled, he braced against his crutches for a dash to the door when he was blindsided by a large woman. Knocking him to the floor, she landed on top of him, her large breasts covering his face. Struggling to breathe, he moved his head back and forth, further working his nose into the crease made available by her low-cut dress. She smelled of sweat.

"Get off me," she ordered.

"Lady, you're on top of me," he said in a muffled voice. He flashed back to his first night in Alamo and his struggle under the massive woman in the muddy street. Panic surged through him... *There must be a fire! I've got to get to the twins!*

"Help me up!" the fat woman yelled. She waited, and when no help came, she rolled off.

Sam scrambled in the opposite direction, barely escaping the crash of her weighty purse. Keeping an eye on her, he picked up his crutches and moved away.

"What's going on?" he asked a uniformed bellboy.

"There's a fire," the boy said.

I knew it, he thought. "Where?" he asked.

"South side," the boy said. "Go outside. You can see it."

Sam pressed a quarter into the boy's hand. "Can you help me? Take the box of food in the buggy in the barn to my room, would ya?"

"Yes, sir."

Outside, the sky to the southwest was aglow. Sam cringed at the memory of Bacon carrying the lantern into the barn with a pain in his chest. If there was time, he'd go back to check on him. At the hospital, the nurse at the front desk recognized him and sent him in the direction of the Labor and Delivery Room. He met Dr. Elliott coming out of the room.

"Your wife is in labor," he began. "It's early, but nothing would surprise me in this situation. I'm going to send word for Dr. Hunt. If anything goes wrong with the delivery, the separation surgery may have to commence immediately."

"How long will the labor be?" Sam asked.

"I don't know. It may go on for a while."

"Can I see them?"

"Yes, they're resting."

Sam knocked on the door and stuck his head in.

"Sammy, come in," they said.

"Hey, how're you doin'?" he said.

"Good," Chastity said. "I've had two contractions, about an hour apart."

"Does it hurt?"

"Yeah, but not bad."

"How about you?" he asked Prudence.

"No, silly," she said, slapping his hand. "The baby's over here. Where have you been?"

"There's a fire," Sam said. "It's gettin' big fast. It's in the direction of Bacon's house. Last I saw him, he was carrying a lantern into the barn with pain in his chest. I'm worried about him."

"Oh dear," Prudence said. "You should go back and check on him."

"What about the baby?"

"How long did it take you to get there?"

"Maybe forty-five minutes," he said. "There wasn't no fire then."

"This is going to take a while," Chastity said. "You should go. You still have the buggy, right?"

"Yeah, but…"

"I'll wait for you to get back." She smiled. "There isn't anything for you to do here anyhow but sit and worry. You go now while you might still be able to do Bacon some good. We love him!"

"He sent some food. Should I get it?"

"No, we can't eat while we're having a baby," Chastity said. "Now go! Hurry!"

Sam maneuvered through a small group of students walking toward the maternity rooms. He moved quickly to the hotel then around back to the barn. The buggy's bay gelding pricked up his ears and gave him a sideways glance as if to say, *I thought we were done for the day.* But he whinnied and pawed at the ground when he got outside and saw the orange glow in the sky. Sam stood next to him, scratched his nose, and stared in disbelief at how much the fire had grown in the minutes he'd been inside. The smoke smell was intense, and ash was wafting down from the sky like snow.

"Come on, old son," he said. "Let's get closer. We don't want to miss anything."

They drove a distance toward the conflagration and faced a stampede of people fleeing the flames. A man stopped Sam and yelled, "You can't get through. The fire's on both sides of the road. On both sides of the river too. I'll help you turn around."

He grabbed the horse's headstall and turned the outfit to the north. "Get up here!" Sam yelled to him. "I can take you."

The man climbed onto the seat next to Sam and asked, "Where are you going?"

"De Koven Street," Sam said.

"You'll have to go around miles to the west. The fire's huge."

Sitting close, Sam had a chance to see that the man was scorched and black with soot. His hair was singed, his cheek was burned through to the bone, and the grimace on his face told the story of the pain within.

"My God, man, what happened to you?" Sam asked.

"My house burned. My wife didn't make it out," he said and started to cry.

"I'll take you to a hospital. Where's the closest?"

"Go left two blocks. It's on your way."

Sam reached under the seat and felt around until he found the box of Bacon's food. The bellboy hadn't taken it. He groped through it until he touched a bottle of number 1 and pulled it out. "Here, man. Take a couple swallows. It'll help your pain."

The charred figure took a short then a long pull and seemed to relax immediately. "What is it?" he asked.

"I don't know," Sam said, looking over his shoulder at the racing flames. "It helps with pain. I got it from a friend. I got a bad leg, a burned leg. I take it every day."

"I think I feel better. Turn in here," the scorched man said. "This is Meridian General."

Sam pulled up to the portico then turned away from the chaos in front of him back to the street. "Here you are," he said. "I'm sorry about your wife."

Thanks," the man said. "Stay west if you want to get around the fire. But I don't think it's a good idea."

More panic. The burned man was right; this was a bad idea. He was off on a mission to help a friend who was probably dead when his wife and her sister were having his baby. If it was a clear and beautiful night, it would be different. This fire changed everything. The pledge he'd made to these women and himself to get them here could not be ignored. He had to get back to the hospital.

The horse had shown great heart this night facing the mass of fleeing people. He was lathered and scared, and stomped and jerked at his harness. Sam jumped down to calm him, landing on his weakened leg and falling under the carriage. The movement further spooked the horse, and he jerked ahead, rolling the buggy wheel over Sam's ankle. Feeling no pain, he stood, collapsed, and rose again to move to the horse's head dragging the leg.

"Easy, old son. We're going home," he said, rubbing the soft and whiskered nose. "You'll be fine. Nothing here to worry about."

His head in a fog, Sam hobbled back to his seat and climbed aboard. He looked down at his injured leg and saw that it was caked with blood.

"Jesus Christ," he said, reaching into his pocket for the pill bottle. He shook two out, tossed them into his mouth, and reached for the number 1. He took a long gulp of the powerful medicine to wash down the pills, and he was ready to go. He slapped the reins on the horse's back, and the rig jumped forward. Blind and disoriented, Sam turned left then left again into a blind alley and raced toward a hundred-foot wall of fire.

68

Autumn 1871

Sheriff Walter Becker, John Walker, and his son, Johnny, arrived in Spanish Fork on the 4:00 p.m. train. They were all strangers to the town. The older two had been the law there two decades ago, and young John had come with his mother, Zelda, several months earlier. Now it was early October. The cottonwoods and aspens were turning yellow, and there was frost on the ground most mornings. There would be mild panic in homes that hadn't finished stacking their winter's supply of hay or firewood. Days were getting shorter, and there was never enough time.

"Do you remember this place, sheriff?" John asked.

"Of course I do," he answered and laughed. "Do you suppose the new sheriff will let us sleep in his jail?"

"I suppose if we cause enough ruckus, he won't have a choice," John said. "Let's get you a room and something to eat, then I want Johnny to take me to his ma."

They walked through town taking in the changes and found their way to Brigham's Inn. Walter had slept most of the way from Alamo to Spanish Fork, and if he didn't know he had a snoring problem, the absence of anyone willing to sit near him even during the day should have tipped him off. Still, he was alert and enjoying himself when he was awake and pleased to be back home.

According to the hotel clerk, Heaven's Café was still a going concern and the best eatery in town. John let the former sheriff lead the conversation as they strolled down main street, young Johnny enjoying the stories and descriptions of events older than himself. The restaurant was filling up for the dinner meal, and they took a table by the street window so they could watch the traffic. A portly waitress with gray hair tied in a bun and tucked into a bonnet arrived to take their order. She looked at Johnny and put her hand over her heart and stuttered, "Deputy, you-you never got old. I-I don't believe you ever…"

"Sarah, I'm over here," John said, smiling. "This is my son, Johnny, and you'll remember Sheriff Becker."

"Oh…oh, of course." She blushed. "I'm so embarrassed."

"Please don't be," he said, reaching over to pat her hand. "This happens all the time. And I still owe you for a glass of buttermilk and a hard-boiled egg."

"Oh no, deputy." She smiled. "That was my privilege. It's so nice to see you all again. And to meet you, Johnny."

The men all nodded, and John said, "We'll all have the supper special. We don't even care what it is."

"I'm sure you'll like it," she said, looking back and forth at the Walkers. "My Lord…"

"Sheriff, we'll take you up to the ranch, but I gotta see Zelda first," John said.

"I can get up there," the sheriff said. "I got a letter a few years ago that said some of the Jordans was livin' there. I oughta just give it to 'em. They ain't got shit."

"You got no kin left?"

"Not since Ma died," he said. "They's all buried in that red-dirt hill."

Their supper truly was special, and John made sure the tip more than covered the cost of the extra portions Sarah had added to his meal two decades ago. He looked to the kitchen before they left and saw her standing in the doorway watching. It saddened him to think how often she might have stood there over the years waiting for someone to come through the door and smile at her.

The sheriff left the café to walk the streets and was soon caught up in a conversation with an old friend.

"He'll be all right on his own tonight. He has lots of friends here, and they'll take care of him," John said. "He won't remember where the hotel is, but there aren't many options, so somebody will get him home. Where are we goin'?" John asked as they walked toward the livery to rent a buggy.

"Do you remember Lupita Hernandez?"

"No, I don't," John said. "I really didn't know many folks in Spanish Fork. I knew your ma from school."

"Ma promised Lupita she wouldn't tell anyone she's here. She's pretty scared," Johnny said. "She saw the Colonel in Salt Lake just like Lloyd did. He knows she would come back here. He has another railcar."

"How do you know this?"

"I got a letter before I left San Francisco," Johnny said. "I was working for the Box brothers."

They drove down the East Road, past the Chatham place, and beyond to the Green Apple Farm. Pickers were busy in the trees; the branches heavy with fruit were sagging to the ground. Smoke drifted from the chimney of a cabin in the center of a long row of similar little buildings. Johnny drove to it, jumped out, and wrapped the horses' lead rope around a rail. He walked to the front door, knocked, then stepped back to watch his father climb down from the carriage. The door opened, and he was hugged from behind by his mother as she spoke to him in a tearful voice, "You found him."

"Yeah Ma," he said. "He's here."

Zelda broke away from her son and walked forward to embrace her husband of twenty years. "Oh my Lord, John," she cried. "What happened to our lives?"

"That's over, Zelda. We'll never be apart again," John said, staring into her eyes.

Their nights of wedded bliss began as if they were still in their teens and continued unabated for a month. Johnny worked on the farm in the orchard, enjoying the interaction with the Spanish pickers, rapidly picking up the language. He met and fell in love with a girl with long black hair and big brown eyes from Hermosillo and made plans to marry her. Former Sheriff Walter Becker found the family ranch in far better condition than he'd expected, with two families of Jordans living there. They'd developed an irrigation system and were growing vegetables to sell on main street in Spanish Fork. The families agreed to create a living space for him in the tack room and keep him fed and warm in exchange for a deed to the property when he died. Walter preferred to stay in town, however, where he held court in the general store most days, telling stories that bordered on the fantastic until he remembered no one's name, including his own. Walter lived almost a year. When he died, the county's appreciation of his service was evident by the great number of its citizens who joined the funeral procession up the road to the red-dirt ranch. He was buried next to his mother, with the rest of the Beckers nearby, on the little hill above the farm.

The letter from Chicago came on a Monday. Dr. Hunt had gathered as much next-of-kin information from the twins as they could offer, naming their older sister Zelda as the primary guardian in their lives.

Dear Zelda,

It is with a heavy heart that I send you news of the deaths of your sisters Chastity and Prudence. It has been my privilege to know them for this too-short time, during their quest to become separated. They were remarkable together and would have been remarkable individuals.

Before I continue, you should know Chastity died in childbirth. There is a beautiful baby girl here waiting for you. She was born premature and has been in intensive care for two weeks but is strong and growing and will be moved to the nursery soon.

After the baby was delivered, Chastity began to hemorrhage, and nothing we did would stop it. An emotional Prudence said goodbye to her sister, was sedated, and the separation surgery began. Dr. Elliott and I and our team of medical students operated for six hours. Prudence lived for three days but never regained consciousness. We are all still devastated by our failure.

Samuel Maxwell, Chastity's husband, left the hospital as his wife's labor began to check on a friend and was never seen again. It is feared he was consumed by our Great Chicago Fire.

As you might imagine, news of the twins' presence in Chicago and the planned separation were the talk of the city. There is a great sadness here at the news of their passing, only rivaled by the grief at the tremendous losses of our city. No funeral arrangements have been made for your sisters pending your notification.

I have a handwritten will signed by both naming both you and Samuel Maxwell as corecipients of all their possessions. I am the executor.

A Colonel Kasper Cobb has come forward to claim the bodies. He presents papers dated in 1849 that name him as legal guardian, signed (he claims) by their father, a man named Chatham. He is suing in court for his right to possession.

Please wire me at St. Luke's Hospital with your thoughts as soon you can. I don't expect a legal ruling on Colonel Cobb's claim for at least a month.

Sincerely,

Dr. J. R. Hunt

The letter overwhelmed Zelda so that she lay in bed and cried for an hour. John boiled water for tea, brought her fresh apple cake, and sat beside her holding her hand.

"What do you want to do?" he said.

"We must go to town and send a telegram immediately," Zelda sobbed. "Then we will go to Chicago to bring the baby home. I want to bring the girls back here to bury. That monster would put Chastity and Prudence in his circus."

"I'll hitch up the buggy."

They drove to Spanish Fork, Zelda alternately crying and cursing. "His railcar was here for a week a month before you came," she said. "He asked around town about me and the girls, but nobody knew I was here."

"Did you know what the twins were about to do?" John asked. "Did you know about the baby?"

"I knew they had talked about separation, and I knew Chastity was pregnant," Zelda said, blowing her nose. "They sent me a letter from Alamo. They never said anything about when these things would happen though. I wrote them back but never got an answer."

Zelda wrote and sent the telegram:

DR. HUNT,

HUSBAND JOHN AND I WILL LEAVE FOR CHICAGO TOMORROW. WILL BRING TWINS HOME FOR BURIAL. COBB MUST BE STOPPED!

ZELDA WALKER

69

They rode the train to Salt Lake City, where they bought tickets to Cheyenne, Wyoming, and would purchase additional fares as they traveled. With layovers, they were told it could take as long as ten days. Zelda would send telegrams to Chicago along the way.

That night, John went to see Lloyd Clark to ask for money. Over two hours and several beers, he recounted the years of his search for his wife and the twins and the devastation the Colonel had brought to their lives.

"Now he wants to put those twins in his circus when they're dead," John growled. "I can't tolerate it. I'll pay you back, Lloyd. You know I will."

"I know you will, and I'll look forward to a full report when you get back," Lloyd said, laying his hand on John's shoulder. "Let's walk back to my house."

On day 9 and train number 6, they pulled into Chicago. The final few miles to the station were a shock to see, and they rode into the city mouths agape. The destruction was enormous, and they wondered at the skyline they would never see. But even as they were shocked, they were impressed by the activity around the destruction. Debris was still being removed, but there were repairs being made and construction everywhere. As they pulled into the trainyard, both searched for the railcar they knew to be there. Without saying anything, they spotted it at the same time and turned to look at each other.

"He won't stop us," Zelda said.

"No, he won't," John replied.

They hired a carriage to take them to St. Luke's, and the driver described the fire and its race through the city in detail. He had lost his home and a cousin, but his business had been so good since the fire that he had to buy another horse. He recommended the Windy Sailor's Lighthouse as a reasonable place to stay, so they dropped Zelda off at the hospital, and John went to the hotel to check in. When he arrived at the hospital, he was taken to the nursery where Zelda was rocking the baby girl and humming a lullaby.

"She looks just like them," Zelda said. "These blue eyes and look at all this hair."

"Yeah, she's beautiful," John said. "So small. What will you name her?"

"I don't know," Zelda said thoughtfully. "Something that represents everything we've all been through in the last twenty years."

John laughed. "That would be a long name."

"And hard to spell." Zelda smiled, nuzzling the tiny face.

"The doctor will see you now," a young nurse said entering the room. She took the baby from Zelda and walked away.

"It's nice to meet you both," Dr. Hunt said, and rose from his chair to shake their hands. "How were your travels?"

"It's a long way," Zelda said. "I've had lots of time to think and a lot to think about."

"Yes, I'm sure," he said. "I really admired your sisters. As it turned out, they were right about wanting the separation considering the pregnancy. We were at least prepared to go forward with it at the birth. It was Prudence's only chance after Chastity died. Being attached to her dead sister could have been a long and excruciating death for her."

"What can you tell us about Samuel?"

"He was a quiet young man," Dr. Hunt began. "Apparently he traveled with them from Montana. They said he saved them from a fire. All three of them had scars to show for it. Samuel had a wound on an ankle that had never healed from the event. Dr. Sholes performed a skin graft on it while he was here."

"Where was he during the birth?"

"The girls said he left to check on a friend of theirs at the beginning of Chastity's labor," Dr. Hunt continued. "It was a long labor, and they never quit asking for him. The fire was raging at that time, and there's no telling what he might have run into. I'm quite sure he would have been here if possible. He seemed devoted to them."

"I never knew him," Zelda said. "John met him in Alamo."

"He was only sixteen, but a tough kid," John said. "You saw his scars."

"Yes, I did."

"Doctor, we could spend the rest of the day telling you the unbelievable story of our lives with those girls," Zelda said with moist eyes. "Now we want to take them and their baby home. What do we need to do?"

"I will contact Judge Conrad Cornfield today to let him know you are here," he said. "I expect this matter will be settled quickly. I also wanted to ask you if you wanted to see your sisters."

"Yes, I would," Zelda said, looking at John.

"Yes," he said.

"I can arrange that right now. I will get one of my students to take you to the morgue," he added. "I would also suggest having the bodies embalmed if you plan to take them to Utah."

They all stood, and Zelda thanked the doctor for his time and attention. The medical student arrived, and John went with him to the basement morgue. He was shocked at what he saw. The bodies were gray, unrecognizable, and looked as if they had never been alive. The smell was already so overwhelming that he almost vomited.

"Zelda honey, you should not see them," he said emotionally. "Keep your memories of them as they lived. It would be unfair to remember them like this."

Zelda cried and could not speak. She held John close, and they climbed the stairs to the nursery. They sat together with the baby for a while then walked to the hotel. Later that night after dinner and in their room, John said, "Zelda, you know I'll do whatever you want, but would you consider burying the twins here? Taking them 1,200 miles back to Spanish Fork where no one knew them doesn't seem right. At least here they were admired and would be well-remembered."

She looked at him but didn't say anything.

"You will have their baby to love, and you will remember them every day when you look at her."

She nodded and hugged him, and they went to bed.

70

The meeting with Judge Cornfield went well. He read the will, asked John and Zelda a few questions, then spoke to Dr. Hunt quietly at the bench. Colonel Cobb's document was considered in his absence and ruled invalid. Zelda was granted possession of the bodies and full guardianship of the unnamed daughter on Chastity Maxwell. The judge expressed his condolences at the loss of the sisters and congratulated Zelda at the addition of a new daughter.

"Dr. Hunt, thank you for all you've done for my sisters and our family," she said back in his office. "I haven't decided what I will do with the bodies, but I'd like to have them embalmed. I think it's undignified to move them anywhere in their current state. The caskets will stay closed regardless, but I cannot tolerate the odor of death."

"Certainly, it's been a privilege to know you, your sisters, and Samuel," the doctor said. "I'll send a messenger to Dickens Funeral Chapel and see that Mr. Dickens takes care of it. I know the child will thrive under your care."

John and Zelda stopped at the nursery and made arrangements to pick up the baby the following day. They stopped at a dry-goods store where Zelda purchased basic baby supplies, and John carried them back to the hotel in a large satchel. After an early dinner, they relaxed in the hotel dining room and talked of their life possibilities in Spanish Fork. "You know, John, if it's not too expensive, I think the twins belong in the place of their birth. I have yet to go through their things, but I know they had money."

"That's what we'll do then. We'll take them home."

John nodded in quiet agreement, then they went upstairs to their room and went to bed.

An hour later, Zelda was lightly snoring in a rhythm John had learned to love. He quietly left the bed, removed the pistol from his duffel, and left the room. A footman at the hotel's entrance referred him to the front of the hospital for a cab, and he set off in that direction. The driver relived the days and nights of the Great Fire in a practiced description as he drove, but John barely heard him. He stopped the man a mile from the rail yard, paid him, and walked the rest of the way.

Locomotives moved boxcars to loading docks at the north end of the tracks where the night crew waited to load them with freight. John kept to the shadows, leaving the commotion behind as he walked to a siding at the south end. He approached a dark-red caboose with dim light leaking from two rear windows and quietly climbed the steps. There he was. Sitting at a table reading a book, a small cigar in one hand, he raised his head but did not look surprised when John pushed the door open and stepped inside.

"I see you found your wife, the whore," the Colonel said. "Easy enough. Just follow the stink of her nasty parts." He laughed and laid down the book. "Not so easy finding me, I guess."

John pulled the revolver from his belt, cocked it, and pointed it at the old man. "You're right," he said. "It's taken far too long."

"There's a taxidermist in St. Louis who tells me he can recreate those Siamese twin girls into an attraction that will draw customers for miles to my new circus," he smiled. "I expect to deliver them to him in a fortnight."

"That's not going to happen, you jackass," John said. "Maybe he can do the same thing to your stinking carcass while your soul burns in hell."

The Colonel laughed again. "Earl, push that shotgun into his back a little harder so Mr. Walker can get an idea what's coming up next for him."

John felt the pressure of the barrels in his back and heard the click of the hammers as Earl cocked them both. "Lay that gun on the table, boy, then get down on your knees," the Colonel continued, as

John complied. "After I get rid of you, I'll have the lovely Zelda in here tomorrow. I've got plenty of her favorite tonic onboard."

"I'm here now," Zelda said and walked through the open door and went directly to the table.

The Colonel smiled then lost his amused look when she stepped forward and leaned over the table to fire a small-caliber pistol into his heart. He stared in disbelief for a second then slumped forward to the tabletop, his cheek landing on the still burning cigar.

Earl, also surprised, took a step back and leveled the shotgun at John and Zelda. They stood together facing him but did not speak.

"Do you remember me, Walker?"

"Yeah, I do," John said, looking at the wooden peg that supported Earl's right leg. "That foot got shot off in San Francisco."

"That's right," Earl said. "Then you used my belt to tie a tourniquet around the leg. Then you gave me pills that took the pain away. This was after me and Benny almost killed you. I been walking on this wood stick ever since. I ain't never forgot you."

"Yeah, well, it was nothin' personal. I just wanted to get away and find my wife."

"I know," Earl said. "And now you got her, and now's your chance to get away. We're even."

Earl let the hammers down slowly and pointed the shotgun toward the floor. John and Zelda looked at him then to each other and turned and walked out the door.

71

John and Zelda sat next to each other quietly, lost in the power of events just played. John drove the buggy north, past the skeletal remains of scorched buildings silhouetted behind the foundations of new structures. The odor of burned wood and ash melded with the fresh smell of cut lumber and cement. It was time to leave this city of motion and return to a more relaxed setting. After a couple miles, John broke the silence and asked, "Where'd you get the gun?"

"Cecil Box. He showed me how to use it and said to keep it close."

"Where'd you get the buggy?"

"I rented it while you were in the morgue. It's been in the hotel stable."

"You're better'n most, you know that?"

CPSIA information can be obtained
at www.ICGtesting.com
Printed in the USA
LVHW021705200221
679520LV00004B/343